THERE'S ALWAYS TOMORROW

JIM CARR

THERE'S ALWAYS TOMORROW

ISBN: 978-1-989425-03-9

CHAPTER ONE

"It will change your life forever."

Sommer Kappel didn't know what to say. Her mathematics professor at McGill University, Dr. Siegfried Fuhrman, smiled as he folded his hands on top of his shining mahogany desk and waited for her reaction.

He still spoke with a German accent, even after 12 years at McGill in Montréal. Some of his students used to imitate his accent. He caught them unawares one day and just smiled. Even his parrot, his sole companion, imitated him. But Sommer was different. Her parents were German, and she understood him in a way the others did not.

"Your scholarship to study under the great German mathematics genius, Professor Friedrich Albrecht, who will introduce you to a world that you never dreamed of."

She just sat there with her hands folded on her lap with no expression of any kind as she tried to digest exactly what it meant. She had light brown hair, like many German women, with high cheekbones and darting hazel eyes that seemed to delight at every new thing in her life. Her father kept telling her she needed to put more weight on and that her breasts were not big enough, but her mother, who ruled the household, told her she would fill out in the next five years. "Don't pay attention to him. He still thinks young women should focus on getting a husband rather

3

than learning to add and subtract."

Her mind snapped back to Professor Fuhrman, who was speaking to her. He was such a kindly man who loved mathematics the way some men loved women. His greying mustache twitched when he was excited as he was now.

The pride in his voice was unmistakable. "I was a junior professor at Bonn University before coming to Canada and always delighted in talking with him. He was a person with great ideas. Frederich is a genius, as you will soon discover. He is what you need today."

Sommer wondered what her parents would think. For her mother, Sommer was the focal point of her life and her sense of purpose. She could also hear what she would say when she told her mother.

"I will never forget you, Professor Fuhrman, or what you have done for me." She lowered her eyes and thought about her father. He would never say much. Her mother did all the talking. He would be against it. She knew that without thinking, but she also knew her mother would pressure him and that everything would be fine.

Professor Fuhrman stubbed out his cigar in the glass ashtray on his desk and looked at the books that covered the wall on his left. He loved the smell of books, which had become a constant companion in later years. He would miss Sommer and her delight in learning new things. He never had so gifted a student in all his years. There was no doubt that one day she would be awarded the Fields Metal and achieve great things in mathematics that were beyond him.

"Thank you, professor," she said in a small voice, rising from her chair.

"One thing before you go, Sommer. Ottawa has somehow got wind about your scholarship at Bonn and would like to talk to you before you leave."

"What for?" she suddenly felt apprehensive.

"Someone in Foreign Relations, as they call it," he added, passing her a small piece of paper the size of a business card. "They said to call them direct before you come."

"I know this sounds foolish, but I don't have a good feeling about any of this, and I can't really tell you why," she said.

"I understand, Sommer. I felt the same way when I left Bonn. So I would advise you to go all the same. We are living in the midst of the Great Depression. Jobs are not plentiful these days, and who knows where this could lead."

She was about to get up when he stopped her.

"The university has asked for your picture, and I have sent it off to them already. I hope you do not mind. Someone will be at the Bonn train station and need to know what you look like. Here is the documentation for all your trips," he said, passing it to her, "including your return train ticket from Ottawa."

He stood and shook her hands. "One favour to me, if you would, Sommer. Would you look up my sister, Jundt Fuhrman, should you find yourself in Berlin? Be sure to tell her I think of her every day, especially now."

He saw her to the door. "One more thing, Sommer. I keep forgetting things these days." He reached into his trouser pocket. "This is a magic key. It could save your life one day. Ask my sister about it."

***

She was brushing her shoulder-length hair at the train station when she realized she had not called in advance. She took a taxi from the station to 26 Sussex Drive to meet someone by the name of André Proulx. It was the first time she had ever taken a taxi, and she smiled. She knew intuitively it would not be her last. The world was opening up to her, and she knew that she would do many things she had done before. The taxi was just a symbol of what she would do and accomplish.

André Proulx's office was located at the back of the building. It was not large and looked faded and out of date. He was shorter than she had imagined, with dark brown hair and a mustache that he kept pinching as he listened to her.

"I understand that you're headed for Germany. Someone in the foreign office in London would like to chat with you before you embark for Germany."

"What is this about, Mr. Proulx?"

"I'm not sure, mademoiselle, other than there is some urgency to the matter." He paused. "I understand you speak German without an accent."

Sommer nodded. She didn't feel good about any of this.

He sat back in his chair, lit a cigarette, and thought about the new model train he had bought for his basement railroad. He told his wide it would be for his son, but she knew it was really for him. He was in his mid-30s, a lawyer by training and stood erect in a stiff way. His eyes were as dark as his hair, and he tended to smile a lot.

His office looked out onto the garden filled with tulips dancing in the wind and the road that connected Ottawa and Québec. His black telephone sat on an end table next to his desk. There were two stacks of paper on each side, an ink bottle, and an ink blotting card for handwritten messages on the centre of his desk.

Sommer didn't wait. "Do you have any idea why they want to see me?

Proulx nodded. "But that's really for them to tell you. In the meantime, I've taken the liberty of creating a package for you. A chauffeur will wait for you outside Customs and take you to your hotel. Any questions?"

"For some strange reason, I suddenly feel apprehensive. Is there a reason why I should?"

Proulx smiled again. "Let us get a taxi for you."

***

The doorbell rang about an hour after she arrived back in Montréal. She went to answer it to see her mother and father standing with a grim look on their faces. Her mother didn't waste any time. Sommer has no sooner taken her coat when she started.

Sommer saw fire in her mother's eyes for the first time in her life. "I don't know why you feel you need to do this. Your place is with us."

Her parents had arrived on the evening train. First, a train journey from their small town in northern Ontario, where they operated a small farm, to Toronto and from Toronto to Montréal. It was a long trip, and they were tired. Sommer could see it in her father's face.

Her mother broke into tears. "You've had enough education. It's time to come home."

"Come with me," said Sommer. Her eyes misted, and she knew she would break into tears if they carried on."

"Your mother is right, Sommer. Forget Germany. It's not a place for you, especially now."

"I had a letter from your aunt Gerda, who tells me the Jews are being rounded up and shipped in cattle cars to God only knows. Anyone who disagrees with Hitler and his Nazi party is marked and disappears. It is not a safe place for you, Sommer.

"I will be at a famous university where no harm can come to me." She stopped, not sure what to say next.

"That may be, Sommer, but I want to see you every morning when I wake up. I have mussed you. So much."

"After two years are up, I will come home to stay. But this, I think, I must do for myself. Just this once."

"So be it, Sommer. Surely, I do not need to warn you about drinking liquor. It makes you do crazy things sometimes," said her mother, casting a sidelong glance at her husband. "That includes letting your defences down and waking up in the morning with no recollection of what happened."

Her mother's washed-out blue eyes looked tired, and her greying hair was tied in a bun behind her head. She reached out and smoothed Sommer's long hair. She wanted to cry but knew intuitively that it was the wrong time and that she needed to be strong and show it.

Jacob Kappel, his face more lined now than she remembered, shook his head and looked away.

***

There was an air of excitement as she entered her cabin on the second level. She opened the porthole and looked out at the harbour as the Empress of England started to move, gradually picking up speed as it left the harbour area. An hour later, she went on deck to see her last glimpse of Canada. It was getting dark, and she shivered.

"First time leaving Canada," said the man standing beside her – an Englishman with a black mustache and smoking a pipe. "Tomorrow, we will be at sea with no land in sight." He relit his pipe with a lighter and smiled. "Don't know about you, but I'm going in. It's a bit chilly out here. Coming in?"

Sommer followed him into the ship's fast-food café. Straton Wilcox was at least a head taller than Sommer and seemed on good terms with about everyone. He pointed to a table beneath one of the café's lights. He sat opposite her. "My name's Straton, by the way, and you are?"

"Sommer." She eyed him wearily. "You seem to know everyone, Mr. Straton."

"Wilcox. My first name is Straton." He smiled, showing a dimple and bright dark brown eyes that seemed to smile when he talked. He was wearing an Irish tweed cap and a grey tweed jacket. "This is my fifth trip to Canada in the past year and my last, hopefully. You get to know people when you travel on the same ship after a while."

"Let me get you something, Mr. Wilcox," she said, rising and walking across the tiled floor to a do-it-yourself, where she unloaded three croissants and jam and poured two large mugs of tea. She placed them on a tray and set them on the table. The tables could easily seat three or four people and their tops shined in the reflection of the lights above them.

"I got you a croissant, too, Mr. Wilcox. I've heard about them and wanted to try them. This is my first time," she laughed.

"I'd feel more comfortable if you called me Straton."

He spoke with an educated voice and sounded a lot like one of the professors who taught English at McGill. Over the next few days, they saw a lot of each other at meals. Otherwise, Sommer kept to herself and the ship's library, where she looked for any German books or magazines. There was only one book – a copy of Goethe's poems, which she found haunting. Some of the lines echoed in her head. He could make German sound so beautiful. She shared supper with Straton most nights. He was the only person she knew on the boat, aside from a few friends he introduced her to.

She asked one of the waiters about him at breakfast on the day of their embarkation.

"No one seems to know much about him other than he seemed to spend a month in the U.S. and Canada four or five times this year. A refined gentleman in every regard."

"I hear we should dock shortly after lunch," said Straton as she sat beside him. Straton's face looked thinner, and his eyes looked tired. They didn't talk much. When they finished, Sommer noticed a number of the other travellers gathered their things together.

"I think it's time to go," said Sommer.

CHAPTER TWO

She lifted the receiver. "Miss Kappel?"

"Yes."

"My name is Myles Brookfield. Would it be convenient for you to see me today?"

She suddenly started breathing hard again. "What is this about, Mr. Brookfield?"

"We would like to make you an offer." A short pause. "What about it, Miss Kappel?" Brookfield had a deep, commanding voice that made her feel uncomfortable.

"We'll send a car for you. It will be at St. Ermines in an hour."

The line suddenly went dead. Sommer got out of bed slowly. Her back was sore, and it took her a few steps to feel better. She liked the room with its wide bed and thick comforters and the signs on them, the radio on the right side of her bed, and the black telephone on the left. The walls were green with yellow wooden trim and pictures of the English countryside and the Tower of London. She looked in the mirror of the dresser at the foot of her bed and made a face.

She wondered if it were safe to meet some man who telephones her out of the blue. She had an uneasy feeling about it somehow. She tried to apply the makeup her mother had given her, and her hands shook. This is stupid, she thought. She was smart, probably smarter than he was. She would have preferred if he had told her what it was about.

She got dressed and went down to the lobby ahead of

time but didn't feel comfortable sitting in the lobby by herself.

A man dressed in a charcoal-coloured suit approached her about 15 minutes later. "My name is Winton. I'm here to take you to your appointment with Mr. Brookfield. I'm your chauffeur," he added. He led the way, walking with a slight limp. He saw her looking at him. "A souvenir from the last war," he said with a laugh. He had deep blue eyes and dark hair with grey streaks and carried himself with a military bearing.

She followed him to the black Rolls parked outside. She sat in the back while he carried in a rolling commentary of the sights they were passing, like Trafalgar Square and the Parliament buildings. He wheeled into a side street, stopping a few feet from the main street. He got out and opened the door.

"Do you know what this is all about? I have to admit, I'm a little nervous. "She could hear the anxiety in her voice.

"Mr. Brookfield asked me to take you directly to his office. It's a bit of a warren in here," he added as they entered a building that had seen better times. They mounted the stairs to the second floor. "It can be confusing the first time you come here."

They stopped at Room 234. Winton opened the door and ushered her inside. "Miss Kappel to see Myles."

The lone secretary rose and rapped on the door to the left of her desk. A tall man with a cigar and a glass of brandy opened the door. He had long chestnut hair and a dimple that deepened when he smiled. The dimple reminded her of Straton. He waved her in, held out her hand, and held hers in both his hands as he helped her to a plush chair in front of his desk. He sat in the other next to her.

He looked at her for a few seconds, rose from his chair, cigar and brandy in his hands, and sat beside her. "I hate talking behind a desk."

Sommer had never seen so many books in an office before. Except for the window behind his desk, both walls on either side were overflowing with books. A large framed picture of Churchill was on the wall next to the door.

"Like books? I have never been able to part with any of them. There's one," he said, getting to the wall left of his desk, "is my prize. It was printed in 1699. *History of Rome and Greece*. Here, have a look." He passed the brown-covered book to her. Sommer's hands shook. "I felt the same way before I became acquainted with it."

Sommer held it in her hands for a minute before opening it and seeing the printing date and the dedication. She skimmed through it, looking at one of the drawings originally pasted into the book and the dedication again. She passed the book back to him. "Why do you really want to see me about Mr. Brookfield?"

"I understand your parents are German and emigrated to Canada from Engen, South Germany, after the Great War. And that you can speak German with a South German accent."

"What exactly is this about?"

"I also understand that you will be attending Bonn University." Another pause. "We would like you to be our eyes and ears and tell us what's happening in Germany while you're attending university."

"Are you asking me to spy?"

Brookfield shook his head.

"Because I know absolutely nothing about this kind of work," Sommer said. "And I'm sure I'd disappoint you greatly. To be honest with you, I'm not sure what this is all about."

Brookfield lost his smile. "You're a very intelligent lady, Sommer. Before I go any further, you must promise never to reveal what I am about to tell you to another living soul."

Sommer nodded and felt her hair with her left hand.

"We have every belief that Germany will attempt to invade its neighbours before this decade is out and trigger another world war. We need people on the ground to tell us what's happening – to act as kind of an advance warning signal if you will, so that we're not caught with our pants down."

Sommer listened with an open mouth. She couldn't believe what she was hearing. Another world war. No. It was impossible. Then she recalled her parents' warning that things were unsettling in Germany now and to be very careful about everything she did and said. But studying under the great Dr. Albrecht was something she just couldn't give up, no matter what. She had the feeling she was on the brink of something monumental. She didn't know what exactly other than it was going to change her life forever. At that moment, she understood what Professor Weber was trying to tell her.

Brookfield watched her carefully. "You don't need to make up your mind now. All I ask is that you come and see me when you return from Bonn and give me your answer then. Deal?"

"Deal."

"Before you leave, I would like you to meet two of my operatives." He pushed a red button next to his phone.

The door opened. Straton Wilcox and a blonde-haired woman entered smiling.

"I believe you know Straton. He travels between North America and London quite frequently for us. I asked him to be on the lookout for you on the Empress and ensure you reached your hotel. St. Ermines, I believe. A grand old place. The blond lady with him is Vera Winters, who teaches at a Berlin upper-class girl's college. A number of German army officers send their daughters for a classical education.

Vera reached out and shook her hand. "I teach Latin and Classics. I hear you're a whiz at math. We must talk sometime."

"We understand that you're heading for Dover tomorrow morning and thought you might join Vera and me for a tour of London," said Straton. He glanced at Myles, who shook his head.

"Maybe next time. Tonight I have to see the minister, for God alone knows what."

Everyone laughed, and Sommer immediately felt better.

"Too bad about Myles," says Straton. "He's the life of any party."

"Where are you staying?" said Vera.

"St. Ermines."

Vera laughed. "Everybody stays there. I think he owns shares in it."

"In case you forgot, I am still here. Sounds like a great evening. The three of you get moving. I've got work to do before I see the minister."

Sommer looked around at the shops and the constant movement of people. Strange place, she thought, for recruiting spies. In the foyer, Straton snapped his fingers and Arthur, Sommer's chauffeur, suddenly appeared.

"What would you like to see first?" said Arthur.

"How about the Tower of London? It's getting closing time," added Straton.

"Charles Dickens' favourite tavern is on the way. Should we stop for a pint? Who knows, if we're lucky, we'll be at one of the tables where Dickens sat."

"Another time, Arthur. The Tower is something most tourists want to see," said Straton.

The Tower of London was about to close when they arrived. Straton talked to one of the guards, dressed in red and carrying an ornamental spear. His eyes seemed to glitter when he looked at you, and his white mustache curled upwards when he talked.

"Where was Anne Boleyn's kept?"

The guide nodded and led the way. Her cell was barely large enough to contain a bed and a place to wash. "She was able to see them building the platform where she would be beheaded from this window," said Stratton.

Sommer shivered. She had a romantic notion about Anne Boleyn in high school. The cold reality of the stones that surrounded her cell changed that in a hurry, and she began to understand the awful power of despots and how it could ruin lives with a twist of the mouth.

"The poor woman."

Next, the crown jewels. It was coming onto seven when their guide took them upstairs and the way out. "I think it's high time we stopped for dinner," said Vera. Then turning to Sommer: "Perhaps the next time we meet, we can go shopping together."

Sommer smiled but did not respond. She was thinking of her mother and how she darned and remade their clothes to save money.

Two hours later, tired and worn out, Arthur took Sommer back to St. Ermines. "I'll be waiting for you here at six sharp tomorrow morning to take you to the train station for Dover."

The outing was different from anything she had ever known, and she suddenly felt guilty. In her room, she knelt to offer her rosary for her mother. She knelt and started, "I believe...

***

Sommer was packed, checked out and ready before six when Arthur appeared in the lobby. It was deserted, except for the odd person checking out and two maids changing the flowers and sweeping the floor with an old vacuum. The clerk was standing behind the desk, covering his mouth when he yawned. Arthur saluted and took her suitcase, the one her father bought in Germany to come to Canada. Vera

Winters was already in the car and opened the rear door for her.

"Myles asked me to keep you company as far as Germany, where I will take a different train to Berlin, and you will head south to Bonn. He thinks of everything," she laughed, a deep, throaty laugh that made you laugh with her. She had fox fur around her shoulders and wore a light blue wool suit and a cap.

"Except for a departure at this ungodly hour." Then, looking at Sommer: "I normally walk for an hour every morning before breakfast. Rain or shine."

Vera talked non-stop to the train station. Sommer could see Arthur smiling as Vera rolled from one topic to another without stopping and winked.

"What car and compartment are you located in?"

Sommer handed Vera the ticket from her package. "Too bad. You're in an entirely different car." Then, as an afterthought: "Hopefully, we'll be located in the same car and compartment when we board the train in France for Germany. Maybe we'll be able to lunch together," she said, kissing Sommer's cheek and almost falling on her high heels as she tried to steady herself as she mounted the stairs and disappeared into her car.

"A lucky break," said Arthur with a hidden smile. "Let me help you find your car." Two minutes later, she was mounting the stairs and waving to say goodbye to Arthur. There were three others. A clergyman, who had his coat collar up and his hands in his brown coat; a tall young woman, sitting opposite the clergyman, wearing bright red lipstick and rouge and wearing a floral dress; a middle-aged man, wearing a grey suit, a crisp white shirt, a college tie, with dark piercing eyes and dark hair turning grey at the temples, who kept smoke one cigarette after another, who sat beside the clergyman, who had his head turned away from him.

***

"Are you hungry?" Vera demanded when we met after leaving the train. "I'm dying of hunger."

Sommer looked around to see other passengers boarding the boat. The sea looked choppy, and the sun, bright and glorious, was already past noon.

"Let's go," said Vera, pulling Sommer's arm. It took 10 minutes to board and head for the ship's cafeteria. Vera ordered for both of them: Bacon and egg sandwiches and coffee. She was right about the sandwiches, but the coffee was the strongest Sommer had ever tasted. A young woman behind the counter was trying to put a scoop of ice cream into a cone without success as a young man kept chiding her.

The ship suddenly hit rough water, and her sandwich slid down the table before she had a chance to grab it. The woman with the monkey fell against an older man with silver hair and a ruddy face who was trying to light his pipe.

Vera talked to everyone she was close to, laughing at their jokes and getting to know them. There was the woman with a monkey. Vera reached out to pat it, but the money reached out and grabbed her earring. Vera rubbed her ear as the woman scolded her monkey and demanded he surrender the ring. The men were laughing, and Vera joined them, shaking her head

A few hours later, when they boarded the train for Germany. "You probably think I'm a scatterbrain," said Vera, putting their suitcases above their seats in the compartment. One last one, a small carrying case, was causing her a problem, but she kept pounding at it until it finally found a place beside Sommer's suitcase.

"It's calculated. I did this little demonstration to show you that people are not always what they seem. Usually, people write me off as a threat and tell me things they wouldn't tell ordinarily tell a stranger. Would you guess by the way I just acted, I was a British spy? It serves my purpose."

It was an eye-opener for Sommer. She suddenly thought of Brookfield and understood his cleverness for the first time.

CHAPTER THREE

The train slowed as it approached the railway terminal at Bonn. Sommer opened her purse and re-read the letter from the university for the 20th time, informing her that she would be met at the train station by someone from the university. When the train jerked to a stop, she grabbed her purse and bag, made her way down the aisle, and waited until the seven people in front of her left the train before stepping slowly down the stair to the platform. She looked around for someone who looked as though they came from a university.

She missed Vera's company and her cleverness. Before they parted, Sommer began calling her the Chameleon Lady. She always had an answer. She grabbed her purse over her shoulder, picked up her bag, and headed for the station to wait for her contact there. She was met at the door by a young woman, holding up Sommer's picture in her left hand. Sommer nodded, and she suddenly found herself being hugged by two young women. "I'm Gretchen Moller," said the taller one. "The university has asked me to take you to your room at our dorm."

There was another young woman beside her. "My name is Katrina Meer." She had an angelic face and looked like a carbon copy of Gretchen in how she dressed and walked, only shorter. The other young women ignored her when they discovered she wanted to become a nun, even though Gretchen invited Katrina to her parties.

Gretchen threw back her head defiantly and smiled at Sommer with hypnotic blue eyes. "Your room is on the same floor as ours. Can't wait to have parties together." She had a special way of walking that was suggestive and enjoyed a generous allowance from her parents that made the other women in the dorm envious.

"Our dorm is a 10-minute walk from the university. You'll love it here. And I'm not outgoing," said Katrina in a soft voice. "Before the others tell you, I would like to become a nun."

"Then why are you here?" said Sommer.

"I keep telling her she's crazy," said Gretchen, buttoning up her light brown coat. "She's a beautiful young woman who should live life to the fullest."

Sommer didn't respond. She looked at Katrina and touched her hand. "I understand."

The room was a surprise – a large bed, a window that overlooked a garden filled with fall blooms, a small desk with a lamp and a picture of Bonn University's Science Building over the foot of her bed.

They helped Sommer unpack. "What's this?" said Gretchen.

"A brick of maple sugar. My mother must have packed it without my knowledge. Try it with your coffee. You'll love it."

"We shall. Just as soon as we finish helping you unpack."

***

"I was expecting you at 3.30." When she entered his office, Professor Albrecht was writing a math equation on a moveable chalkboard to the right of his desk. His desk was

19

piled with books and papers and a large glass ashtray with three cigar butts. In the left corner behind his desk was a large glove of the sky and in the other corner, a large telescope. There was a single high-backed chair in front of his desk. She stood, but he never invited her to sit down.

No one ever told her about Professor Albrecht's temper or obsession with time. She put it down to his age. He was in his late 60s, but you'd never guess it, except for his white hair, faded blue eyes and protruding stomach. There was a time when his voice commanded attention but less so now, despite his brilliance. He brushed off his tweed jacket and sat down behind his desk.

"According to your friend, Professor Fuhrman, you're a very gifted student. I must warn you. Have a look at the problem on the chalkboard beside me. It's difficult. Do you think you can solve it?

Sommer smiled as she glanced at the board, "No one can. There are a few incorrect entries. But, of course, you already knew that."

Professor Albrecht suddenly became very serious. "You are undoubtedly a very intelligent young woman but don't let that go to your head. The other students in your class are also very intelligent. You all have much to learn this term, and some of you will not be here next year."

He stood and shook her hand in a formal manner. "Good luck, Sommer Kappel. Make us all proud." He turned and suddenly asked her what she thought was her biggest gift in mathematics.

"Solving complex equations other people find hard to do."

"It is mine, too," he said with a smile.

There was a knock at the door, and two younger men entered. Professor Albrecht smiled. "Let me introduce our latest student. Sommer Kappel from Canada, Professor Nikolas Zimmerman, who lectures on logic, and Professor

Marius Klessner, our expert on Quantum Mechanics. You'll be taking classes with them. You never know when you will need their knowledge."

***

Back at the dorm, one of Gretchen's parties was in full swing. Someone had brought a bottle of brandy, which was added to the coffee. Sommer and Katrina found a quiet corner to drink their coffee. There were calls for Gretchen, dressed in a tight-fitting outfit that showed off her figure, to do her imitation of Marlene Dietrich. She is reluctant, but someone starts singing one of her popular songs, and Gretchen joins in with the words – in a voice you'd swear it was Marlene Dietrich in person. It ended with enthusiastic clapping and shouts for more, and Gretchen lifted her leg on the seat of a chair and showed her leg's calf.

There were cheers for more and more. Then, suddenly, in the silence that followed.

"Heil Hitler."

The music and the laughter suddenly stopped. The faces around Sommer suddenly looked strained, and many had lost their colour.

"Hitler can be good for Germany. We'd be begging for crumbs for other countries if it weren't for him. Everyone is working again, and everyone has money again and no infla-tion. Most of all, he has given us hope to dare again," said a young man standing in the centre of the room surrounded by the others. His suit jacket and trousers were cut in the latest fashion. His blond hair was cut short, and his bright blue eyes seemed to take in everyone at once.

"But at what cost?"

"Who cares?"

A young Jewish woman, whose room was on the floor below, quietly got up and headed for the door, where Gretchen caught her. "Where are you going?"

"Who cares," said a second voice. "She's a stinking Jew,

and she doesn't matter."

Gretchen stared him down. "I think she does."

Sommer was surprised at how authoritative Gretchen sounded when she was aroused. She smiled at Katrina, who squeezed her hand.

"That young woman was here at my invitation and as my guest. I think it is time to say good night. We had a wonderful thing going on tonight, but you had to ruin it. If you don't like my friends, your absence will not be missed."

The room slowly emptied. The young woman hugged her and wiped the tears forming in Gretchen's eyes. It was a Gretchen Sommer had never seen before.

***

There weren't a lot of parties after that — just a big one at Christmas, which was held at the university's gymnasium. The men brought the beer, and the women, sandwiches and other goodies.

The men were already into the punch by the time they arrived. Sommer couldn't believe what she was seeing as the table filled with sandwiches, sausages and even a big ham, with a chef to slice it along with potatoes. There was a big Christmas tree in the centre, and someone was playing Christmas carols on the piano.

There was a lot of laughter, and one of the men was lighting candles encased in pine wreaths and singing carols as he did each. Sommer looked around the room. There was a huge fire sizzling in the great fireplace in the centre of the back wall, and red and green streams strung diagonally across the room.

Gretchen took Sommer and Katrina to a pastry table, where they gorged on the cake and other pastries. Sommer sat with Katrina on a bench near the fireplace, giggling and watching one huge log after another send flames to new heights. The men gathered around them and started to sing to the ladies, accompanied by a piano near the fireplace. There was a lot of laughter with the men inviting the women to dance with them under the mistletoe.

When it was time to leave, Gretchen bought four boxes of different pastries to take home with them. "We'll bring three of them to the Christmas party. Since the three of us will be staying over for Christmas, the other one is for us, Christmas morning," she said as they headed out into the cold.

Gretchen was wearing a light coat but didn't seem bothered by the chill. Sommer buttoned up her jacket, and her face became reddish from the north wind that sent shivers up her body. Katrina folded a scarf around her mouth and throat and shivered.

They sang Christmas carols and laughed all the way back to their dorm.

Sommer never felt happier and made a mental note to find some small gifts for Gretchen and Katrina.

About 20 other women from the dorm joined them, singing Christmas carols all the way home. One of the policemen guiding traffic doffed his hat as they passed, shouting *Frohe Weihnachten*.

When they returned to their dorm, the three of them decided to sleep in Gretchen's room. "I've been saving this," she said, producing a bottle of Champagne from her icebox. She quietly poured three glasses and passed one to Katrina, who shook her head.

"Katrina and I do not drink alcohol. You know that, Gretchen."

"In 30 minutes, it will be Christmas. Let us celebrate Christmas in grand style. Who knows if the three of us will celebrate Christmas ever again?" She pressed the glasses to them.

They raised their glasses and said in a loud voice: *Frohe Weihnachten*.

Gretchen put her mattress on the floor, got two blankets from the bed, and covered them. "Good night ladies and *Frohe Weihnachen*."

Gretchen hogged all the quilts, and Katrina got up, went to her room, and returned with quilts for her and Sommer. They finally got to sleep around two.

Sommer and Katrina woke up before Gretchen and started to hum *Ave Maria*. Gretchen woke up, and they hugged each other. "I've got something for you," she said, passing a wrapped gift to Katrina and one to Sommer. "Open them."

"Katrina and I pooled our money and brought you a gift from the both of us," said Sommer.

Katrina passed a small box to Gretchen. "Now it's your turn."

"Gold earrings," she said, holding them up to the light, "I will wear them at special events only and think of this Christmas and you both every time I put them on.

"And thank you for our gifts," said Sommer. But now, Katrina and I must get ready to go to mass. We'll celebrate when we come back."

"Wait, and I'll go with you."

They met five minutes later at the entrance. "It's starting to snow," said Gretchen as they started. Gretchen grabbed their arms. "This is the best Christmas I've ever had."

CHAPTER THREE

Gerda knew it was Sommer as soon as she stepped off the train. Sommer had a lot of her mother's features, and Gerda would know her anywhere. She started waving her arms and calling out her name when Sommer headed in her direction. Gerda hugged her for almost a minute.

"I have a taxi waiting for us," she said, putting her arms around Sommer. "You and your mother are the only family I have left, and I want nothing to happen to you in Germany." She looked around her before continuing in a whisper. "Germany is going through a difficult period at this time and doing things to its citizens that will haunt us for decades. Enough," she said. "Our taxi awaits."

Back at her home, she got Sommer a cup of tea and showed her a picture of her son, who was arrested for belonging to a protest group and has never been seen since. Gerda does not know if he is still alive or dead.

"Tell me about you. I know your mother is very proud of you."

Sommer tells her about her math scholarship to study under a famous mathematics professor at Bonn University. "He's very demanding and makes you stretch yourself in ways you never thought possible. I owe him much for the knowledge I learned under him."

She looked around Gerda's parlour – a cuckoo clock on the wall on the right side of the fireplace; the lace curtains that had not been washed in years; the fireplace, made from stones for their farm; the dark varnished rocking chair; and her threadbare sofa and needlework canvass of a cavalier sitting on a bench in a garden. The worn linoleum floor shone in the light from the window on the opposite side of the room.

"Have you encountered many Nazis?"

"At dorm parties, but no one pays much attention to them."

"And the girls you room with?"

"I've never heard them speak and can't offer any opinion. If anything, I'd say they think Hitler is a very evil man and stirs up trouble for Jews."

"Do not say such things, Sommer. Walls have ears, and there is no shortage of tattletale ears in Engen. She looked around in a way that suggested she feared as though something was wrong, and her actions reminded someone of someone who was no longer with them.

Gerda patted her hand. "I want you to stay with me for a while, Sommer. When do you have to go back?"

"At the end of the week. We have finals the week after."

Gerda went to the kitchen and started making coffee for them. Sommer followed her and sat on the side of her table, covered by a worn cloth. The window and door at the rear of the kitchen showed the back porch.

Gerda's hands shook as she brought Sommer's coffee over to her and tried to smile. The lines on her aunt's face were more pronounced in the light streaming in from the side windows over the sink.

Sommer waited until she sat and reached out for her hand. "What's wrong?"

Gerda broke into tears. Sommer rose and held her in her arms until she felt better.

She took a sip of coffee and set her cup down. "I don't know how quite to tell you this."

"Just start."

"Come with me."

Her aunt led her to her bedroom, where a baby was lying in the centre of her bed.

"It can't be yours. Whose is it?"

"About a month ago, I discovered a young woman hiding in my woodshed. She was pregnant. "She asked me if I was Gerda Weber. I nod. *Thank God I've found you*, she whispered. *I need your help. My time is near to give birth. Can you help me?*

"I brought her inside and helped her deliver her baby. A boy, when I suggested going for the help of a midwife, she became alarmed. She said she was Jewish and her baby would die."

She paused to take a mouthful of coffee and then started to cry. "It was only after she told me she was my son's wife and that it was his son."

"Where is the mother now?"

"Dead. She would go out at night and steal milk from peoples' doorsteps for the baby. Two weeks ago, she did not come home, and I heard stories about some woman trying to steal milk and who was shot dead by a policeman. I haven't slept at all since then. I don't know what to do. Your mother said you are very smart. Tell me what to do." Then, as an afterthought, "I would like to bring him up myself."

"The one thing I learned in mathematics. There is always an answer if you look for it. I am going out for a short walk to think. I will be back in less than an hour. I don't want you to leave your grandson by himself. You never know with babies."

Sommer left her aunt staring at her coffee and walked out into the cold March wind in her face. She walked on the cobblestone street and passed several houses, some painted yellow or green with white trimmings, towards the church. Sommer went inside. The interior had a haunting beauty about it she would always remember. The kneelers felt hard on her knees, and Sommer shifted them as she tried to pray. Fifteen minutes later, she was walking back when an idea struck her.

"I have an idea that may work. Leave a note for your milkman that you have a guest from Bonn, your niece, staying with her baby for a month. Would it be possible for him to leave extra milk for the baby?"

"But what happens when you go back?"

"Tell him I have returned to Bonn, leaving you to look after her baby."

***

The next few months flew by without incident after she returned. There was the odd letter from her aunt about the baby and how she had to make a crib for him because he could now roll off the bed. There were also letters from her mother about how she missed her and was counting the days before she came back to them.

At Gretchen's parties, she met other students from the same dorm and got to know them by their first names. She studied hard and did everything in her power to please Professor Albrecht, who never seemed to be satisfied with anything she did, even though she thought it was better than the others.

"He's taken a special interest in you, stretching you to your outer limits," said Gretchen when she broke into tears on the way back to their dorm. Gretchen was in the same class and one of the brighter students. "You're far beyond anyone else in our class. You are his star student. And, yes, he is tough on you. I'm surprised you didn't figure that out for yourself.

Spring came and went, and the term was nearing an end. To her surprise, she also enjoyed the lectures of Prof. Klessner on Quantum Mechanics, especially when he talked about how they related to physics and math.

***

The big night everyone had been talking about for weeks finally arrived. The Fuhrer was coming to the university to give an address.

"You're coming, aren't you?" said Gretchen. They say everyone goes wild when they hear him speak, and a military band will play marches and Nazi music. It's going to be just wonderful. And who knows who we're likely to meet there."

They left an hour earlier, just in time to get seats midway in the Great Hall. Gretchen's eyes were everywhere. She caught the look of a young soldier, but Gretchen turned away.

"She's after the young officer she met at a party two months ago. She's been pining for him every day since then," said Katrina.

Thirty minutes later, the auditorium was packed, and people were standing in the aisles. The whole room rose in a frenzy the moment Hitler appeared on the stage. A solid row of soldiers armed with machine guns stood below the stage with orders to kill anyone who tried to get on the stage.

There was magic in the air as soon as he started speaking. The fire in his voice carried a conviction Sommer had never heard before. By the time he had finished, there was no doubt in his mind or your mind that Germany was about to rise from the ashes like a great phoenix.

At the party afterwards, Sommer noticed a young man with burning eyes staring at her. He wore a Nazi armband and waved at her. Sommer looked away. A few minutes later, she could feel his presence. Then, without a word, he pulled her to her feet and put his arms around her. She was gliding over the floor with him even though she had never danced before.

"You're quite sure of yourself."

He laughed. "Not really. I was shaking in my boots when I walked over to your table." Then, when the music stopped, he kissed her in front of everyone.

Sommer kept thinking about it all the way back to their dorm. She didn't even know his name. She had never been kissed before, and she liked it. An hour later, she pulled the covers over her head and drifted off.

CHAPTER FOUR

Sommer blinked. There he was, sitting three rows away from her, except she had never seen him before. For the first time, she noticed his curly light brown hair and blue eyes. He saw her looking at him and smiled back. She can feel her face burn.

Professor Albrecht stopped mid-sentence. "We are here to study mathematics, not to make eyes at each other. If you cannot keep your mind on mathematics, I suggest you find another course of study."

Gretchen, who sat opposite her, hid a smile behind her hand.

Professor Albrecht, who liked to wear a long, black taler, pulled the corners to his throat and went on to the complex equation he had written on the chalkboard. Two other students beat her to it and by the time, they were done, the young man was heading out the door. Sommer planned to stay a few minutes after the class was dismissed to apologize to Professor Albrecht.

He waited for her a block away and spotted her immediately in the rows of faces that emerged from the main exit. She had a special way of walking that made her stand out in any crowd. He waved to her, and without thinking, she waved back.

"Before you say another word, tell me your name."

"Felix Wagner. I know who you are. Anything else?"

"How could you possibly spot me in that crowd?"

"You have a distinct way of walking."

"You mean there's something wrong with the way I walk?"

"No, it's just different, and I love it."

They were walking towards her dorm when he invited her for coffee. "There's a Kaffee place right next to your dorm."

The coffee house was busier than usual, and they had to wait for almost 30 minutes for a table. "What about Professor Albrecht today?"

"He's a bit gruff at times," said Felix, "but he's a genius, no doubt about that, and loves people who share his passion. I don't have your abilities when it comes to math. In fact, I've been thinking about dropping out."

"Watch your step," he said as they stepped down the recessed floor, which creaked when you walked on it. The room smelled of pastries and coffee and the sound of loud voices. A young woman, wearing her blond hair in a net, and a flashing smile, escorted them to a table near the diamond-shaped windows near the end of the room.

Felix held out her chair.

"I could help you, "

Felix shook his head, sipped his coffee, and looked up to see two friends enter. He waved them over.

"So that's why you've disappeared on us," said the tall, clean-shaven one.

"You could at least introduce us," said the other.

"My name is Sommer Kappel. I am studying mathematics at Bonn University under Professor Albrecht."

"So that's how you connected," said the latter one. "My name is Anton, and my anxious friend here is Lukas."

Felix didn't know quite what to say. "Great rally the other night."

"Germany has been transformed under Hitler. He is another Frederich the Great, and Germany is in great need of him now," said Anton, winking at Sommer and pushing his light brown hair from his eyes.

"Glad we ran into you, Felix. We're joining the SS. Why not join us."

"Now is not a good time for me right now, Anton. Perhaps later."

They looked at Sommer and smiled.

They were without words as he saw her to her dorm. He was about to turn when he said: "The three of us have been together since we started school. I have an uneasy feeling that Germany will be at war soon and that I should be with them."

***

Gretchen knocked on her door and peeked in." Party time. Just you, me and Katrina. My room at 7 p.m. Be there." She glanced at her wristwatch. "Five minutes from now."

Sommer was at Gretchen's door five minutes later with a box of cookies. She knew Gretchen had a sweet tooth and that it would please her.

Gretchen had her mind on other things. "What's he like, Sommer?

"Two of his friends are joining the SS and want him to join them. He's thinking about it."

"Forget that for the moment. I have to ask. Is this the first time you've been kissed?"

Sommer nodded. "And probably the last."

Katrina sat in silence, feeling like an outsider for the first time.

"I came here to study mathematics, and that's what I

need to concentrate on now and in the coming weeks."

"When are you meeting next?"

"He didn't say."

That came two days later when he waved to her from the next block. "Ever been to an opera?" He didn't wait for her answer. "I have two tickets to Wagner's opera, *Tannhauser*. You'll love it."

"What about my books?"

"We'll drop them off at your dorm, have a fast supper and take the tram to the opera house."

They arrived at the theatre where the opera was being held. The movie screen at the centre of the theatre had been rolled up, and the orchestra pit players were tuning their instruments. It was like music to Sommer. She looked around with mounting excitement. The doors were framed in curtains, and the seats were a plumb shade. The aisles were carpeted in a brown shade with scenes showing singers and actors. Ushers in dark blue uniforms and flashlights walked up and down the aisles, directing people to their seats. The theatre was filling up quickly, and the noise level was rising by the minute. Her heart was pounding. She glanced at Felix, who was sitting back and taking everything in.

The orchestra was tuning up as they found their seats at the back of the theatre. Once the opera started, Sommer knew this was something she would love forever and wondered why no one had ever told her about it. She had never heard a tenor voice before and how it could take your breath away.

"It was composed by Richard Wagner," he whispered.

She nodded and touched his hand. "Later."

Sommer was silent as they walked back to her dorm. The music was still in her head, and she could still hear the tenor. It made her heart race. She knew she would remember this night for the rest of her life.

Felix watched her out of the corner of his eye. "It's time

to come back to reality," he said, leading her to the Koffee House across from her dorm.

"Thank you for tonight, Felix. You've opened up a new world for me." She was sitting opposite him, reaching across the table and squeezing his hand.

The moment was broken by two brown shirts going from table to table and asking people for their papers.

"They're looking for Jews," said Felix. "You're not Jewish, are you?"

Sommer shook her head. "And if I were?"

The two brown shirts, both in their early 20s, towered over their table and asked for their papers. They studied Sommer's papers for a few minutes. "How long do you plan to stay in Germany, fraulein?"

"Next year, when the spring term comes to an end."

He returned her papers and turned his attention to Felix. "Why aren't you enlisted? Got a rich father? We need true Germans; Germany needs all her sons to answer the call."

CHAPTER FIVE

Gretchen and Katrina joined Sommer for an opera night in Flex's rooms.

"How can you afford all this?" said Gretchen, inspecting his small kitchen, his bedroom and large living room, returning to examine his record collection. "Do you have Italian opera as well? I love *La Bohème*. Do you have it?"

"There are a couple of arias, one with the great Italian tenor. They're in the other stack."

Gretchen, Katrina and Sommer sat on his blue-covered sofa while Felix sat on the floor in front of them. He never looked better than he did at that moment, thought Sommer. His wavy brown hair shone in the light from the arched window to his left, and his eyes seemed to dance in time with the music. He wore a red sweater over a white shirt.

Katrina eyed the freshly cut pineapple plate and whipped cream bowl behind him. "I've never tried pineapple before," she said, her bright dark eyes already tasting it.

Felix looked around. "See what a poor host I am. I completely forgot to put the coffee on." He rose and headed for the kitchen. "In the meantime, why don't you look over the record labels and see what you like to hear? It's not often that we encounter people who like classical music."

He returned a few minutes later to add chunks of pineapple and heaping spoon-filled whipped cream that swirled into each bowl. "Does anyone like Cognac with their coffee?"

Gretchen nodded. "You never did tell me how you came to afford all this." She looked around his apartment to emphasize her question.

"No secret. My father happens to be a very rich merchant in Munich, and I am his only son. He refuses me nothing." He smiled and poured some Cognac into her cup.

Katrina didn't look up until she had finished her pineapple. Felix filled her dish with pineapple and whipped cream before passing it back to her.

"How about you, Gretchen or you, Sommer."

Gretchen, like Sommer, shook her head. "My father is also a merchant," she began, "and a member of the Nazi Party."

Everything seemed to change from that night on.

***

It was the week of the final term, and everyone was cramming for their finals when something happened that brought everything all home to Sommer.

Katrina and Sommer took the same course in philosophy with Professor Hoffmann when a squad of brown shirts suddenly entered the classroom, slamming the door behind them with a violent crash that made everyone in the room jump.

"You," said one of the brown shirts. "Yes, you. Are you Hoffmann, the Jew?"

"We don't want to wait for an answer," said another brown shirt.

"I am. But I am not a Jew. I am a Catholic. Ask my parish priest. You can't go by a name."

Everyone believed he was Jewish, even his students.

"I go to mass regularly. Please, I beg you, ask my parish priest."

One of the brown shirts swung his club and hit him on the side of the head. Blood ran down the side of his face as they dragged him out of the room, laughing and clubbing him a couple more times for good measure. Sommer watched from the window as they threw him into the back of a van with bars on it.

The other students quickly joined her to see what was happening. Some were appalled at what they were witnessing. Others began to clap and chant: "Germany for Aryans. They zeroed in on Sommer. "That includes you, too, fraulein. You are Aryan and German. Join us." They surrounded her and kept chanting. Sommer covered her ears with her hands and closed her eyes.

Felix stopped him without thinking. "Back off." There was no mistaking that he meant it. They scattered around the lecture room, singing Germany is for Aryans. One of the chanters aimed his fist at Felix, who ducked, and threw him to the ground. "I said Back Off, and I mean it. Back Off."

One of them stood up to Felix and tried to stare him down. "Everyone has something to hide, and that includes you, Wagner. We won't forget tonight or what we owe you."

Sommer cried all the way to her dorm. Felix put his arm around her to comfort her. He held her at the door and kissed her tonight, running his hands through her hair.

***

After that, Sommer and Felix kept to themselves, going to Kaffee shops or listening to classical music in his apartment.

Professor Hoffmann surfaced in many of their conversations. "If that is the Third Reich, I want none of it," the professor was often heard saying.

Felix put his arm around her. "It's part of the price we Germans must pay to be respected by our peers again. I know the Jews are being unfairly treated."

"Convenient scapegoats, if that's what you mean."

"For us, Sommer, the Third Reich is everything, and

each of us, including you, has a role to play to see that it will last 1,000 years." He paused, unsure how she would take what he was going to say. "I have to be honest with you. I feel very guilty about not enlisting with my friends."

"But surely not the SS."

"Maybe I can convince them to join the Wehrmacht instead."

Sommer sat back, no longer feeling as sure of him as she had been.

"Have a Cognac with me," he said, pouring it into her coffee. "Smell it before you drink it. And be forewarned, it's strong."

He was right. It does have a wonderful aroma, Sommer thought as she finished the cup. She held it out to him. "I would like another."

"Cognac as well?"

She nodded and smiled for the first time since they sat down. Felix leaned across the table and kissed her again.

Later, they went back to his apartment to listen to classical music. They sat down on the floor as he selected Beethoven's *Emperor Concerto* to show her that "not all of us are barbarians."

He poured them another coffee and Cognac. They were sitting against the sofa and listening to the music. "Beethoven could have been a great mathematician."

When she woke up in the morning, she saw him asleep next to her.

***

It was three weeks later when Professor Albrecht announced that Sommer had made the highest marks of any student he taught. It was also the same day she realized she was pregnant. Her first instinct was to tell Felix after class. He would be waiting for her. She spent many of her nights with him at his apartment now and loved his cooking.

The sight of someone being thrown into a police van

made her almost sick. It was the final straw. She knew she had to leave Germany and would not tell Felix she was pregnant. All she knew was that she had to go now.

What would she tell him? She would say her mother had mailed her to come home as soon as possible because her father had a bad heart attack and wanted to see her before he died.

Felix had news of his own. He waited until after supper, and as they shared a coffee and Cognac, he announced in a soft voice: "I've enlisted in the SS with my friends. I am very, very sorry to hear about your father." Then, after a pause, "When will you be coming back?"

"Not sure. It depends on my father."

She rose and left him sitting there.

CHAPTER SIX

"So you've come back to us, hopefully with a decision," said Brookfield. He sat back and spun the large globe beside his desk with a whack of his hand.

"How did you know?"

"I can see it in your eyes, Sommer."

"I've seen enough to stop me from being an innocent bystander."

Brookfield sensed there was something more and did not comment.

"I'm also pregnant. The father is a German student who decided to join the SS the day before I left."

Brookfield nodded knowingly. He had a broad face, one that crinkled when he laughed. There was a scent around him that reminded her of his books. "Have you really read all of them?"

He nodded and smiled at her again. "Are they seeing to you properly at St. Ermines?"

Sommer nodded. "The inciting incident that brought me here is seeing what they did to one of my professors. They accused him of being a Jew and struck him on the head with their clubs. The side of his face was bleeding as they dragged him to a van with bars."

She held her face in her hands for a few seconds. "All because Professor Hoffman was suspected of being a Jew. He told them he wasn't a Jew over and over, but they weren't listening. They didn't care."

"And your baby?"

"I didn't want my baby born in a country like that. My mother used to say: Evil spirits walk among us. I understood what she meant that day and knew I had to leave. I would like my baby born in England."

Brookfield reached out for her hand. "Not in Canada?"

"My mother would die if she knew I was pregnant and had no husband."

"If you haven't seen a doctor yet, I have an old friend from my Cambridge days who may be able to help you. He's regarded as the best baby doctor in Britain. I'll call and schedule an appointment with him if you wish."

"I would appreciate that."

"Then leave it in my hands. My assistant will give you the address." When he returned, he added: "Can you make it this afternoon? Say 3 p.m."

Sommer nodded and lowered her eyes, surprised she was able to speak so bluntly about being pregnant to a man old enough to be her father.

"And have you thought about where you'll stay while waiting for the baby to be born?"

"I haven't thought that far ahead," she said, drawn by

the smell of his books. It made her feel comfortable like she was again in an academic environment.

"I have an old family friend who would love your company. She lives in a small village called Shere in Surrey. I'll ring her this afternoon and tell her you'll be staying with her for a while. Go back to St. Ermines, pack your suitcase, and take the train to Shere. There's one at 6. Knowing Perdita, she'll probably have supper waiting for you."

***

Dr. Thomas Regan had a long face. "I don't have good news for you, Mrs. Kappel. There might be a problem with the birth."

"In what way?"

"The way your baby is positioned in your uterus. Often these things solve themselves, but I wanted you to be aware of it in case it doesn't right itself."

Dr. Regan loved being a baby doctor and bringing new life into the world even more, so the world seemed hell-bent on another world war. His long, thin fingers sought out the baby as he massaged her stomach.

He was taller than he seemed, sitting behind his desk. He asked his nurse, who had assisted him in his examination, to provide Sommer with vitamins and information on the exercises she should do every day.

"Do you know if it's a boy or girl?"

"At this stage, only God knows, Mrs. Kappel."

On her way back to St. Ermines, she decided not to tell her mother about the baby. She would never understand, especially after her parting words about alcohol and men. Somehow, she felt guilty and knew in her heart that her mother would have to know one day.

***

Sommer was waiting on the train platform for Surrey for some minutes when she became aware of the presence of someone behind her. She turned without thinking and saw a young soldier about her age. She turned quickly and could feel her cheeks burn.

"I hope I didn't startle you, miss."

She ignored his comment and focused on the approaching train. When it stopped, he followed her to her compartment. "It seems we're destined to meet," he said with a broad smile. "Let me put up your suitcase," he said, lifting it from her hands and reaching on his soles to make sure it fits snugly into the compartment.

She turned away from him and wished she had a newspaper or a magazine to read. Instead, she looked out the window.

"You're going to get a sore neck if you look out the window all the way. Where are headed?"

She turned slowly and tried to smile. "To a place called Shere. Ever heard of it?

"So am I." He smiled again. "You have family there?"

"No. I just want to spend some time in a quiet village and get away from things for a while."

"Where are you staying?"

"At the home of Mrs. Perdita Matthews. Do you know where she lives?"

"I do. Allow me to drop you off at her home when we arrive."

The train took a large curve, and she almost feel into his lap. He grabbed her arms and helped her straighten up and sit back in her seat. There was a loud whistle as the train neared the next stop.

Sommer turned to the window again. She had to admit that part of her problem was that he was good-looking in a boyish way and how his brown eyes talked to her. But she had enough of handsome men to last a lifetime. They stirred something inside her.

"Where are you travelling from? You don't sound English."

"From Germany, via Canada, where I was born."

"Smashing." He smiled in a way that he knew what she was thinking.

"I hear Germany has become a police state, and Jews are packed in rail cars without food and water and shipped off to POW camps."

She suddenly burst into tears as she told him what happened to Professor Hoffmann and how some students began clapping when they saw him being clubbed, dragged into a van, and driven away.

"The same day I discovered I was pregnant. The father never knew because I knew he would try to stop me. But I did not want my child born in Germany." It came out without warning. And she felt sheepish and didn't know what to do or say next.

"I think Germany is preparing for war," he said suddenly.

"Faster than you think," she said, suddenly finding the words and thankful that he had ignored what she had blurted. She could feel the tears forming in her eyes, and she looked out the window to hide them. "I don't know why I'm telling you all this. I'm not normally this forthcoming. "The day I left, my boyfriend told me he had decided to join the SS with his friends."

He offered her his handkerchief. She took it and wiped her eyes again. "Why don't I drop you off at Perdita's."

She shook her head.

"No, really. If you're worried about what she might think, don't be. She's my aunt."

"I don't even know your name."

"Andrew Bartlett, Lieutenant Andrew Bartlett, East Surrey Regiment, at your service," he said, saluting her.

When they reached Sphere, he helped her off the train and carried her bag to the taxi stop. "My car is around the corner. Let me drive you there."

Sommer shook her head.

"I won't take no for an answer. My aunt will have my hide if she hears that I made you take a taxi." He took her suitcase. "Follow me."

Perdita opened the door, expecting to see a young woman and was surprised to see Andrew with her. Perdita was in her early 60s and had a smiling face with black dancing eyes when she smiled. There was an irrepressible joy in her voice that drew people to her. Since her husband died two years ago, she suddenly seemed older. Her call from Myles had her humming as she polished everything in her kitchen and the room her guest would occupy upstairs.

"Here's your company, auntie. We met on the train, and when she told me she was coming to stay with you, I just had to ensure she didn't get lost."

Perdita smiled at Sommer. Don't pay any attention to Andrew. He's a born flirt. You can go now, Andrew."

"I'll pop by tomorrow to see if you need anything," he said as he disappeared from the doorway.

"Andrew is a nice boy. He joined the army two years ago and seems to love it. My sister despairs that Andrew will never amount to anything. I tell her over and over that he will find himself if he stumbles on the right challenge. And don't let his foolish banter of his fool you. There's a lot to that boy that has to be awakened."

Perdita helped her upstairs with her suitcase. "You shouldn't be lifting heavy things right now."

"So you know I'm pregnant?"

Perdita gave her a mother's smile and hugged her. When they came downstairs, Perdita made tea for her. "May I offer a suggestion, Sommer? In a few months, you'll be showing. It may be time to think of a cover story about yourself and why you're pregnant."

"Like what? I've been thinking about that, too."

"How about this? Your husband was in the RAF and died in a plane crash in the Channel. What do you think?"

"It's a winner. Is there anything you can't do?"

"If anything, it will keep Shere's idle tongues from becoming overtaxed."

"You're very kind, Mrs. Matthews."

"Perdita. Please call me Perdita. "It's been very lonely here since my good husband died. You are the blessing I prayed for." She smiled, showing a missing tooth near the front of her mouth.

Her greying hair reminded Sommer of her mother and thought of Brookside and how he seemed to know exactly what to do in everything he did. "How do you know, Mr. Brookside?"

Perdita put a footstool under Sommer's feet. "Myles is my husband's cousin. He used to visit us quite often in the old days, especially when he was at Cambridge." She felt silent and looked as though she was ready to cry.

Sommer rose and put her arms around her.

"Your mother must be very proud of you."

"I don't think so, Perdita. I've made a mess of my life."

"Let me tell you something, Sommer. Don't underestimate your mother. If I had a daughter and she told me she was pregnant and unmarried, I would give anything. And always remember, Sommer, no matter how dark things may appear now, there's always tomorrow."

Sommer tried to smile.

"Forgive me. In all this, I have supper on the stove. We'll have a bite, listen to the radio for a bit and get you to bed."

Perdita's stove had a warming tank attached to it and a warming compartment above. She saw Summer looking at it. "My husband and I bought this stove when we were first married. I can't bear to part with it."

"We have one just like it at home."

There was a window over the sink opposite the stove and a wooden icebox on the other side. The floor was covered in knitted rugs that were warm to her feet, and there was a bird in a cage next to the door.

"I love chicken?" Perdita said as Sommer sat down at the kitchen table. The kitchen was painted a deep green, and there was a fireplace where the fire was dying.

"Right now, I could eat a horse."

Perdita poured her a glass of milk. "One before and one after you're done."

"You're too good to me, Perdita."

Nonsense. In a way, this will be my grandchild, too," she said, putting a plate of chicken, mashed potatoes, and gravy in front of Sommer.

Perdita turned on the BBC. Gracie Fields was singing, and later, they listened to a BBC drama. Sommer was getting tired, and later, when she closed her eyes, she fell asleep without saying her prayers.

***

The Vicar of the Church of St. James visited Perdita the next morning. "Heard you had company. Thought I'd stop by and welcome them to Shere and St. James."

"How thoughtful of you, Vicar. Sommer will be down shortly. She had a long day yesterday. " She paused, not sure how to tell him this next. "I understand the young lady is a Catholic. Her husband was an RAF pilot and lost his life when his plane crashed in the Channel."

"All God's children are welcome, no matter what their faith, especially those in great need."

The next three weeks went by quickly. By the end of the month, Sommer received a letter from her mother, forwarded to her by someone in Brookfield's organization. Her hands shook as she tried to open the envelope. It was short and to the point.

I am so happy to hear that you are finally out of Germany and harm's way. Gerda mailed me and told me how you helped her and that everything was fine now, thanks to you.

I have some sad news to impart to you. Your father was putting new shingles on our roof and slipped and fell. He was in the hospital for a month before I brought him home. He has been bedridden since then. I need you here. I cannot work the farm on my own.

There was also a short note from Brookfield: *Heard from your doctor. He said he would like to see you when you come to London next.*

CHAPTER SEVEN

It snowed the week before Christmas, with drifts a foot high in some places. Sommer walked around the village. It felt like home for a few brief moments, and she thought about making angel wings in the snow as she did as a child. Her baby bump made her think twice.

She returned to find Andrew there, trying to get a large Christmas tree through the front door. Once in the living room, he went to the basement to make a stand for it and returned with a saw, a hammer, and a handful of nails.

It's the biggest Christmas tree this house has ever seen," said Perdita, clapping her hands and humming *God Rest Ye Merry, Gentlemen*, and a joy in her voice that spoke of Christmases past. She played Christmas records on her phonograph and hummed along with them. Sommer suddenly remembered the Christmas with Gretchen and Katrina, drinking Champagne and the incredible pastries they devoured after mass, and the carol singing with the other students when they left the university on the way home. Life was so simple then.

"Help me trim the tree, Sommer," Andrew said, passing her a box of Christmas ornaments. "You take the other side, and I'll finish here."

They sat down for tea afterwards. Andrew sat next to her. He never looked so handsome with his dark brown wavy hair and eyes that sent messages to her. Sommer turned away to check if the single strand of lights was still on.

Andrew stood, straightened his tunic and clicked his heels. "I have an announcement to make – an invitation to join my mother and me Christmas Eve, for dinner. Cocktails at 6 p.m. Come early."

Perdita looked at Sommer, whose blue eyes sparkled in the light from the Christmas tree and smiled.

"All agreed? It's a date. And bring your collection of Christmas records, auntie."

***

Eleanor Bartlett, dressed in a deep purple dress and a silver broach that many Bartlett women had worn since the early 1800s, met them at the door. She kissed Perdita on both cheeks and stepped back to look at Sommer. "How lovely you look. I wished I had looked as pretty when I was carrying Andrew. He was such a troublesome baby," she said with a light laugh.

Andrew took the occasion to take Sommer on a tour of his home – the drawing room decorated with pictures of previous Bartletts and paintings from the 18th Century.

Sommer looked around. "Is your portrait here?"

"No, just the Bartletts from the 1800s. That picture over there is Ranger Bartlett, the founder of Bartlett Estate, who made a fortune in the brass business in Birmingham. The Bartletts have lived here ever since.

"I'm the last surviving member in direct line of Sir Roger Bartlett. He was later knighted. How about you?"

"My mother and father came from a small town in Southern Germany and immigrated to Canada after the Great War. They saved enough to buy a small farm. They discovered that there was no math problem I couldn't solve in high school, even problems above my level. I was lucky. I went to McGill University in Montréal on a full scholarship to study mathematics, which helped me get a two-year scholarship to study mathematics under the great mathematician, Dr. Frederich Albrecht, at Bonn University."

Andrew whistled. "No wonder Brookside wants you on his team. I must tell you that I'm not good at math. My great strength is the classics, but it doesn't prepare you for much. The army was my only option. I got a commission as a lieutenant and hope to be a general one day." He stopped walking. "You've been in Germany for two years. From what you saw, do you think war is imminent?"

"Yes."

"In a year or sooner?"

"I'm not sure, but I should probably say very close."

They returned to the dining room. Eleanor and Perdita were already seated. Eleanor eyed them suspiciously. "We were about to send out a search party."

"I was showing Sommer our paintings."

The table was set with a lace tablecloth. They sat at the far end, leaving the balance of the table uncovered. Crystal glasses sparkled in the candlelight, and the silverware had a lustre all its own. The high-back chairs were far from comfortable, but it didn't stop her servant, dressed in a grey uniform with a white collar, from serving them from the sideboard near the table.

"Please sit down." She turned to Sommer, who was seated opposite Andrew. Perdita, who sat next to her, squeezed her hand. "I understand you're from Canada," said Eleanor, who was watching her carefully. What is the weather like there now?"

"Cold. Very cold. You can't imagine how cold because you've never spent a winter in Canada. It's what makes us strong. If war comes, you'll be glad of that strength."

Eleanor made a face. "I also understand that your family comes from Germany and that your father met with an accident. Can't be helped. I suppose you would not agree,

Andrew."

The servant poured tea for them along with the plumb pudding. Andrew finished his in a matter of seconds when the others barely tasted theirs.

"I'm also a Catholic," added Sommer.

"So I hear."

"And pregnant."

Eleanor almost dropped her tea cup. "Now that I can see you in this light, I can see you're showing," she added, offering a weak smile and raising her eyes to Perdita, who occupied herself with the goose meat on her plate. Eleanor had a mean streak ever since she was a child, and Perdita often wondered why George Bartlett ever married her.

"Her husband," said Andrew, "was an RAF pilot and lost his life when his plane crashed into the Channel."

"You probably read about it in the paper. It was also on the BBC. I know I did," said Andrew.

When he drove them back, he waited until Perdita left the car and said: "Count on me for anything you need, Sommer. I will always be here for you." He kissed her hand and wished her Merry Christmas.

Perdita shook the snow off her coat and got out of her winter boots. The first thing she did was turn on the radio. "If you're not too tired, Sommer, listen to the radio a bit for me. My husband and I used to listen to their Christmas music on Christmas Eve until he died."

Sommer sat on the sofa while Perdita sat in her rocker. Sommer didn't pay much attention to the music. She knew he was occupying her thoughts too much lately in a way no one had before. The last thing she needed at that point was a romantic entanglement.

Back at Bartlett Park, Eleanor didn't like what she had seen. She was nothing much to look at, yet she had never seen him so besotted. She shivered at the thought of him getting involved with a woman like that, and she had doubts about her husband's death if a husband really did exist.

Breakfast was also over when Sommer decided to talk to Perdita about Andrew – where he went to school, what he studied at Cambridge and the kind of music he liked.

"He's a scatterbrain at times but a fine young man at heart. He needs someone in his life to keep him grounded. I must tell you that I have never seen him so attentive to another woman as he is with you. He hangs on every word you say. And I'm glad to see it. I know you would be good for him."

Sommer lowered her head. She was becoming more confused by the minute.

"And don't mind Eleanor. She's a bit of a pain at the time and a gossip. But deep down, she has a good heart. I suspect that she thinks you were never married. Did you notice how she looked at your ring hand? The next time you go to London, buy a wedding band. She won't know what to think then. You can't afford anyone nosing about your business right now."

Sommer bent down and kissed Perdita's forehead. "And never forget," she whispered in Perdita's ear: "There's always tomorrow."

***

Eleanor Bartlett could not keep her thoughts to herself and asked her son point blank if he were interested in Sommer as soon as he sat down at the breakfast table. "She hasn't any money, her manners are unspeakable, and she dresses like a peasant."

Andrew clipped the top of his boiled egg with his knife and dipped a piece of toast into the yolk. "I haven't given it much thought, mother."

"She's not like your other lady friends, Andrew. She's not the kind of woman you can suddenly drop when some other woman comes along who fascinates you."

"No. She's a mathematics genius whom Myles Brookside has big plans for."

"For the life of me, I can't understand why." Her eyes burned, and she began to cry, "Mark my words, Andrew. She will come at a very high price, which could cost your life very well."

"You're becoming very melodramatic."

"And that child she's carrying. I, for one, don't believe she was ever married. Can you really picture yourself rearing another man's child with a woman like that?"

"Let's not quarrel, mother. I received word to report for duty. There's intelligence that the Germans are moving troops in large numbers to the Polish border."

"Oh, no, Andrew. I hope it doesn't come to war. Mr. Chamberlain –"

"Mr. Chamberlain, my ass. We need someone strong who knows how to stand up to dictators." He paused. "And Myles Brookside wants to see me this afternoon."

He stopped to see Sommer on his way to the train. "the news is not good, Sommer. It would appear that Germany is getting ready to invade Poland. Our ambassador in Berlin has asked Herr Hitler what his attentions are. We are still waiting for an answer. And I have orders to report for duty."

✳✳✳

The next morning, Sommer received a call from Brookside asking her to take the noon train to London. "I have news for you," he said before handing up.

Brookside opened his door as soon as he heard Sommer's voice at reception, waved her inside, and took a seat opposite him in front of his desk. "Andrew told me he talked about you and what the Germans are doing. But I also have some good news. There's a plane leaving for Halifax tomorrow morning."

He searched her face for a reaction. There wasn't any. "I thought you'd be jumping with joy."

"I am. But I will miss Perdita. She has become a real mother to me."

"And Andrew? You know he's absolutely bewitched by you."

"If he is, he certainly hasn't mentioned it to me." She could feel her cheeks burn.

"He's stopped seeing his other lady friends; the only person he talks about is you."

Brookside sat back in his chair, and his face suddenly changed. "When do you think you can return to us?"

"By August. I will need time to nurse my baby. And Hitler?"

"He will have to wait until you get back. I still think he will show his hand sometime in the fall. He hasn't made any visits to his troops at the front. At least, not yet. But he will. That's when I'll know." Then, after a pause. "The person we need at the helm at a time like this is Mr. Churchill. If he had been PM, he wouldn't have come back with a piece of paper. I can't say anything more. I hope you understand."

"What about the plane? Where do I get it, how do I get there and when does it leave?"

"It leaves at 7 – so they'll have daylight all the way. Andrew will come to your hotel to pick you up at 6. Make sure you're packed and ready. You should be in Halifax in time for supper."

"Then what?"

"A long, tedious train ride from Halifax to Toronto. And when you're ready to come back to us, call this number," he added, passing her a slip of paper. "We'll also need to contact Perdita and ask her to pack your things and make sure it gets to St. Ermines before midnight. Le's call her now."

He picked up the phone and dialled Perdita's number. It took seven rings before she answered it. "I'm the bearer of ill tidings, Perdita. Can you pack Sommer's suitcase and make sure it gets to her room at St. Ermines Hotel before midnight."

"Is anything wrong with Sommer?"

"No. Here, you talk to her.

"There's a plane leaving London for Canada tomorrow morning." She paused. "I will miss you, Perdita. I thought about what you told me about my mother. Thank you. I will never forget you." She passed the phone back to Myles.

She felt lightheaded when she left the elevator and passed through the revolving door. She was about to call a cab when a black Austin stopped in front of her. The driver opened the door. "I knew it was you," she said, still standing on the curb."

"Hop in. We're having dinner tonight at the Dorchester."

"That's quite an end-off," she said, sliding into the seat beside him. "You must be eager to get rid of me."

"Anything but —"

He suddenly realized she was teasing him.

All the waiters seemed to know him. "We haven't seen you in quite a while, Lieut. Bartlett," said Maurice, the head waiter. He led them to his favourite near one of the corners, where they could speak privately. Sommer looked at the incredible triple-tiered chandelier at the centre of the room open-mouthed. She had never seen anything like it before and turned to Andrew and smiled.

There was also a bottle of Champagne waiting for them on the table.

"They both shouted "Brookside" at the same time.

CHAPTER EIGHT

Sommer wondered what her mother would say when she saw she was pregnant. She had never lied to her mother before and felt guilty just thinking about it. She was waiting for her mother at Union Station. Her mother's train was due in 10 minutes, and she could feel her heart pounding in her ears, and with each passing minute, the thudding grew louder and more pronounced.

She looked at the clock. Her mother would be arriving in one minute. When she looked back, she saw her mother getting off the train. Her mother spotted her, and Sommer ran towards her. When they met, her mother hugged her for almost a minute as Sommer kept whispering how much she loved her. She could smell the cheap perfume her mother always used. It brought back memories of happier times when his mother and father took her to the fall fair in town to get supplies for the winter.

Sommer led her to the Royal York across from the station and to the horseshoe-shaped counter for a quick bite in the basement of the hotel. As they sat on the stools, her mother noticed that she was pregnant.

"You never mentioned you were pregnant or that you were married. This is not like you, Sommer. You always told me everything, but you've changed since you've been away."

I didn't have time to write you because I've been working on a secret for the British government, and with the baby coming, I have been more tired than usual."

Her mother's hair was greyer than she remembered, and there were lines on her face now, and her eyes seemed smaller and colder.

"Your father has been sick with worry about you and asked me every day, *mama, has Sommer written us?* Why didn't you write, Sommer." when I told him you were coming home, his eyes lit up, and he looked like his old self.

The next day, they boarded the train for the five-hour trip, where they would leave the train and take the bus to their farm. When they entered their home, her mother made coffee and sliced bread and asked her to take it to her father. Sommer mounted the stairs she had seen in her dreams only more slowly since she had become pregnant. Her father was propped up in bed against two pillows, and his eyes lit up as soon as he saw her.

"You've come back to us," he said to her in German. It is all your good mother, and I have been praying for months now."

Sommer sat on the edge of his bed and passed his coffee mug and toast to him. He put them on the nightstand next to him and opened his arms to her, holding her tight and repeatedly saying, "tell me you'll never leave us again."

She soothed his forehead until he fell asleep and crept downstairs.

"What would you like for supper? I cooked a ham before I left. It's in the iced box."

That night, as they were listening to the radio, she thought of Perdita and felt she needed to tell her mother at least a cover story about her pregnancy and her work in mathematics for the British government.

The next morning, she made an appointment with Father Kelley to see him in the afternoon. St. Mary's was a 30-minute walk from her home, and her mother reminded her that snow was forecast for later in the afternoon. She tied on her snow boots and her old winter coat, which was a bit snug now.

"Here, take my coat," said her mother, passing her coat to Sommer along with her father's heavy woollen scarf. "You may need them. My coat looks as though it was made for you. You didn't eat much for breakfast. Let me make some French toast with a slice of ham from yesterday. You used to love it when you went to school. You need your strength, and it's also important for your child."

She paused at the door as she prepared to go and smiled at her mother. She looked at the kitchen one more time. It was the largest room in the house. The big iron stove with the warming oven above made her think of Perdita's. There was a window over the sink with no tap but a pump. They got all their water from that pump, including water for a bath. The back wall had a small window next to the door, which they used to feed the chickens and milk the cows. The linoleum had changed, thank God, she thought. It had never changed in all her memory.

"Ask Father Kelly to bless your baby."

As soon as she stepped from the back door, her face felt a rush of air from the north wind. She draped the scarf around her face. She had forgotten just how cold Canadian winters could be as she headed onto the snow-covered highway. She was just a few minutes out when she felt the first flakes before they gradually thickened.

The drifting snow was getting thicker by the minute, falling every few feet on a slippery path of ice beneath the snow, and he wondered if she should turn and go back. She decided to carry on, and a few minutes later, it was almost blinding. She could barely see six feet in front of her. She increased her pace, but it only made her fall even more. She felt sore as she struggled to her feet and felt her baby move inside her.

Suddenly, there was a momentary patch of clearing in

the snow. The rectory. She would be there in 10 minutes and tried to increase her pace. The snow suddenly swirled around her, biting her face and eyes now. Her fingers felt frozen in her mittens. She turned her back and tried to walk backwards, but that didn't work either. After righting herself, she tried running, shielding her eyes in the direction where she last saw the rectory.

Father Wes Kelly could barely make out the lone figure struggling toward him. He put on his winter boots, coat, and goggles. His legs, strong from cross-country skiing, carried him to her in a few minutes. It was a woman. She helped her to her feet.

"Sommer Kappel. I thought you were in Europe." He grabbed her left arm and walked her slowly back to the rectory. Inside, he helped her out of her coat and snow boots and left her in his rocking chair while left to get her a hot coffee.

"I put a drop of Brandy in it. You're half-frozen, and you need it now. I can't believe it's you, Sommer. I talked to your mother about you two weeks ago. So you've come back. Your mother has had a hard time of it since your father fell. Here," he said, helping her rise, take my easy chair and stretch out." He stopped, noticing her swollen stomach. "You're pregnant. Wonderful."

Sommer looked up from her coffee cup. "That's not all, Father. It was important to see you because I needed to talk to someone about myself and what to do if something happened.

She didn't know where to start, so she started with Felix, spending the nights with him, how they became friends, and what happened after Professor Hoffmann had been beaten until his face was bleeding. "It was a big joke to them. That's when I decided I didn't want my baby born in a country like that, and when he told me he was going to join the SS, I decided not to tell about the baby."

"How did she react about the baby?"

Sommer shook her head. "She's very rigid, Father. I made up a story about it but decided not to use it."

Father Kelly cocked his head to the left. "Don't you think she deserved to know the truth?"

"Of course, Father, but I'm afraid how she'll react."

"She may surprise you."

Two hours later, she awoke with a start. She suddenly felt very tired and closed her eyes. She sat and looked at Father Kelly, his smiling hazel eyes and how he tapped the tips of his long, tapering fingers together when he answered a question.

"I've called your mother and told her I would drive you home once the storm ends. She was worried when you didn't return and was imagining the worst.

Sommer tried to get up from the easy chair but fell back. "Stay where you are. Your body needs to rest now." He cocked his head again. "Is there anything else you'd like to tell me?"

"Yes, and what I'm about to tell you, Father, you must never tell another living soul until the war ends. I have been recruited as a spy by the British government. They want me to return to Germany before the end of the year. I have undertaken to be their eyes and ears on German weapon developments." Then, after a pause, I do not want my mother to know this."

"Understood. But I feel you should tell your mother the truth about your baby."

***

"You've changed, Sommer. You're not the daughter that left us two years ago. You used to tell me everything. Now, it seems an effort for me to talk to you about anything."

Sommer didn't respond. They were sitting at the kitchen table, eating her mother's home-made soup, when she suddenly broke into tears. Her mother, who was in the process of pouring her a glass of milk, put the glass down and put her arms around her. Her secret was gnawing at her stomach, and she was finding it hard to get a good night's sleep.

The tears ran down Sommer's cheeks, her body shook with convulsive sobs, and she couldn't stop. Her mother put her arms around her and wiped her cheeks with the edge of her apron, the way she did when Sommer had skinned her knee or when some girl at school had made fun of her.

"It's all right, Sommer. It doesn't matter. Did you think I wouldn't understand? You and your child are more important to me than anything else on this earth. When you feel up to it, you can tell me then. Remember, no one else in this world is more important to me than you and now, your precious child."

She wiped the new tears from Sommer's eyes with her apron again and walked to the wood stove to get them a coffee. "Do you know what you need now, Sommer?"

Sommer looked up. Everything was the same as she had imagined on lonely nights in Bonn, even the pale yellow wainscoting that now looked tired. The stove pipe that never quite fitted the chimney still looked out of place.

"What if I make you buttered toast smothered in hot milk? You always wanted to make it when you were sick."

Sommer sat back in her chair. "I feel a lot better now, mother, but I'm still open to tasting your milk toast.

***

"Just relax and lie back," said Estelle Cranston, a midwife everyone called on in their village whenever there was a birth. "Don't forget that I've brought you into the world, screaming your head off."

Estelle had a loud, high-pitched laugh, a neck that reminded Sommer of a giraffe, and in a commanding voice, gave her mother a raft of orders.

"When do you think the baby will come?"

"No two births are alike. Just know that your time will come, and you'll experience a lot of pain when it does. Scream your head off for as long as you want, but when I tell you to push, push with every bone and muscle of your body."

Sommer closed her eyes, and when the time came, the pain was unbearable but not half as bad as Estelle had made it out to be. Then, what seemed like hours later, she heard her mother say: "She looks like my sister, Gerda."

"They named her Andrea."

***

Her father laid Andrea beside him and kept kissing her forehead. He died a week later from the flu. It was her mother's time to cry, and Sommer made all the funeral arrangements with Father Kelly. Her mother was never the same after that, and Sommer helped her to make all the meals and did all the chores, including cutting wood for kindling in the woodshed and starting the fire in both the kitchen stove and the big heater in the living room. She did her best to console her, but nothing seemed to give her any peace. Except for Andrea.

Then, a week later, Andrea got sick, wheezing when she breathed. And her skin was red and hot to touch.

"We need to take her to the hospital."

"It's snowing again, mother. No taxi will come out here in this kind of weather."

"Then call the hospital and ask them what to do."

"They think it's the flu and send an ambulance to get her. We can go with them."

Her mother swung into action immediately. "You get the baby ready and keep watch for the ambulance. You pulled through. And so will Andrea. You won't remember because you were still very young, but you got very sick

62

when you were about five years old, and your father had to walk six miles into town in a snowstorm to get medicine for you.

Two hours later, they were waiting for the doctor to tell them about Andrea.

"Good thing you got her here when you did. As a result, we were able to reduce her fever, and we've given her a new drug called Penicillin, which seems to work miracles. It would be better if she and you and your mother stayed here overnight. You can take her back home if her fever's down by the morning."

*****

Over the next three months, Sommer got to know her mother in a different way. They were more like friends now. When July came, she knew she had to tell her mother that she had to return to England in August.

"But why? There's a war on, and people, even old friends, are saying bad things about Germans these days. They hate us."

It's something I promised to do. You know what happened at Dunkirk. Worse things are about to happen. I must go back to help."

"How? And why?"

Please do not ask me anything more. Please listen carefully. Tell them I have become a nun if someone should come looking for me or where I've gone. Nothing else. They will want to hurt me, even kill me, to stop what I must do."

Her mother broke into German. "I will say the rosary for you every day."

"I need you to look after Andrea for me until I come back when the three of us will be together forever."

"When will that be?"

"When the war is over."

Three weeks later, she knocked on the door of a convent in Toronto and asked to be admitted.

"Why do you wish to be admitted?" The mother superior, now in her early 70s, had doubts about the young woman sitting before her. She suffered from Arthritis in her legs and shoulders and found it difficult to work on rainy days.

"I have sinned and wish to do penance. I have given birth to a beautiful baby girl, am not married, and failed to honour my parents. I would like to spend a week with you and the other sisters, fasting and praying for forgiveness."

"This is somewhat irregular for us. We are a community of women devoted to the love of our Blessed Mother and her Blessed Son every hour of the day."

"I understand, Mother. It is your devotion that draws me to your community."

Mother Superior's pale blue eyes watched her, looking for clues about how she might fit in with the other sisters. Her lined face made her look older than she was. She was tired, waking up three times every night to pray. She sat back on the old chair behind her desk and wondered if the young woman in front of her loved God enough to follow their way.

"Spend the rest of the day and night with us, and if you still feel the same way, then stay the rest of the week with us."

When the week was up, Mother Superior blessed her. "Go in peace."

One thing, mother, should someone come looking for me, tell them I am not permitted to see visitors. "

Mother Superior raised her hand.

"Before you say anything, Mother, you need to know a secret I hope you can never reveal to anyone else. Only Father Kelley knows. My mother does not know, only that I am going to spend some time with you. I am a spy for the British, and I will be sent to Germany to provide the British with information on new weapons the Germans may be launching. So if anyone else comes asking about me, it will be to find out if I am a spy."

The first person she called when she checked into the Royal York was her mother to ask about Andrea.

"Better than ever. And don't worry about her. I've done all this before."

"I won't be able to call you once I leave Canada. Don't ask why. It's better if you do not know."

She replaced the receiver and looked for the number Brookfield had given her to use when she was ready to return.

CHAPTER NINE

Sommer looked out the window. The fog was thicker than she remembered, and she wondered if her plane, an ageing Armstrong Whitworth Whitley, would be able to land in London after all. Her military transport had aborted three attempted landings. One of the airmen crawled back to tell her to buckle up, that they were going to make a "now-or-never" descent, and if she knew any prayers, now would be a good time to say them.

A few minutes later, she could feel the increased pressure as the plane descended steeply. A few seconds later, she could hear the wheels bump and rise in the air three times before landing for the final time. The pilot slammed on the brakes, sending the plane off the runway before crashing into a petrol truck.

"Everyone out. Now. This thing could explode in

flames in a matter of seconds. Hurry."

Sommer unbuckled herself, grabbed her suitcase and crawled to the exit door.

"Push the damn handle," said the deep male voice behind her. "Here. Let me." He pushed beside her and booted the door four or five times before it sprung open. He grabbed a metal ladder next to the door and flew down it in five seconds. "Turn around and climb down as fast as you can. And then run like hell."

Sommer threw out her suitcase first and hit the ground in seconds. She grabbed her suitcase and ran in the direction of an approaching truck. It stopped a few feet from her. An arm shot out and lifted her.

"My suitcase."

"To hell with it," said the driver.

"I'll get it for you," said the voice behind her.

She turned. It was Andrew

"I told you I would be waiting for you."

He jumped out, grabbed the suitcase and climbed back in. "Drive like hell, driver."

They reached the station a few seconds before her petrol truck exploded, taking the aircraft with it.

***

Myles Brookfield raised his glass and smiled. "You look ten years younger, Sommer. The same way you looked the first time we met. You've told your mother, I see."

Sommer nodded and glanced at Andrew, who smiled back.

"And your baby?"

"Her name is Andrea. I fell in love with her the first time they put her in my arms. She favours my aunt, Gerda, who lives in Germany. The same eyes, the same curly hair, even the way she sneezes." Then, after a pause, "I suspect you want to talk about other things."

They were in a private room at St. Ermines. The waiters left as soon as they served each dish.

"You always go to the point, Sommer. It's what I admired about the first time we met," he said with a smile, adding a touch of Brandy to her coffee." Then, as an aside: "I hear Churchill is a bottle-a-day man, bless him."

"I remember your picture of him on the doorway wall. So you got your wish after all."

Andrew's hand found her beneath the table. Sommer looked at him and smiled.

"As you know, all our worst fears have come to reality." Brookside paused to take a small pinch of snuff and sneezed. "Great for clearing your head. As I was saying, anything that could go wrong has gone wrong. Dunkirk, terrible as it was, was our only bright spot. Herr Hitler now controls most of Europe. We're next on his lift once he has command of the skies, and that, thanks to our gallant RAF pilots, he has not been able to manage."

"We heard about Dunkirk on the radio at home."

"All of which brings me to the purpose of our little reunion and why we're meeting here. German spies are everywhere. They know where my office is and keep tabs on everyone who comes to my building. I do not want them to see you entering my office – for I'm sure they or take pictures of all the people who come to see me.

"During our last meeting, we briefly discussed our training school for agents in Herefordshire. All of you will go there under assumed names – for each of your protection. You'll be trained with four others. If any of you are discovered and forced to tell the terms of the others, you will remember their assumed names only.

The truth. "Each of you will be given other names again when you head out on your assignment — everyone except you. You will assume your proper name in the field because there are many people who know you by that name in Germany and you have a wonderful cover story to tell. Any questions?"

"About the others –"

"Trust no one. Not even the people who train you. And definitely not any one of the people who train with you. At Herefordshire, you'll learn Morse code and how to protect yourself using Judo, a gun, a knife, and all about explosives. Even how to find your way around a French or German kitchen just in case you find yourself in that position."

Sommer's mind drifted to her family kitchen and the legs of their kitchen table, which had been green since she could remember.

"Tomorrow is a holiday for you two. But be ready by 10 a.m. to be driven to an old manor house in Hampshire."

He looked at his pocket watch. "I see duty calls. The next time we meet, Sommer, check into the Devonshire. Until then." He raised his coffee cup and finished the contents. "I leave you in Andrew's eager hands."

***

A young-looking soldier opened the car door and helped her out before reaching for her suitcase. He led her through the iron gates and to the entrance to Beaulieu Estate. Standing just inside the lobby, a grey-haired officer extended his hand to her.

"I'm Col. Elliott Winslow. Welcome to Beaulieu Hall," he said, extending his hand to her. "We're informal here. If you have any problems, my door is always open. In the meantime, Cpl. Bennett will take you to your room so you can settle in and rest before dinner, served at sharp. Please don't be late. We're also informal here about rank and the way we dress."

Sommer looked out the window onto the incredibly green lawn and the flower gardens near the greenhouse. She sat on the edge of the bed and opened the end table next to her bed, which had the highest box springs and mattress she had ever seen. Her feet couldn't reach the floor when she sat on the edge. Her bedroom was larger than those at St. Ermines, and the larger windows had lace curtains. The walls were painted a faint green, with light green mouldings along the floors and windows casings. A hunting scene looked down at her from the opposite wall.

She lay back on the bed, suddenly tired, and drifted off to sleep. She woke two hours later with a start, a little confused for a few seconds, before remembering where she was. The clock on the mantle showed 5.45. She got out of bed immediately and went to the adjoining bathroom to prepare dinner. It had a huge mirror that stretched all the way to the bathtub and next to the mirror, an object she had not seen before. She brushed her hair, which was starting to turn a darkening blond colour. For the first time, she spotted the hint of a line around her chin. She made a face and shook her head.

Sommer looked up and down each side of the corridor, painted bright yellow with paintings of former owners at intervals. She tried to remember what side the stairs were on until a young woman emerged from her room three rooms down. Sommer waved to her, and she waited until she reached her. She was about the same age as Sommer and introduced herself as Madeleine Préfontaine.

"I was one of the lucky ones," she said in a soft, accented voice as they reached the stairway. "I managed to escape on a fishing boat about a week before Dunkirk." Madeline had long brown hair, which she kept tossing to get it to land the way she liked. "It's almost impossible some days to get my hair to behave."

"What's it like here?"

"The meals are fabulous, and so are some of the instructors we met informally last night. Everybody is friendly. I arrived on Monday and the others on Wednesday." They started down the stairs. "They're a good crowd."

Sommer heard voices behind her and turned around to see two men and a woman about six steps behind them. The woman had a loud laugh that you hear through three cement walls.

Col. Winslow stood at the bottom of the stairs to welcome and introduce her to the others. "Ladies and Gentlemen, our new comrade, Perdita Hastings."

Sommer smiled and sensed Brookfield's sly hand.

"What a beautiful name," said the man behind her. "Perdita. It suits you, *bella donna.*" He introduced himself at Elio Giordano. "I come from beautiful Napoli, where everyone has a beautiful voice. He was short, had a fat face and looked harmless. His large brown eyes had a way of rolling when he talked.

"On your left," added Col. Winslow, "Alex Greenwood, who's fluent in German and French as well as being an expert on explosives. Everything about him looked nondescript, which made him perfect for his assignment. Greenwood nodded.

The woman next to him smiled. She tossed her dark hair, laughed at her joke, and started talking in Italian. "I am an entertainer and come from Milano. "They call me Bonfilia Marchetti, and I am anything but bona filia." her blouse expanded as she took a deep breath and began to sing *Torna a Sorrento.*

Gérald Dangler was the tallest of the group. His thin face and dark eyes make him look as though he hadn't eaten in a month. He kept drumming his fingers and smiled. "I have a lot of nervous energy."

"And now, ladies and gentlemen, the chef is getting impatient. Please take your seats," said Col. Winslow, who took his seat at the head of the table.

After dinner, everyone gravitated to the front room in front of a giant fireplace. "We have a different film every night," said Madeleine. "Last night, it was about Berlin with special footage on the Gestapo Headquarters and the HQ for the Wehrmacht. Tonight, we'll see the U Boat bases along the French coast and their fortifications."

Col. Winslow suddenly appeared. "A word, Miss Matthews."

She followed him to his office. He waved her to the chair next to his desk. "Anything wrong, Colonel?

"A bit of advice. Don't get too chummy with anyone in your group. It could save your life one day. "

Sommer raised her eyebrow.

"We suspect that one of your group is a German agent. We brought that individual here on the pretext of becoming a spy and learning all about our operations in order to study him or her very carefully."

"Any suspects?"

"Hopefully, we will know before you leave. You seem surprised, Miss Matthews. Don't be. This is what war is like. There are no rules. Just winning and losing. We're out to win."

CHAPTER TEN

"Welcome, ladies and gentlemen. My name is Sgt. Mike Mason. You'll be spending the next three weeks with me as your Morse code instructor. You'll learn Morse Code, how to send messages and how to decipher the ones you get. And last, use the radio transmitter and receiver each of you will take with you.

He wrote his name on the blackboard in Morse Code and turned, tossing a piece of chalk in the air and catching it as he turned. "It's as easy as that."

He went to his desk and pointed to an object on his desk. "This is the radio transmitter/receiver you'll take. Guard it with your life. It's your only lifeline to us. But first things first: You need to know how to open it." He stood behind the radio transmitter and placed his hand on the machine's upper part. You can open the cover by prying it loose from the top like this."

Bonfilia giggled. "I can't find the place to remove it."

He walked down to Bonfilia's desk and turned her machine so everyone could see it. "Place your fingernails here, press down, and it will pop open automatically. Now, each of you try it 20 times so you can do it with your eyes closed.

"Next," he said, standing beside Bonfilia's desk, "here's how you replace it. Ok. Try it."

Bonfilia was able to do it on the first try and looked around and smiled at everybody.

"Now, open it again," he said to everyone. "Now that the cover is off, I want you to find a cardboard folder, which you will find here," he said, showing a small niche on the right side of the machine. He held it up so everyone could see how to open it. "It shows the dots and dashes die each letter. Actually, they're on-and-off clicks or short and long signals. The short signals are dots, and the long signals are long ones. Any questions?"

Everyone was trying to type each of the letters on their desk. Some were quicker than others. A couple tried to use the key in the radio transmitter, but that made everyone laugh.

"That's for another day. At the moment, I would like each of you to practise them repeatedly until you get them down pat. Your life might depend on it one day.

Next, she showed them how to use the key to send a message and recognize the short and long signals when they heard them.

"That's it for today," he said, looking at his wristwatch. "This afternoon is yours to practise each of the 26 letters so you can try to send messages to someone using the key."

Their lunch plates were filled with vegetables. Bonfilia picked at them hesitatingly. "Does anybody know how to make spaghetti here beside me?"

Everyone laughed, including Bonfilia. "I don't think they'll ever get the hang of it. Just don't serve me noodles and catsup. That's where I draw the line and pretend it's spaghetti."

"It could be taught better," said Madeleine Préfontaine in almost a whisper. "What do you think?"

Sommer shrugged. "It's all new to me. I'll have to study much harder than the rest of you."

"We've only got three weeks to master it. I'm not sure I can," said Gérard Dangler. "What happens if we can't? We can't?"

"What do you think, Alex?' said Madeleine.

Alex Greenwood shook his head and smiled. "I take the attitude that if someone else, someone like Mason, is an expert at it, I can, too."

They broke early in the afternoon. Sommer went to her room and laid out the cardboard folder she had in class. She then took out a pad and wrote down the code for A, then B and C and D and E and F. She wrote a dot and a dash for A; then a dash and three dots for B, and then two dots, a dash and then a dot, and then the code for D, E and F. She memorized over and over, testing her memory at every stage. Then the codes for D, E and F repeating the process over and over until she had mastered the entire list.

Sommer loved learning new things as much as she loved a challenge. It's what made mathematics so fascinating.

Downstairs she joined Madeleine at the bar. She could hear Brookfield's voice as he warned her not to trust anyone and Col. Winslow's comment about a German agent in their midst. He must be wrong, she told him later. "The only one who stands to gain from this is Alex Greenwood, but I just don't see him as a spy."

"But if I'm right, Sommer, that person will know each of you and your lives could be in danger if he or she should suddenly come across you in France or Germany."

***

"I notice you pray the rosary every day at the outdoor fountain every morning," said Madeleine.

"Only on good days."

Madeleine had met her on the ground floor. The corridor had a series of alcoves with seats with large windows that let in the sunshine along the entire length of the passage.

"Such a beautiful sight," said Madeleine, looking out at the gardens and lawns surrounding Beaulieu. "You'd never think a war was going on not far from here."

Sommer got up to leave.

"Do you know where they're sending you?"

Sommer shook her head.

"What are you good at? We never did learn, or is it all high-hush?"

"My gift is that I'm nondescript and blend into any place." Sommer made up stories of her childhood and the major events in her life and looked forward to her assignment to bring excitement into her life. "And you, Madeleine?"

"I'm good at electronics. But that Morse code business gets to me." And then, unexpectedly: "I hope we meet again after the war. "

Elio Gordano led the class. "Italians excel at everything," he shouted as Sgt. Morison shook his hand.

***

What Sommer dreaded most was using a gun and, most of all, how to kill someone with a knife. Surprisingly, it was Madeleine who was the best shot. "French women also excel in everything."

In the final week of their training, only Madeleine and Bonfilia could succeed in the assignments they were given. Sommer made a point of failing. Her mission was to steal the formula for a new explosive. She was able to memorize it in a matter of seconds but purposely got caught with the formula in her purse.

Madeleine's assignment was to sabotage the production process in an electronics factory. She posed as one of the workers and closed down one of the tube–making lines by using a hairpin." I could have closed the entire factory and set back production for weeks," she told Col. Winslow when she returned to Beaulieu.

Bonfilia was ordered to destroy a heavily armed cement guard post just inside a POW camp to free prisoners.

"How were you able to manage that?" said Alex Greenfield when she returned.

"I told the guard I was there to entertain the POWs," she said with a toss of her blond hair. "They believed me after I sang *Torno a Sorrento* for them. I took off my gloves and slapped their cheeks with them. The guard post was easier. There were only four soldiers and they, too, wanted me to prove I was an entertainer. I started to do a strip tease, and somehow my bra got loose and flew over their heads. They all dived for it. And while they were fighting over it, I managed to fit a dummy explosive where they would never look. It was timed to produce a lot of smoke about 15 minutes after I left."

She tossed her hair again. "Italians excel at everything."

"How about you, Sommer?" said Madeleine.

"I was caught when they stopped me, dumped out the contents of my purse and saw the formula I was asked to steal."

The next day, they were grilled by someone they had not met before, dressed in a German uniform. Sommer was first as the others watched.

"Your name?"

Adalie Fontaine."

"Your ID says you're a secretary. Why are you here."

"I have a week's leave. My boyfriend will be joining me tomorrow."

"His name?"

"Armand Archambeau."

"Where will you be staying while in Provence?"

"Chien d'Or."

Report to us when you leave Provence. Understood?"

"A word, Sommer," said Col. Winslow. "You seemed a bit too sure of yourself. Most people do not share your confidence in dealing with German officers.

***

Then, the final day. A special dinner attended by Lord Montagu, their trainers and Brookfield. Col. Winslow rose and tapped his water glass for attention. "Now, ladies and gentlemen, it's time to hear from someone we all know. Myles Brookfield."

There was a polite round of clapping as Brookfield stood, laying his freshly lit cigar in the glass ashtray to his left.

"How wonderful to see all our faces and hear your voices again. Thank you for joining us in our crusade against tyranny. You have been given the best and most up-to-date training in the world today. I hope it will serve you well in the field.

"My parting advice: Above all, be careful. Take no unnecessary chances that could put you in harm's way. If you feel your cover has been blown, send us a message, and we will create a new persona for you and move you to a new area."

Madeleine Préfontaine raised her hand. "What if we see one of us in the field? Do we pretend we don't see them or what?"

"You will have to decide that yourself. Just don't compromise yourself or the other person because you want to hear a friendly voice. Tomorrow morning each of you will be driven to a different place, where you'll await your assignment."

Sommer was the last to leave the table. She felt cold and very much alone, knowing her only contact with London was through a box.

Brookfield met her at the stairs. "These things are always downers. So don't let it get the best of you. You'll meet new people and do things you've never dreamed of before. And you'll come back to us, perhaps a bit wiser and prepared for even greater things in your life, knowing you made a difference.

"Thank you, I needed that."

"We will meet again in three days in London to talk about your assignment, which in many respects is the most important of all. Call me when you check into St. Ermines." Brookfield's hazel eyes smiled at her, "My car is waiting to take me back to London."

It was time to leave. They all hugged each other, knowing they might never see each other again. Bonfilia had large tears in her eyes as they promised to come to Beaulieu after the war and spend the weekend with each other. They had become close friends during their four months together, and Sommer couldn't imagine any of them as German agents.

Madeleine was waving to her from the head of the stairs. "Let's share a coffee and chat before we go to bed and go our separate ways in the morning."

Sommer followed her to her bedroom. "I'm going to feel a bit lonely after this. I lost my parents when the Germans came to our village. They were gunned down by a gun-crazed soldier, who had to be stopped by his comrades after he had killed seven people."

"Why are you going back, then?"

Madeleine looked up, her large blue eyes were staring at the window and the darkness outside. "To get even."

CHAPTER ELEVEN

Brookfield took a pinch of snuff and stirred his coffee. "I've brought Andrew along so he knows your assignment and where you'll be going should something untoward happen to me. He will be the only one who knows, at least at this point.

Andrew saluted her and smiled.

"You look different somehow. It's your uniform. You've changed it."

"I've transferred to the Royal Marines. There's talk that Mr. Churchill is planning a special commando unit. I expect to be appointed captain when and if it's established."

"But first, Sommer," said Brookfield, do you have any questions before I begin?"

"Yes. Col. Winslow mentioned that he suspected one of my associates at Beaulieu was a German agent. Do you know who it is or might be?"

"We have suspicions but are not positively sure. You've been with them for four months. Who would be the most likely candidate in your mind?"

"At first, I suspected Madeleine Préfontaine. She was always asking me questions about me and my life. I lied to her, of course, but something she confided in me after our farewell dinner changed my mind."

"What was that?"

"When I asked her why she was going back to France

after escaping from it, she said: *To get even*. I could see it in her eyes. A German soldier had murdered her parents and five others."

"We will get to the bottom of it. You can be sure of that. And when we do, we will find a way to warn you and the others. Now you understand why they know only your assumed name."

"You discussed something about a special assignment."

"A rather difficult one, I'm afraid." He paused. "The Germans are working on a secret project. We don't know what it's about, but they've assembled a team of high-powered mathematicians headed by your old professor, Frederich Albrecht. You are the only one we know who could possibly gain entry to this elite group.

"Unlike the others, you will go to Germany using your real name. You've already established an ID there, and the authorities know who you are and that you studied under Dr. Albrecht. You speak German fluently with an authentic South German accent, which establishes you as one of them. But before you do anything, put together a bulletproof story to tell everyone. It must be based on absolute truth as much as possible just in case the Gestapo gets it into their heads of administering their famous truth serum. Have that story down pat, including returning to Canada to see your dying father and having your baby born there – just in case they check up on you there as well. They'll look under every stone if this project is as big as I think it is."

Where would you like to go to dinner?" said Andrew. "I'm starving."

"I'd like to join you, but I'm promised elsewhere. But I'd like your suggestions on how best to get Sommer into Germany. Parachuting her is out. Her sudden appearance would only raise more questions about how she was able to return to Germany unnoticed in the midst of a war."

Brookside consulted his pocket watch and made a face.

"It's getting late, I'm afraid. In the meantime, Andrew, give my last question some thought."

He left a few minutes later. Sommer stood and looked out the window to see Brookfield's driver suddenly wheel up to the hotel's entrance. She turned to see Andrew looking at her. "What are you thinking?"

"That I will miss you when you leave. I hate to see you leave after not seeing you for months. But what about dinner? There is an old tavern I used to frequent in my younger days. Their food is plain, but the taste stays with your forever."

"Give me 15 minutes to get ready."

An hour later, they sat in a private alcove at the Admiral's Quarters tavern. "This is England I always imagined," she said, reaching for his hand to kiss. "I will remember this night for the rest of my life."

***

She woke to the phone ringing and reached out to grab the receiver without thinking. It was Brookfield. "Some unfinished business you need to know. If you could arrange breakfast for three, I would be eternally in your debt. I'll be there in 15 minutes."

She was showered, dressed and ready when she heard a knock. It was Brookfield who sat down at the table next to her bed. "Sorry, Andrew had to bail at the last minute. Duty calls, and that was it."

There was another knock at the door. Her heart leapt. She was about to say Andrew but stopped just in time to see the waiter, dressed in a white shirt and a black bowtie, wheel in another table prepared for three people and prepared to serve them eggs, bacon and cold toast how she longed for hot-buttered toast. There was also a flagon of coffee. He poured each of them a coffee and left as silently as he entered.

"He did have time to mention an idea he has to get you into France without causing a problem. Instead of being unnoticed, to have you very clearly noticed instead. I said I would fly it past you."

"Go ahead."

"Go by boat across the channel and have the Germans discover you trying to land."

"Sounds great, except I don't know anything about boats."

"Here's the plan. We will arrange for you to steal a motorboat and head out for the coast on your own. Andrew will go a short part of the way with you and show you how to start and steer it, even how to speed it up and slow it down. Then he will leave you by a rowboat attached to the motor boat once you leave the harbour."

"When would this take place?"

"Two days from now. At one a.m., when no one's around, especially the owner of the motorboat. By the time you know how to steer and operate it, Andrew will leave you. All you need to do is steer East and land on France's coast. We'll even arrange for the owner to report his boat stolen and have it reported in the newspapers, just in case your friends in Berlin check out your story."

He took a pinch of snuff on the bottom of his hand. "So, what do you think?"

"Not ecstatic."

"But in our estimation, it's the fastest way to get you to Berlin without encountering any problem en route. Your story will have much more credence if the captain of one of their patrol boats tells them."

He dug into his eggs and bacon and washed them with two cups of coffee. Sommer replaced his coffee and tried to smile while Brookfield dipped his toast crusts into the coffee.

"What aren't you telling me."

"Your radio transmitter and receiver. In a parachute drop, it's easy to drop it with them. But that's impossible in your case."

"So what do I do?"

"I've been thinking about that. It occurred to me that the one place you can go without raising suspicions is a church."

Sommer was about to say something but was stopped by Brookfield's raised hand. "Hear me out before commenting. One of the great Catholic Churches in Berlin is St. Michael's. Go there for mass every Sunday and sit in a row – what's your age?"

"Twenty-four."

"Sit in row 24 from the front and leave a holy card of St. Michael on page 157 in one of the prayer books."

"If they have missals, I'll put the card on page 157 in one of them."

Brookfield nodded. "If the card is no longer on page 157, it means you have made contact. You will be contacted a week or two later. In the meantime, your contact will confirm that you are in Berlin."

"Let me repeat. Do not try to seek them out. Otherwise, you might be compromising both of your lives. Remember, unless they have been arrested, they will find you when you least expect it."

CHAPTER TWELVE

A ndrew was at her door three days later. She opened it to see him smiling. "Why didn't you call me?"

"I wasn't able to. We were on manoeuvres with no contact with the outside world."

"It doesn't matter. You're here now." She paused, not sure how he was going to take it. "I leave tonight. After midnight."

"I know." He didn't know what to say next. "I'll take you to the boat and show you everything, so you know how it works. You'll have enough gas to get you to France."

"I'll be all right," she said, reaching out for his hand.

Fog will drift in tonight and help you make a clean escape. It can get cold at night in this weather. So bring an extra sweater and a jacket with you just in case."

"One more thing. The Royal Navy patrols the waters outside the harbour during the day and night. Try to avoid them at all costs. The last thing you need is to have your mission aborted before you start. Pray instead to be picked up by a German patrol boat."

Sommer shivered in the cold wind from the North Sea as she guided the boat outside the harbour. She blessed Andrew and held him for a full minute. He looked at her face and then hauled in the rowboat. He levered himself into the boat and started rowing back. Seconds later, he had disappeared into the darkness and the fog. Loneliness rose like a wave and washed over her. She shook her head and knew she had to get back to business.

Steering the boat was easier than she imagined she thought it would be, and So was regulating the speed. She kept an eye on the compass for five minutes or so to ensure she kept the boat heading East.

About an hour later, she thought she heard a sound of a motor and stopped the engine immediately. She peered into the darkness and thought she saw a glimpse of a black object close by in the swirling fog. Waves lapped against the hull of her boat. She turned the boat in a different direction to see if that would help. She sat down and felt hungry, remembering the box of sandwiches and a thermos of coffee Andrew had left for her. She thought what an extraordinary gift he was in her life, wondering if he liked classical music.

Sommer shivered and looked for her jacket when she heard a motor starting. She held her breath and waited until the sounds of the motor of the other boat faded into the blackness. She started her engine and headed out into the fog.

The rest of the way was pure monotony. It was only when the fog had lifted, and in the light of the morning sky, Sommer could see land in the distance. She kept on course, and after she got closer, she spotted a boat heading towards her at full speed. She looked down and picked up the binoculars Andrew found for her in the cabin and saw a German flag flying from the mast of the approaching boat and a man in a white cap pointing at her.

A few minutes later, the German patrol boat manoeuvred beside her. Four sailors pointed machine guns at her as two others jumped aboard, setting her craft rocking back and forth,

"Identify yourself. And where are you going?"

"My name is Sommer Kappel. I am on my way to Berlin to answer the call of the Fatherland," she said in German.

"You're German?" said the captain, who had jumped aboard when she had heard her speaking German.

Sommer shook her head. "I am Canadian, but my parents are German. They came to Canada from Engen."

"I thought I heard a South German accent," he said, taking off his cap.

"I studied mathematics at Bonn university for two years. I had hoped to stay longer, but my father fell off the roof at home and was badly injured. My mother wrote me that she feared for his life and he wanted to see me before I died. He did two weeks after I arrived back home. Before he died, he made me promise to answer the call of the Fatherland."

Two of the sailors reached down and pulled her aboard the patrol boat. "My things," she said, looking at the captain, who nodded, and two sailors jumped aboard the returned with her suitcase and purse. The patrol boat turned left, churning up the water in its wake. Sommer looked at her boat bobbing on the waves, deserted and alone. It was the only connection she had with Andrew, and now it was gone, and her mother and daughter. She seemed to leave them all behind in the motorboat.

The captain approached her. "When we land, we will take you to the Gestapo. They will decide what happens to you."

***

"If you don't have an ID or a passport, we can't verify you are who you say you are," and Capt. Reinhardt Weisz commanded the Gestapo office in a small town near Calais. "Your German is perfect. And you appear to have friends in high places who have not yet gotten back to us. In the meantime, you will be placed in one of our cells until we decide what to do with you."

Weisz had dark grey eyes that closed when he laughed,

86

which was not often. He had grown a large stomach in recent months and was on another diet, which put him in a bad mood. He lost his temper easily, and the staff tried to avoid him as much as possible.

The first call was from Bonn University. It was Professor Albrecht who asked where Sommer was now.

"In one of our cells," said Weisz in a gruff voice.

"Get her out immediately. We need her to work with us on a new secret project ordered by the Fuhrer.

"Can you vouch for her?"

Professor Albrecht was shouting now. "Of course, you idiot. What do you think I've been trying to tell you."

"I will see to things immediately, Herr Professor." Weisz made a mental note to wait for his other calls before doing anything. At the end of the day, he ordered Sommer released.

"I gather Capt. Weisz talked to Professor Albrecht," said the guard, who unlocked her cell and nodded. "May I advise you to play up to the captain. He is a very vain man, and you will need his goodwill until you reach Berlin."

Sommer smiled a thank-you and followed him to Weisz's office. Weisz had just finished combing his grey mustache and looking at himself in a desk mirror. He had a large desk gleaming in the sun's light from the window to his left. It was completely clean of any papers or folders. A large picture of Hitler dominated the wall behind her.

"That mustache looks as though it were made for you, captain. It makes you look so distinguished, don't you think so," she said, cocking her head this way and another as if to see him from a different angle."

Weisz smiled. "Thank you, fraulein. He put the mirror inside his desk. "I have talked to Professor Albrecht at Bonn, He tells me you were his most brilliant student and needs you for a project he is heading for the war front. Others have also told me that." I told him we were sending you to Gestapo Headquarters in Berlin. They also wish to talk to you."

"One thing, captain. I have no money and no place to lay my head tonight,"

Weisz was nodding as she spoke. "You will spend the best hotel in town. Order whatever you wish. You are the guest of the Third Reich." He closed the folder with her name on it and turned. "Heinrich," he said in a loud voice.

A SS private sitting outside his office stuck his head inside.

"Escort Fraulein Kappel to the hotel and make sure the owner understands he must obey any request she has." He smiled and touched his mustache. "Before you go, fraulein, you should know that Heinrich will be escorting you to Berlin to make sure nothing happens to you.

***

The phone was ringing as Sommer emerged from the bathroom. It was Heinrich. "I'll be ready in five minutes."

Heinrich was waiting in front of the hotel's wire–caged elevator. He took her suitcase and had a driver take it to the railway station, where soldiers are alighting from a train nearby.

"What's this about?"

Heinrich shrugged. "I heard there were troops arriving today, but I have no idea where they're going. We're often the last people to hear about things." He looked at a train on the opposite track. "That's our train," he said, leading the way. He helped her up and followed her down the corridor. "We are in the last compartment on your right."

They sat down on well-worn seats wide enough for three people. The floor of their compartment was covered in mud and dust to the point where she could barely make out the design. Heinrich relaxed. He sat in the seat opposite her and lit a cigarette. He offered her one, but she shook her head.

Later, when he was thirsty, he hailed down a passing steward and ordered sandwiches and four coffees – "one for now and one for later."

Soldiers passed their compartments on their way to the dining car. One of them slid open their door. Heinrich waved to them. "You've got it easy, "he said to Heinrich, eyeing Sommer."

"Where are you headed?"

"No one knows. But there is talk about the Russian front. And you?"

"Just escorting this young lady to the Gestapo in Berlin."

"Lucky you," the soldier said, closing their compartment door and disappearing down the hall.

Ten minutes later, their train started with a sudden jerk as another troop train arrived. You could hear their laughter from their compartment. Sommer made a mental note to tell Brookside about it. But how to reach him?

Five hours later, the train rolled into the Berlin railyard just as a siren started to wail. Heinrich grabbed her suitcase. "We need to get off the train now and run for shelter as soon as the train stops."

CHAPTER THIRTEEN

Gestapo Headquarters occupied the art museum on Prince Albrecht Strasse. Sommer could feel her heart beating rapidly in her ears as she walked by the columns on either side of the entranceway and becoming even more rapid as she mounted the wide staircase to the second floor.

Heinrich asked for Col. Reinhard Jager and was directed down a long corridor to Room 189. She spotted him as soon as Heinrich opened the door. Col. Jager, tall, slim, and energetic, was talking on the phone. His secretary, a blond wearing ruby red lipstick, laid down her cigarette. "Col. Jager is busy now but is expecting you. Have a seat over there," she said, nodding to the seats against the other wall.

"Mission done, Heinrich, And thank you for getting me here safe and sound."

His face reddened. He rose and clicked his heels. "Good luck," He left a minute later, glancing back at her as the door closed behind him.

"You're from Southern Germany?" said Jager's secretary.

"No, Canada."

"But you talk with a southern accent."

"My mother and father came from Engen."

"So do I. What are their names?"

"Kappel. Jacob and Wildfreida. My aunt, Gerda Weber, still lives there. I visited her a year ago."

"I know Gerda. It really is a small world. My name's Hilda, by the way."

Jager's office was furnished with three modern wide chairs covered with white cloth showing signs of Germany's conquests and capable of seating two people. There were pictures around the world showing scenes of German troops marching on the streets of Paris and Warsaw and a very large portrait picture of Hitler.

Hilda glanced at Jager's office. "Good luck with your meeting with Col. Jager. He's looking over your file now." There was a short buzz. "He's ready to see you."

Sommer was not sure what to expect. He left her standing while he finished reading her file. Five minutes later, he closed her file and waved her to the chair in front of his desk. "I see your parents come from Engen. So does my secretary."

Sommer smiled. "She knows my aunt."

Jager stood and extended his hand. He was about to sit down when he offered her a cigarette. Sommer shook her head. "Smart lady. You've had a child, and the father doesn't know." He looked up. "I see you describe him as a smooth-talking RAF pilot."

"I never told him. I returned to Canada to have my baby; I did not want my child to be born in England." Sommer could feel her cheeks burn. Just talking about it made her feel uncomfortable.

"You should have come to the Fatherland. We would have welcomed you in every way."

Sommer kept nodding as he talked. "When you're alone and in a panic, you don't always think clearly. Besides, my father fell off the roof of our home, and my mother sent me a letter to come home to be with him before he died." She paused. "He died two weeks after I came home, but before he died, he made me promise to answer the call of the Fatherland in his name. "Another pause. "Jacob Kappel reporting for duty and ready to serve."

"We're glad you think this way. I've taken the liberty of calling Col. Erwin Schwartz at Wehrmacht headquarters. He needs your math skills. Professor Albrecht at Bonn University says you are his most brilliant student ever. Schwartz needs someone with your math skills just now."

He stood and offered a Hitler salute, which she returned, laughing. It felt strange and awkward, but she also realized she had better get used to it.

It was a cold fall day, with a fierce wind from the north as she walked to Wehrmacht headquarters, only a few office buildings away. Inside, she could feel the difference. Less tense but with a heady sense of a place where things were made to happen. It was also warmer.

"Col. Jager recommends you highly," said Col. Horst Schwartz. His office was filled with pictures of groups of soldiers, metals and Wehrmacht generals. A picture of Hitler was on his desk. Schwartz had a broad face, black hair and dark eyes that made you feel you were the only person in the world. His soldiers loved him and nicked named themselves *Schwartz's Hellions.*

He glanced at her file and laid it down on his desk. "I'm assigning you to our coding department. Let me introduce you to Zelda, who runs our office." He rose from his chair, dusted off a few cake crumbs from his tunic and led her to a shapely young woman who had been typing out field orders for much of the day. She blew an aberrant lock of brown hair from her forehead and looked up as Schwartz approached.

"Zelda Thiessen, meet Sommer Kappel. She's going to work with us on coding for a while."

Zelda eyed her suitcase and asked her where she was staying.

"I haven't solved that problem yet."

"You're welcome to stay with me until you get your

own place. Unless you…"

Sommer shook her head. "I would be very grateful."

Later, on their way to her home, Zelda suddenly stops. "My friend, Lotte, may have a spare room. Her husband is in Czechoslovakia with the SS and doesn't get home all that often."

At lunch the next day, Zelda leaned forward as if to impart some great secret." She was a bit hesitant but will see us after work."

Everyone liked Zelda. Her large black eyes had a language of their own, and her hands were never still. "We'll take the tram. You'll love her. If she likes someone, she'll do anything for them. Her husband is insanely jealous of her."

It took about 20 minutes to reach her house. She had prepared some sandwiches for them and hugged Zelda as soon as she opened the door. Lotte was in her mid-30s, tall, slim and with a sparkle in her eyes, men found attractive. "So this is the young woman you've been raving about."

"Her name is Sommer Kappel. She's insanely brilliant. Everyone at the office likes her."

"What a wonderful name. Sommer Kappel. You have very beautiful eyes." Like Zelda, she punctuated her comments with her hands. "I've made some sandwiches for us. I so love parties. Do you like parties, Sommer?"

Sommer didn't quite know how to respond. "It depends on the party."

They laughed together. Sommer found her light spirit exciting.

"I never get out anymore. Since my husband left for Czechoslovakia, I haven't stuck my nose out the door. I have no one to go with. When my husband is here, we go to a party almost every night to dance the night away with other SS officers and their wives." She paused. "Tell me about yourself, Sommer. I'll go on forever if you don't stop me."

"Not much to tell. My parents are from Southern Germany and immigrated to Canada after the Great War. Before my father died, he made me promise to answer the call of the Fatherland and put myself at its disposal."

Both Zelda and Lotte smiled. Lotte passed her and Zelda another sandwich. "With rationing now, it's hard to get any food," said Lotte.

Sommer nodded and tried to smile. "So I found out on my first day on the job. By the way, how close are you to St. Michael's Church? I like to go to Mass every Sunday."

"It's a bit of a distance."

"No problem. My father always wanted to see it before he died."

"I think we will have a great time together, Sommer Kappel. So will my husband, especially after he hears you go to church every week. Let me show you the room. It is a small room in the attic. "If you like it, it's yours."

"I have no money. Can you wait until payday?"

"I understand, and it's no problem. It'll be a treat to have someone to talk to other than the walls and the radio."

***

Oberleutenant Konrad Becker waited until the end of the day before seeing Col. Jager. He knocked and opened the door.

"You wanted to see me, Becker?"

"About that Kappel woman. Why did you send her to the Wehrmacht to do coding?"

"She can't do any harm there. Why are you asking, Becker?"

"I'm not sure. Not something I can put my finger on exactly but something in my stomach tells me there's a lot more to her and why she's here more than she's not telling us."

Jager inserted a cigarette in his ivory holder and lit it. "I don't know more I can do. We've checked everything she's told us, and everything checked out. We even checked her story about stealing a motorboat to get to us. Our agents in London reported that the boat was reported stolen to the London police at that time."

"What about her pregnancy?"

"That, too, checks out. Women are like that. She's embarrassed by the whole thing. On top of everything else, Professor Albrecht, her old teacher at Bonn, thinks the world of her and wants her for a special project initiated by the Fuhrer. But she declines to tell us the name of the father. So tread carefully."

Becker saluted and left, shaking his head. His gut had never been wrong, and it was working overtime since he heard Sommer's story. He straightened up. His stomach was never wrong, and it wasn't wrong now. He was strong, muscular and had an impressive bearing. Women liked his close-cut light blond hair and authoritative manner. He decided to stay put for the time being and watch her closely, find out who her contacts were and the names of the friends she made. He will bide his time and when it was time to strike, he would bring her to justice.

CHAPTER FOURTEEN

It took only 30 minutes by tram and a short walk past a magnificent garden and the canal to reach St. Michael's. She felt immediately at peace as soon as she passed the entrance guarded above by a statue of St. Michael and into the church. She looked at the Way of the Cross and up at the statues of saints in alcoves under the great dome and knew she was home again. She dipped her finger in holy water and made the sign of the cross before walking up the aisle on the right until she reached the 24th pew. She knelt and prayed for guidance.

A middle-aged woman arrived with three small children in tow. She smiled at Sommer and grabbed her youngest, who was trying to crawl beneath the pew.

The organ above her at the back of the church burst into song with a sound she had never heard before. The familiar sound of a Latin high mass transported her back to when she sat between her mother and father as a child. For a second, she thought of Andrea, and wondered if her mother was already taking her to mass.

When mass ended, she opened the Missal from the rack in front of her, turned to page 157 and inserted a holy card of St. Michael from her purse. The woman with the three children stood and started to leave. The woman smiled at her again before marching her three toddlers out of the church. Sommer suddenly felt self-conscious and decided to wait until the church was almost empty before she left.

A week later, the holy card was gone when she opened the Missal. Her heart almost leaped out of her body, and she smiled inside. She no longer felt alone. It meant Brookfield knew where she was and how to contact her. She took a deep breath, inserted another holy card to the same page, and quietly left.

***

Becker couldn't believe at first that the old man with the thick grey mustache was a spy. They brought him in for questioning when one of the Gestapo's plainclothes officers saw him talking to a British agent known to them. It was the second one they napped that week, and Becher couldn't help feeling pleased for himself.

They beat him first with a club and then gave him the water treatment before administering the truth serum. All they learned was that he was not married, had no living relatives, felt sorry for Jews and didn't believe what Hitler was doing. He held up his hand and started to beat him again. Blood poured from a broken artery in his head, spattering it over Becker's face and tunic. Becker withdrew his gun and shot him between the eyes.

He walked into Jager's office with a swagger. "Just came back from killing a British agent. In the end, I shot him between the eyes, which brings me to Sommer Kappel. I must admit she's made a difference at the Wehrmacht, but if it turns out she's a spy, think of the damage she may already have done."

"My hands are tried, Oberleutenant. You know that. I cannot do anything unless there is clear evidence to the contrary. In case you don't know, she's staying at the home of an SS officer and has become friends with his wife."

Jager lit a cigarette and sat back in his chair.

"Then let me add this before I quit talking about it. The

old man attended the same St. Michael's Church Mass as Sommer Kappel. I had both of them watched to see if there were any connection."

"Was there?"

Becker shook his head. "But in my books, you must admit it's more than just co-incidence."

"When you questioned the old man, did you ask him?"

"He denied it."

"Did you believe him?"

"Not sure. All I know is that something in the pit of my stomach tells me there's a lot more to Sommer Kappel than she's letting on. Until we know, one way or the other, I'm not willing to change my mind until this feeling in my stomach leaves. And it's still there."

***

The next stop for Becker was Wehrmacht Headquarters on the pretext of seeing Col. Schmidt about a soldier under his command putting a black comb beneath his nose and raising his arm in a salute.

"Do you have the name?" There was a note of weariness in Col. Schmidt's voice.

"No, but I thought you might be able to find out for us."

"Leave it with me, Oberleutenant. There's no need for you to trouble yourself about it further."

On his way out, he stopped by Zelda's desk and bragged about breaking down a British agent. "We tortured him before he confessed, and then I shot him between the eyes."

Sommer, who worked at a desk close to Zelda's, listened and kept working without raising her head.

"It's always a time for celebration when we uncover the identity of an enemy of the Reich. Don't you agree, fraulein," he said.

Sommer knew the question was addressed to her and looked up. "Congratulations, Oberleutenant." Inside, she felt like vomiting.

Later, when she took the tram home, she realized how alone she was. Even Brookfield's vague words to her – if her contact were ever arrested, he would find her a way to send a message to her – sounded hollow now. That's when she knew Becker was getting to her.

***

She couldn't wait to get to St. Michael's. It was only two days away. Finally, when Sunday came, she hurried to get dressed and head for the tram. She ran from the tram, past the gardens and underneath the entrance, trying to steady herself and walk slowly to aisle 157. She slid into the pew and reached for a missal, quickly turning to page 157. Her card was still there. She sat motionless for the next few minutes, not daring to turn around. She turned the Missal to the beginning of the mass.

The priest entered behind an acolyte carrying a candle. And above her, one of her favourite Latin hymns. It helped her to feel at peace as she concentrated on the mass. "*Ita, missa est.*" She heard the priest say the words and decided to stay and light a candle to St. Jude before she left.

On the tram on the way home, the panic returned. She felt trapped with no chance to escape and, for the first time, regretted meeting Brookfield and being talked into a venture her life was constantly under threat. Brookfield's words kept echoing in her head, and she realized she was the only person she could expect help from. From Lotte, perhaps. Definitely, not Zelda.

If only Perdita were here. Perdita had a way of making her feel better. She closed her eyes. Maybe tomorrow.

***

"Col. Schmidt wants to see you," said Zelda. "There was excitement in her eyes.

"Did he say what it was about?"

"No, but he seemed quite agitated."

Sommer knocked at his door and opened it.

"Sit down. You're making me nervous, Sommer. I have a letter from the Gestapo indicating that we may lose you. It appears that the Fuhrer has launched a special project and has appointed Professor Albrecht to head it. Albrecht has indicated that he wants you as part of his group."

Perdita was right, thought Sommer, feeling the tension suddenly leave her body.

"We'll be sorry to lose you." Then, after a pause, "We don't know when that will be, Sommer. It could be a week, a month, or two or three months. They're just letting us know so we can find someone to fill your shoes." Another pause. "You'll be hard to replace."

Zelda didn't wait for her to sit down. "What was that about?"

"Just a warning that I may be transferred. It seems I'm wanted elsewhere to work on a special project."

"I always knew you were special. You must be very proud."

"It won't happen right away. It's just an advance notice that will happen in the near future." She stopped and tried to smile. "I will miss you all."

"Before you go, will you help me understand the math you use for our work? I promise to study hard."

***

"Does that mean you'll be leaving me?" said Lotte.

"I hope not. I knew that Professor Albrecht – you heard me talk about him – has come to Humboldt University here in Berlin to work on a special project and wants to be part of his team."

"For the Fuhrer," said Zelda.

"This calls for a special celebration. So get your coats on. Sommer will be paying," said Lotte.

There was a small restaurant two blocks away that Lotte and her husband liked and frequented by Gestapo people. The entrance was lit with a neon tube on both sides, and the door had a cut glass pane. Even from outside, they could hear the music and the sound of excited voices.

"I love this place," said Lotte, who knew the doorman. He was dressed in a black suit with a black bow tie and escorted them to a table in the left corner and placed menus on each of their plates. He bowed and left them, returning a few minutes later with three glasses and a bottle of wine. "Compliments of the House."

They saw a few of the officers look their way. One of them, a young recruit with dark bedroom eyes and a face to match, rose and came to their table and introduced himself as Hans Weiner, a freshly minted lieutenant. Lotte introduced herself as the wife of a Gestapo captain, who would soon join them.

He clicked his heels, bowed, and returned to his party. They patted him on the back and went back to drinking. Zelda shook her head. "He was so cute, Lotte."

There was a sudden excitement, with voices rising and clinking glasses to an announcement that the German army was at the outskirts of Stalingrad. Zelda and Lotte clapped along with the others. They looked at Sommer, who suddenly joined them.

"It will be a night we will always remember."

CHAPTER FIFTEEN

"And who might you be?" Steffen Kirshner was a big man, even by German standards, with a red beard, deep voice, and laugh. His associates nicknamed him Steffen Barbarosa. He downed a shot of Brandy in one gulp and smiled at her.

"My name is Sommer Kappel, and I'm just getting back from work."

"So my wife tells me. She seems to like you a lot. Which is good in one way."

"Sommer is very religious, Steffen. She goes to mass every Sunday," said Lotte in a defensive voice as she entered the kitchen.

"Take her with you, Sommer Kappel. Take her with you the next time you go. She's Lutheran. But don't let that stop you." He laughed again, pinched his wife's bottom, and downed another shot of Brandy.

Later, when he thought of their meeting, he had a gut feeling that she was too good to be true and decided to call Jager about her the next day.

After Sommer left for work, Steffan joined his wife at the kitchen table. "Just got off the phone with Col. Jager, you remember him, about Sommer. He says they've checked everything she told them, and she's everything she says she is.

Konrad Becker has some doubts about her. He wants her to be put under 24-hour surveillance for the next few months to see if she does anything suspicious. Could you check her room and report anything that would suggest she might be a spy."

"Sommer is my friend, Steffen. One of the few people I've met in Berlin. I would trust her with my life. I won't do this, Steffen."

Steffen seemed to grow two inches as he straightened up. "Keeping the Reich safe from people who would destroy it is what I do every day. You must help us. You are my wife, Lotte. Your allegiance must be to me and Germany."

A week later, Lotte told her that she had been approached by one of her associates to write down everything she said.

"Have you?" Sommer felt sick to her stomach.

Lotte shook her head. "You've become a real friend, Sommer. Unlike most people I've met in Berlin, who are pretty superficial. I don't know what I'd do if I didn't have you and Zelda. I'm not prepared to spy on anyone, let alone my friends. It's not who I am. I told Steffen that before he left. He didn't like it. But he also told me the Gestapo had put you under 24-hour surveillance."

Sommer didn't know what to say, and she broke into tears and hugged Lotte. That's when she thought about Professor Fuhrman's sister. He had asked her to see his sister if she found herself in Berlin. She had written down her name, address and telephone number in her notebook. It should still be there. She still had Professor Fuhrman's magic key. Maybe his sister, she thought, would know what it was for. And then, just as suddenly, she wanted desperately to be with her daughter and mother and disappeared from everything that frightened her.

Her mind returned to the magic key, and she decided

to see the professor's sister. If she was being followed, how could she without endangering the professor's sister? She decided to talk to Lotte about the professor and his sister.

"Invite her to join us for tea," said Lotte.

"I don't want to put you to any trouble."

"Besides, it'll be a great change for us. Call her now, and let's invite Zelda and make it a real party." Her voice had a special lilt.

Jundt Fuhrman listened as Sommer described herself as a student of her brother, Professor Sigfried Fuhrman and that he asked her to find out how you were. He also asked me to help you in any way I could.

"We'd like to invite you to join Lotte, her friend, Zelda and me for tea on any Sunday best for you."

"I would be delighted. I can't wait to hear how Siegfried has succeeded in Canada."

Sommer gave her the address and hung up. "Do you want me to invite Zelda when I return to work tomorrow?"

***

"How is Siegfried? It's been years since we've seen each other. He was so good to me when we were young. Now, he is so far away." Her voice trailed to some long-forgotten memory.

Lotte passed her a cup of tea and a plate of biscuits to Zelda, who sat next to Lottie. Jundt turned to Sommer. "What was he like as a professor?" Her voice quivered when she spoke his name. "It has been many years since we were together. I used to get packages from him at Christmas, but since the outbreak of war, that is now just a dream."

Zelda passed her another biscuit while Lotte rose to pour more tea for everyone.

"If it had not been for Professor Fuhrman, I would not be here today," said Sommer. He lectured at Bonn University before accepting a post at McGill, where he was head of the mathematics department. He arranged a two-year scholarship for me at Bonn University."

Her face had a few wrinkles around her eyes and mouth, and her dark grey eyes looked tired. "You have such a lovely place," said Jundt, looking around the room.

"My husband is away. He's with the SS and stationed in Czechoslovakia. He manages to leave every three or four months, but it's never long enough. If it weren't for Zelda and Sommer, I think I'd go crazy."

"Do you plan to have a family?"

"We've been trying for a year or two without success."

Around four o'clock, she was getting tired and rose, holding onto the back of her chair to get her balance. "It's time for me to go home. But before I leave, I would like to invite you three lovely ladies to tea at my home next Sunday. I want you to see my garden. It's been a great solace and comfort in these times."

"It must be wonderful, "said Zelda. "I have no room for anything like that except, perhaps, a window box."

"When you come, I want each of you to pick as many blooms as you wish to take back with you."

"I can't wait," said Zelda.

***

Jundt decided to go to mass with Sommer the following Sunday and guide everyone to her home, about 30 minutes away by tram and then a 10-minute walk.

Sommer and Jundt headed out to catch the train. Jundt told her she couldn't walk as fast as she used to. There were within sight of the tram line when Sommer stopped. "I need to ask you a question. When I left home for Germany, your brother gave me a key. He called it a magic key."

"When you come to supper today, I will show you why he calls it magic."

Lotte and Zelda, decked out in colourful fall dresses

and jackets, were waiting for them an hour later when Jundt and Sommer reached them at their tram stop. The tram was packed, and they had to stand for almost 40 minutes to reach Jundt's stop. They followed her down a long street, then left and later right again to reach Jundt's two-storey brick house. Inside, they fell into three large comfortable chairs in Jundt's living room. Their feet ached from the walk. "Next time," said Zelda, "high heels are out."

"It's absolutely beautiful," said Lotte. "This is what I call a real living room. After living in Berlin for three years, you forget things like real living rooms."

The living room was large by Berlin standards, with long lace curtains at the two windows that reached the hardwood floor. There was a large, stand-alone radio in the left corner that was softly playing German classical music.

Jundt smiled and left to put the teapot on. Sommer followed her to help her slice the small cake Jundt had made before coming to church and put out the dishes to put the cake on.

Zelda and Lotte appeared in the doorway. "If you don't mind, Jundt, we're aching to see your garden. Would you mind if we took a quick peek?" she said, beckoning Sommer to follow them.

They walked through her kitchen, past her long table and to the back door. As they entered the garden, no one spoke for almost a minute before splitting to see what flowers they loved first. Lotte bent to smell the brilliant yellow flowers bordering the garden's right side. Zelda paused among the Sunflowers and Mums. Sommer was attracted by the white, purple and blue Asters, which reminded her of home.

"It's so big," said Lotte as they walked back to the house, just in time to see Jundt pouring tea into four China cups and placing white China dishes for the cake on a separate table.

"Everything seemed so substantial, so solid, so pre-war. They felt comforted in a strange way.

"I'll be glad when the war is over," said Lotte.

"But things are going so well for us. The Fuhrer has given us hope again. Every sacrifice we make now is worth it," said Zelda in an emotional voice.

"What do you think, Jundt? You lived through the last war," said Lotte.

"It was not a good time. My mother died during the war. And it cost Germany dearly. It was one of the reasons why I took up gardening. To breathe new life in the ground and us."

"Are you saying you do not believe we will prevail?"

"Do not pay attention to me. I am an old woman, and what do I know about the world?" Jundt smiled weakly. "Would you like more tea?" She stood suddenly. "Where is my mind? It's time to prepare dinner." She turned to Sommer. "Would you go downstairs to bring me some potatoes and a squash? I've been saving them for an event like this."

Sommer found the potatoes but not the squash and looked up to see Jundt coming down the stairs. "I forgot to tell you where to find the squash."

She showed Sommer a half-hidden bottom shelf. She pushed back the potatoes to reveal an almost invisible crack near the bottom of the board behind the shelf. She pointed to it and to the key in her hand. Sommer nodded just as they heard Lotte coming down the stairs. Jundt smiled as she approached them. "You're just in time for us to ask you what else you'd like."

Lotte spotted the parsnips behind the potatoes. "I haven't had parsnips since I left home." She looked to see a can of Danish ham on an upper shelf. "Where in the name of Heaven did you get this? Could I ask you if you have any eggs and if you do, could we have ham and eggs for dinner?"

"I've been keeping the ham for some time. I had hopes that my dear brother would visit me. But that's impossible now. But you three would do just fine."

After lunch, she asked Lotte and Sommer to come to see them and, this time, for supper.

"Actually, I was just about to ask you to visit me next week."

They look their leave an hour later with their arms full of fresh blooms, wrapped in the previous day's newspaper.

CHAPTER SIXTEEN

Zelda came early the following Sunday to help Lotte prepare lunch for Jundt, who had arrived early to go to church with Sommer. Jundt had arthritis in her left knee and hobbled along as best as she could.

"I think we should take a taxi. You'll be in a lot of pain late if we don't," said Sommer.

Jundt ignored her. "Now that we are alone, there is much to talk about."

"But your knee?"

"Perhaps later. We need to talk about the key." She stopped to let the pain ebb away. "It's the key to a special room in my basement, hidden behind the vegetable cold room. Siegfried called it a safe harbour in times of storm and believed we would use it one day. He was also far-seeing as a boy."

She started walking. "If we don't hurry, we'll miss the tram and be late. Getting back to the key. Do you remember the keyhole slit I pointed out to you last week? It's very small and painted the same colour as the wall. You really must know what you're looking for to notice it. When you insert the key, be sure to twist it counterclockwise to open it to reveal the secret room. My father had it built in the last great war."

They were approaching the tram station when Jundt added, "one thing more, the room is equipped with electricity and stocked with food, some dating back to the 1920s. Enough to keep you safe and sound for at least two weeks. During blackouts, I go down there to read."

They reached the tram stop, and waited for a few minutes before Sommer paid for their fares and helped Jundt to a seat. They had the car almost to themselves.

"It's like that on Sundays. But let me continue while we have the chance. Should you ever need a place to hide, even if my home is bombed and I am dead, you know where to go for safety now."

On the way back, Jundt started talking about her brother. Sommer suddenly became serious. "Don't look back. There's a heavy-set man with a sour look on his face. It's the same man I noticed following us last week."

Jundt smiled. "I saw him last week, too. He was sitting in the last pew this week and last."

Lotte and Zelda had different coloured streamers strung from one corner of the room to the other. Jundt stood back to admire it. "It's almost like Christmas. I am so lucky to meet you, young ladies. I cannot tell you how much you mean to me."

"That's not all, Jundt. Lotte saved some party hats from last year's New Year's celebrations."

"As well as a special cake to go with it. We begged and borrowed enough ingredients to make a cake that would bring back memories of the old days just for you," said Lotte.

"And a special surprise we're saving for the end," said Zelda, winking at Sommer, who was helping Jundt fix her party hat. Sommer stood back. " Grey and blue make you look more beautiful than ever."

"Stay right there," said Zelda, who waved a camera in her hands. "I have six shots left on this roll. I've been saving them for something like this."

"Ask your friend, Becker," said Lotte. "The Gestapo always gets anything it needs, including film."

Zelda's face blushed. "You all know I have feelings for him."

"Only God knows why," added Lotte. "He's a bit of a bore."

"Maybe I will ask him," said Zelda, who looked as though she were ready to cry.

Jundt put her arms around her. "I had feelings for someone special once and allowed my mother to talk me out of it. Don't let anyone stop you."

They spend the rest of the afternoon singing old popular songs and new ones, especially *Lilli Marlene*. It was getting time to leave when Lotte announced one more surprise, nodding to Sommer.

Sommer reached inside her purse. "Close your eyes." She withdrew three snapshots. "Now open them."

Jundt started crying as soon as she held them in her hands. All three were pictures of Siegfried with different students. Sommer was in one of them.

"I thought never to see his face again. How handsome he is."

***

Becker showed up at their office a few days later. "Where's Zelda?'

Sommer looked up. "Home sick in bed with a bad cold." She smiled at him and returned to her work.

"I came to invite her to lunch and thank her for all her

wonderful work for the Reich. She is an amazing person."

"She is that and more, Oberleutenant."

"Seeing I'm here, would you care to join me?"

"I'm quite busy on a code. It's needed in a real hurry."

"I'd like to thank you for your work. Your codes are admired all across the Reich's armed forces." Then, after a brief pause: "Get your coat, and we'll lunch nearby," his last sentences sounded more like a command.

They lunched at a small restaurant across the street. It had only a few tables, and they were crammed. There was a bar at the end of the room and a bartender wiping the counter when they entered. The waiter automatically brought two beers to their table and left with their orders.

Becker raised his glass. "To the Third Reich. May it last 10,000 years." Sommer raised her glass and repeated his toast.

"I've taken the liberty of ordering wiener schnitzel. This restaurant is known for it." He patted his stomach. "I think I need to go on a diet."

The waiter arrived with the food.

"I would not say that, Oberleutenant. You look very fit to me," said Sommer, carefully cutting into the wiener schnitzel.

"I still find you a bit of an enigma, fraulein."

Sommer did not respond.

"There are four months that are not accounted for in your story."

"After you left your home and the time we met in Berlin, there are four to five months that are not accounted for."

"I told Col. Jager that I went to a convent when I left home."

"What on earth for?"

"I went to renew myself and find myself closer to God. I wanted to stay a full year, but Mother Superior thought I was ready to leave and make my mark in the world."

"But four months?"

Sommer didn't respond.

Later, when he returned to his office, Becker felt he wasn't any further ahead. Even when she told him about her stay at the convent, it didn't put his mind at rest. Then, there were the codes. He had to admit, she excelled at it. He had to admit she was very clever and of use to the Reich in a big way. He even sent one of his staff to interview Lotte, Steffen's wife, who laughed at any idea that Sommer was a British spy. And Professor Albrecht was the most bothersome of all. He had enormous respect for her and was delighted that she had returned to the Fatherland. With all these things, why couldn't he leave things well enough alone? But deep down, he knew why. His stomach was whispering a different story.

***

A month later, Col. Schmidt passed Sommer's desk, cigarette in hand and laughing at something one of the coders had said. "If you have time, Sommer, I'd like to talk to you."

He sat back in his chair and lit another cigarette. "I've just received orders to transfer you to Professor Albrecht's project."

Sommer couldn't believe what she was hearing. She normally would have given her teeth to work alongside one of the great brains of the century, but at the Wehrmacht, she would have been of much greater use to London.

"I can see by your face that you're disappointed. If it's any comfort, Professor Albrecht describes it as something that could end the war. So are we, but the war needs you elsewhere. You are to report to Professor Albrecht at Humboldt University, Lecture Room 422, Monday at 9 a.m."

Sommer stood. "I've enjoyed working with you, Col. Schmidt. All of us do."

"Before you go, I'd like your confidential assessment of Zelda Thiessen's abilities. I know she works hard, but I need someone to replace you."

"I know Zelda wants to do more for the war effort than just typing reports. May I suggest you give her a try for a month and see how she performs? So that you know, Zelda has been studying mathematics with me for three months. She really wants the job and is capable of doing more."

"Interesting. You paint an entirely different picture of her than I had in my mind."

Zelda put a paper on her desk. "What did he want?" she whispered.

"To tell me I'm being transferred as of Monday."

Zelda's large blue eyes glistened. "Did he say who would replace you?"

"No. But he asked whether I thought you were capable of doing my job. I told him you had been studying math with me and were capable of doing much more for the war effort."

"I could kiss you."

Sommer smiled and marvelled at how her fortunes had suddenly changed.

Later that evening, when she put out the light in her room, her mind wandered back to what Brookfield had told her -- leave the bathroom light on until she heard from someone who would identify as a beauty shop. She had left the light on for ten nights with no word and wondered if it would ever happen.

CHAPTER SEVENTEEN

It reminded Sommer of the first time she met Professor Albrecht. She had a hard time sleeping the night before and woke up early. She had no idea where Lecture Room 420 was and stopped at least ten students before getting definite instructions. In some ways, being on a university campus again was like being at home. The buildings, the quads and the changing landscape of students hurrying to class made her feel like one of them.

The hall was empty, save for a desk and a chair at the front and six student chairs with small moveable desks arranged in a circle around the main desk. She decided to sit in the middle. She opened the door and peeked in. There was a knock at the door, and a woman's face peeked in. It was Gretchen Moller who spotted Sommer as soon as she saw her. Sommer stood as Gretchen broke into a run to hug her.

"I was hoping you would be part of this. I had heard you had left Germany, but I knew in my heart you would return."

They sat down, Gretchen beside her. "I never forgot that Christmas."

Another knock. This time two young men, followed by a woman. Gretchen stood and waved them over, and got them seated. They were about to introduce themselves when Professor Albrecht arrived and strode to the front. They all stood, just as she and Gretchen did at Bonn.

"Welcome, ladies and gentlemen. I see that one of you is missing. Some of you I know from your days at Bonn. I feel very honoured that you are joining me on a quest that could change everything for the Fatherland. We have gathered together the best mathematical brains in Germany. Each of you will be given certain problems to solve, and occasionally, you may need to work in groups to solve particularly complex problems."

"Can you tell us what they are for, professor?" said the woman sitting next to Gretchen and who rose to her feet to ask the question.

"That information was not offered to me, other than our work could change war completely and make Germany the greatest country in the world, including the Americas and Asia. So all of us need to put our hearts and mind into this great adventure."

The door opened, and everyone turned to see who it was. A young man with long black hair and an awkward way of walking that made you feel he was about to stumble at any time. He took the empty seat in the back row.

Professor Albrecht had stopped talking while he took his seat. "As I was saying, for the moment, our task is like walking into a dark room and not knowing where we are or what they want us to do?"

"Are you really serious?" The voice came from the young man who had just arrived.

"The Fuhrer thinks so." Professor Albrecht never liked being interrupted, and his voice's hardness was unmistakable.

"My assistant for this assignment is Sommer Kappel," he said, raising the palm of his hand to get her to stand. "Some of you may already know Sommer. For you that do not, she was the most brilliant mathematics student I had ever taught."

Sommer could feel her cheeks burn and wished she could curl up in the chair.

"I haven't asked her yet. So, Sommer, can we count on you?"

Sommer nodded and took her seat. Gretchen pinched her arm and smiled.

"In my absence, go to her if you're stuck or having a problem. There are only seven of us if that young man at the end measures up to our task."

Now, thought Sommer, this is something Brookfield really needs to know about. It had to be for a weapon of mass destruction. But how to get it to him?

"One thing more. Like me, Sommer has a phenomenal memory. Just remember, if you think you can put one over on her."

"For the rest of the day, let us get to know each other, starting with you," he said, pointing to the woman sitting at the left of the semi-circle.

"My name is Romy Fischer," said an attractive 30-something with a broad smile. "I have a doctorate in mathematics from Humboldt University and look forward to working with you all. It's good to hear you have such a memory. I wish I that that gift."

"My name is Martin Koeln. I hope to become a great mathematics professor like Dr. Albrecht."

"I'm Fritz Cullen. I have a master's in mathematics and believe mathematics will rule the world one day."

"You just read my mind, Fritz," said Sommer offering his a smile.

"Jones Stein. I don't have a formal degree. What I know, I have learned on my own. I've always been intrigued by numbers. I hope this doesn't get me off on the wrong foot with Professor Albrecht because I'm late."

"He's a nut about being on time. That goes for the rest

of you. I know I was late for my first meeting with him, and I can tell you he can be quite forgiving if you love mathematics the way he does."

Martin Cullen shook his head. "Did I hear right?" he said, turning to Fritz. That you didn't go to university."

"No." There was authority in his voice that closed off any discussion.

"If you wish," Sommer started to say.

Fritz Cullen broke before she had a chance to speak. "Some memory. What about the lady sitting beside you?"

"Let me handle this, Sommer," said Gretchen, turning to Fritz Collen, "my name is Gretchen Moller, and you're a very rude young man. I have a master's degree from Bonn, where I studied under Dr. Albrecht. Sommer and I knew each other while we were at Bonn. And I can tell you, and she truly is brilliant the way the rest of us aren't. You'll soon know in a hurry when you're stumped, and she can solve in seconds what you've been trying to solve in an hour."

Professor stood and waved to Sommer to come to his desk, giving her five sealed envelopes. "I would like each of them to take this test. They will have one hour to complete it. We may have to shed one or two, depending on whether you think they can contribute to our project in a meaningful way. We won't have time to teach you things you should already know.

He stood and grabbed his briefcase. "I trust your judgment," he said to Sommer.

"What was that all about?"

"We'll talk about it later. Gretchen. Right now, it's first things first."

Three of the others were talking among themselves.

"May I have your attention?" Sommer was surprised by the firmness in her voice. "Professor Albrecht wants you to undergo a special math exam he has prepared to determine whether you'll be invited to participate. Please sit at your desk. We will provide a pad and pencils, which you will find in each envelope along with his exam," she said, placing a sealed envelope on each desk. Please reseal your envelopes and return them to me before we get together for lunch and get to know each other better."

"What's this about?" said Fritz Cullen again. "I have a master's in mathematics, and you want to test me whether I can add or subtract?"

"If I were you, I'd start working on Professor Albrecht's questions. You've already wasted two minutes."

***

Gretchen stayed behind to talk to her. "Tell me what happened to you after you returned to Canada."

"I went to England to find a boat leaving for Canada, fell for a handsome Englishman, and got pregnant."

"How did you handle that? You told me once your mother was very strict and warned you about drinking alcohol and going out when men you didn't know."

"When I finally made my way back home, my mother could see I was pregnant. She didn't ask me who, how or what? She just accepted it and welcomed me with more warmth than I'd ever known. I gave birth to a daughter, who was born in the same room as I was. My father fell off the roof of our home before I returned and was quite sick. Our doctor told us he had a bad heart and that the outlook was not great. He knew he was dying and made me promise that I would return to Germany and serve the Fatherland."

"What about Felix?"

"When I told him my father had written to me about my father and begged me to come home, he told me he was enlisting in the SS to be with his friends. I have never heard from or seen him ever since."

"Aren't you curious?"

"I wasn't really in love with him."

"Should I ever run into him …"

"Please do not mention my name or even that you have seen me."

"To change the subject. Where are you living?"

"I am staying with the wife of an SS officer currently stationed in Czechoslovakia. It would be so good to be with someone from Bonn again."

"Does she have room for one more? I just got in from Bonn last night. They've put me up with 30 other people in a barracks close to the university. I'd rather be with you."

Sommer cocked her head. "You know, Gretchen, I don't think you've aged a day since the last time we saw each other. As far as Lotte, my landlady, goes, I'll ask her tonight and let you know in the morning."

They left together. It started to rain. "I have an idea. Let's have supper in that restaurant we just passed and wait until it stops."

They entered and caught the eye of two airmen sitting at the next table.

"Come on a date with me – the way we used to when life was simpler. But the men are the same and starving for feminine company, like the two airmen at the next table."

"I don't know, Gretchen. After my experience with that Englishman cured me as far as men are concerned."

"It doesn't matter, Sommer. Christmas is coming, and perhaps we can celebrate it together again."

"What about Katrina?"

"She got her wish finally. She entered a convent to become a nun. I went to see her a couple of months ago, but she was not the same person we knew. She seemed happy, though."

Dinner finally came, and they laughed over some of the people who attended Gretchen's parties.

Over coffee, Sommer looked out the window. "I see the rain has stopped. Will you talk to your landlady for me? I would like us to be together again."

***

"Your professor has been calling for you. He said he would call back," said Lotte just as she finished talking. Lotte picked up the phone and passed it to Sommer.

"Yes, Professor."

"I'd like your opinion of the people who wrote the text with you today. We have room only for the best."

"I've already glanced over their answers, and let me start by saying I'd go with that long-haired young man who came in late. He'd be the first choice. Most of the others seemed to lack that special fire, except him — the same spark and fire you have. And the crazy thing about it is that he's never gone to university. Completely self-taught. And he loves mathematics the way children love Christmas."

"If the others pan out, there may not be room for him."

Sommer put down the receiver, lost in thought. Of all the ones she tested, he was the only one worthwhile. Wait until he hears about the others, she thought.

"I had a hunch you might be dining with someone else. A young man, I hope."

"No, just an old friend from my days at Bonn. Her name is Gretchen. She will be working with me at the university. She's looking for a place to stay and wonders if you would have room for her."

Lotte shook her head. I would love to oblige her; we're a bit cramped. In any event, I've saved dessert for you."

She ate the apple tart, drank a cup of coffee, and talked about her first day.

CHAPTER EIGHTEEN

When Sommer least expected it. Lotte mentioned she had received an advertisement from a beauty salon in the mail a few days ago, offering a special on touch-ups, and saved it in case Sommer was interested.

"If you are, here's the card with their telephone number and address. Sommer glanced at the postcard size card ad and put it in her purse. "Maybe they'll be open after work. "

"It's not that far from the university."

"Do you think I should get a trim as well?" Sommer could feel her heart pounding n her ears.

"Maybe a bit, Sommer, but I like your hair the way it is. Let me know if she's any good."

***

Professor Albrecht was in a fidgety mood. "What is it, professor?" Sommer always thought of him as a strong person, as someone who had everything always under control, and was surprised to see him this way.

"Dealing with politicians and generals who can't add one plus one and get two. They were surprised we had nothing to show them after the first day. We are mathematicians. Not mind readers."

"Just ignore them. Tell them their intrusions are slowing us down."

"Politics at the university was bad enough, but this is something else. Forgive me. I shouldn't be bothering you with this."

Sommer smiled. "On a brighter note, I've been able to see how each member of our team performed on paper and their energy among each other in a party-like setting."

"Any decisions?" He sat down on one of the chairs beside her.

"Just as I told you last night: The biggest surprise was the one who came late. He has no formal training in mathematics. He has never attended university, even at the undergraduate level. Yet he loves mathematics, and what numbers can do in a way the others do not. He is self-taught and proved himself with the questions you assigned him."

He reached into his pocket and withdrew his pipe, tamping it down with his thumb before lighting it. He exhaled blue smoke and sat back. "Anything else?"

"He has fire in his voice when he talks about math.

"How would you rank him?"

"No. 1."

"Above your friend, Gretchen? We both know exactly how gifted she is at mathematics."

"There's no question about that. But she does not have his fire."

"Refresh my memory, Sommer. What is his name?"

"Jonas Stein."

"And the weak link?"

"Fritz Cullen. He did well on some questions, but where imagination and originality in solving complex problems came into play, I'm afraid he just doesn't measure up. He also tends to be argumentative. In a group, that could be unsettling."

"And the lady with the doctorate?"

Romy Fischer. She's above average overall. Strong in

tackling problems beyond the norm and getting the right answers."

He laid down his pipe on the chair beside him. "If you had to eliminate two people?"

"Cullen, for sure, and reluctantly, Martin Koeln, who believes mathematics will rule the world one day. He's a team player and gets along with the others."

"That would leave us with a team of five, counting you." He lit his pipe again. "And special thanks for rescuing me from myself. But these people are different. They think you can build a castle in one day."

"You have given me much, professor. I will never forget that."

At that point, the others started to enter. Professor Albrecht tried to shrink his stomach by sucking in the air as he buttoned his jacket. He sat in front of his desk and smiled as they took their seats.

"Good morning, ladies and gentlemen. Today, we start work on our project. I've already prepared the problem on the blackboard behind me. I would like you all to spend the rest of the day finding the best solution. Take your time. When it comes to our job, take all the time you need."

"How will we know if we're right?" said Fritz.

"You won't. And neither will I. The people on another area of this project will let us know if they're happy with it." Then, after a pause: "I would like each of you to remain at the end of the day. I would like to interview you."

There wasn't much talk as her team worked on the equations they had been handed. By the time lunch came around, sheets of paper from failed equations had littered the floor. "Lunch hour is exactly an hour. But before you go, I'll go around to each of you with a wastebasket, and you can put all your failed answers in it."

At the end of the session, Sommer looked over their final answers before handing them to Professor Albrecht.

"And while you're waiting for your interview with Professor Albrecht, coffee will be available at the rear."

They looked to see two women dressed in white uniforms setting up a table and a coffee urn.

"What about smoking," said Martin.

"It's fine if you keep it to the rear."

Gretchen remained behind. "What did Lotte say?"

Sommer shook her head. "I told her you and I were old friends and that it would be so nice if you could stay with us. She said she would like to, but there's just no room."

Jonas was the first to talk to Professor Albrecht. The interview lasted 15 minutes as Professor Albrecht bombarded him with questions. At the end, Jonas left without talking to anyone.

Romy was next. She patted her hair, reapplied her lipstick, and sat down with the brightest smile she could muster. She left a few minutes later with a secret smile in her eyes.

Fritz Cullen carried an aura of superiority as he sat down. Professor Albrecht reviewed his submission with him. Cullen's face looked strained, and he stiffened as he got up and left without a word.

Gretchen had a short session with him and smiled as she returned. "What about supper?"

"Can't. Got a hair appointment."

***

Liesa's Hair Salon was a 20-minute tram ride from the university, and Sommer hoped it would still be open, peering into the window to see a slim-figured woman in tight clothes styling the hair of a grey-haired woman in Liesa's styling chair. Sommer took off her coat and hung it on a white-painted board with coat hangers. She sat down and picked up a magazine on the chair next to her that featured the latest hairstyles.

"I'll be with you a few minutes," she said.

The other woman left a few minutes later, and Leisa waved her to her chair. "You're new," she added, blowing a saucy curl over her forehead. "How did you hear about us?"

"We got your card in our email address. I thought I'd try you out."

Sommer looked into the mirror to see Liesa comb her hair and begin cutting it. "You really should have it coloured. It needs more than a touch-up."

Sommer nodded as Leisa went on about the latest styles. "Your style is a bit pre-war. It's very hard for us to get pre-war beauty products these days." And then, a sudden change in tone. "I think I'm pregnant. My boyfriend is away in the army, and who knows if I'll ever see him again. I hope it's a girl. Do you think Andrea is a great name? I love it."

"My daughter's name is Andrea," said Sommer suddenly. "And I miss her."

"I know." Then she went on about the beauty business. "I hope you will come to my salon whenever your hair needs help."

She paid Leisa and was putting on her coat when Leisa said: "I think you need something. If you come tomorrow, it will be here. I would like to offer it to you for Christmas."

"No need." Sommer has been warned about being too trusting.

"Why not come tomorrow and decide then."

* * *

There was a faint knock at his office door. Professor Albercht called out "Enter" without thinking.

"Dr. Albrecht," said Col. Reinhard Jager, "I hope I'm not intruding."

"Reinhard Jager is always welcome no matter where I am. I cannot forget your kindness in alerting me about Sommer Kappel."

"I have a problem. A personal problem. I had a call from my nephew late this afternoon that he had not been selected to work on your project. He begged me to ask you to reconsider."

"I am always at your service, colonel. You must understand that your nephew doesn't measure up to our performance standards. He also has a very rude tongue."

They were standing. "Forgive me, colonel. Please sit down."

Professor Albrecht's office, located across the corridor from the lecture room, smelled of old leather and dust-covered books. They sat on a small sofa that offered a view of the quad. "May I offer you something?"

Jager shook his head. "I'm not sure what you mean by he doesn't measure up. He has a master's degree, and despite this, you chose someone who has never been to university. Or am I misinformed?

"You are not." Professor Albrecht smiled as he poured two shot glasses with Cognac, passing one to Jager. "The young man, your nephew, refers to is very gifted in mathematics. He thinks ten steps beyond what we teach at our universities and arrives at solutions that astound even me."

"I do not doubt that, professor. You are Germany's greatest mathematician. Please let me explain something to you. My nephew had led a very sheltered life. My sister has pampered him all his life. He has never had to answer to someone and has never known hardship. When I suggested he join the Hitler You, he flatly refused." He paused. "Too bad. It would have made a man of him.

"Let me get to the real reason why I'm here. I understand that everyone involved in the project, such as you and your team, will receive a special award for your work from the Fuhrer – something that will stay with him the rest of his life."

"I understand fully, Col. Jager. For you, I am always

happy to reconsider. But for your nephew, there will be two conditions – that he obeys my assistant without question and me and controls his tongue. Kindly make sure he understands the conditions fully and understands he will be dismissed if he fails to do so."

Col. Jager stood and shook his hand. "Thank you, professor," he said, turning to the door. "Maybe you can make a man out of him."

CHAPTER NINETEEN

"I was hoping you would turn up today," said Leisa. "I was getting worried and may not have much time left. In war, there is always somebody watching. Get into my chair and let me tease your hair."

Leisa went through the motions and talked to her about her boyfriend, who is now in France. I worry about him. The French girls are so chic. They know how to look great."

"Are you really serious about being watched?"

"Lately, I've been conscious of an unseen presence every time I leave my home," said Leisa. "It was one of the reasons why it was necessary for you to come today. The gift I mentioned to you yesterday is wrapped in Christmas paper, which is hard to find these days. When you leave here, anybody watching will not think too much about it. Christmas is only a few days away. I talk a lot, don't I? That's what my boyfriend tells me."

"Now what," said Sommer as Leisa rubbed her face

with a creamy liquid.

"It will tighten the pores on your cheeks. Your skin is very dry and needs to be moisturized on a regular basis."

Thirty minutes later, she rose from the treatment chair, paid Leisa extra for the facial and started to put on her coat.

"A word of advice do not unwrap the gift until you are home and there are now eyes watching every move we make. Better still, keep it wrapped until it finds its last destination."

Sommer thanked her and decided to carry the gift in her arms.

"Merry Christmas. I hope to see you again in the new year," said Sommer.

They kissed each other on the cheek. "It might be better for both of us if you do not see each other again. May this Christmas bring you great peace."

* * *

Lotte met her at the door. "A gift for me?"

"This one's for Jundt."

"What is it?

"Something for her garden. As soon as I saw it, I knew she would love it."

"You're being very secretive, Sommer."

"It's a special bench. Jundt can either kneel on it for close work or turn it upside down to sit on while weeding."

"That's clever, Sommer."

"They even gift-wrapped it for me. We're invited to her place for dinner on Christmas Eve. Maybe she'll show it to us. Are you giving her something? We can say the bench comes from you and me."

"No need, Sommer. "I've been busy in the evenings, knitting a warm sweater for her. I was able to get blue wool yarn. Her favourite colour. And while we're talking about Christmas, let's invite Zelda and your friend, Gretchen."

"I'll ask her. She and I, and another girl, became close friends while we were at Bonn and spent a memorable Christmas Eve and Christmas Day together. It's one of my great memories."

"I'll call her today. I know she'll be thrilled. It will be like spending Christmas at home for Gretchen and me." Sommer fell quiet, thinking about her daughter and how she'll react when she sees a Christmas tree. In retrospect, it was the right thing to have her daughter at home and good for her mother. She would give anything to hear their voices."

***

Two days later, Zelda arrived an hour before they set out for Jundt's home, armed with two boxes of chocolates – one for Jundt and one for Lotte for our Christmas Day dinner. "How did you ever lay your hands on these? They're gold." She said, swirling her curly dark shoulder-length hair. Her large, dark eyes glistened as she shook her head back and forth with excitement.

Zelda didn't respond. We all knew Becker got them for her. "Wow," she said, looking at the large, wrapped gift for Jundt. "What is it?"

Lotte told her.

"That's a clever gift, Sommer. How about you, Lotte?"

"This is the first Christmas Steffen, and I are not together. I miss him. Him and his deep voice and singing *Minuit Chretien* in French for me. I told him we were spending Christmas Eve with Jundt. And Christmas Day with you, my good friends." She paused for a few seconds. "My gift for Jundt is a sweater. I've been working on it for months. It's all wool and will keep her warm on those long dark, cold nights in January."

"I'm also looking forward to tomorrow," said Zelda.

"Before I forget, Sommer is also inviting an old friend from her days at Bonn."

129

"Her name is Gretchen Moller," said Sommer. "You'll love her. She is working with me now with Professor Albrecht. She's quite lovely and promised to bring us a Christmas surprise for the four of us. "

Forty minutes later, Jundt, who had been watching at the front door window for almost 15 minutes, spotted them as they rounded the corner, and she opened the door before they reached the first step. She hugged each of them and whispered Merry Christmas in their ears.

She led them to the living room. "Since Sigfried left, I've spent every Christmas alone. Having you three girls means everything to me. It's my best Christmas ever."

"Each of us has brought you a special gift," said Lotte.

Jundt wiped her eyes. "If you don't mind, I'd like to open them on Christmas Day. It will give me another day to look forward to and treasure."

Jundt had the start of a nativity scene.

Lotte looked at it. "Where are the things that go with it? Let us finish it for you," said Lotte in a take-charge voice.

"In the bottom part of the sideboard. I'm sorry to put you to work. I couldn't finish the nativity scene and get dinner. You must forgive me."

Sommer, Lotte and Zelda finished the nativity scene in short order. "Do you have any candles we place around the nativity scene," Lotte called out as Jundt opened the kitchen door to see how they were progressing.

"They're in the sideboard, too. I can't wait to see it. It'll be the best nativity scene ever."

They began singing Christmas carols, marching around the living room and dining room before making their way into the kitchen, still singing. Jundt joined in as Zelda picked up one of the pots and began banging it with a long wooden spoon. Five minutes later, the nativity scene was complete.

Two tall silver candlesticks that have not been used since our mother died. They were hidden the sink. "Thought they'd be safe in case someone is looking to steal something." "Now I have a surprise for you," said Jundt.

Zelda and Sommer helped her carve two chickens while Lotte mashed the potatoes and prepared the vegetables. "Look. Zelda, parsnips," said Lotte holding one up.

"What about dressing?" said Sommer. "My mother always made the dressing with chicken in Canada."

Jundt didn't look up but pointed at a white bowl on top of the sideboard.

Finally, everything was ready. They escorted Jundt to the head of the table and seated her while taking seats on each side. The wine had been poured, and they lifted their glasses to her, singing to" the feast and our dearest friends."

"We forgot something," said Sommer. "The candles."

Sommer rose and brought them in from the kitchen. "Now, who's going to light them?"

Zelda said I can, looking into her purse and bringing a small box of matches.

Lotte placed them at the centre of the table and lit them. Jundt wiped her eyes. "Now, who's going to say grace?"

Lotte raised her arm: "I will."

✳✳✳

Lotte woke Sommer up. She had a black comb wrapped in tissue paper and serenaded Sommer with three Christmas carols.

Sommer rubbed the sleep from her eyes. "What time is it?"

"Late."

Sommer leaped out of bed. "I need to call Gretchen before she leaves. I want to make sure she's coming."

"I thought you said she was coming."

"It's a bit more than that. You'll understand when Gretchen arrives."

Gretchen arrived at 12.30, her bags full of Christmas

cakes and candy. Lotte relieved her of her parcels and shouted *Merry Christmas* in her ear.

Gretchen threw her arms around Sommer. "Our second Christmas together. I know this one will be just as special." Her shoulder-length hair, now dark, swirled around her as she shook her head, and her voice had a special lilt that matched how she walked.

"How did you manage all this?" said Lotte, wide-eyed.

"I got some of it in the Christmas market, but it was spare compared with other Christmases. I had help finding the other things."

"She probably won't tell you, Lotte, but Gretchen has a very rich sugar daddy."

"Which reminds me. I've ordered a cooked fat goose with all the timings. It should be here by four o'clock."

Zelda arrived almost an hour later. "Was detained. Sorry." Then, turning: "Who's this?"

"My friend, Gretchen Moller. She was my best friend in Bonn and is with me again, and Dr. Albrecht in Berlin. Gretchen, this is our friend, Zelda Thiessen. We worked together at Wehrmacht Head Quarters before I was sent to Humbolt."

"Welcome to our exclusive club, Gretchen," said Zelda, noticing for the first time the Christmas Stoller cake, the Angel Bread, the Lebkuchen, the Marzipan, and the Gingerbread and chocolate chunk cookies. "Where did you get all this?"

"You must know, St. Nicolaus."

"You're close," said Lotte, and they all laughed.

"And that's not all. She's ordered a fully cooked fat goose to be delivered here by four o'clock."

***

"Your friend is a very nice person. There are a lot of similarities between you. I can see why she became your best friend. Is she always this generous?" said Lotte the next morning over a late breakfast with Sommer.

"Not with everyone. Only to people, she considers real friends. And she's not shy if she feels that someone is not genuine. Her father is a very rich businessman. He joined the Nazi party early on and is a genuine admirer of the Fuhrer."

"And here I was thinking her rich sugar daddy was her boyfriend."

"We knew, and that's why we laughed so hard."

"I also heard from Steffan early this morning. Probably just checking up on me to make sure I wasn't celebrating Christmas somewhere else. He called to tell me he had been promoted and would be coming home on a one-week leave, starting Dec. 30. Can't wait to see him."

"I need to see Jundt today," said Sommer. "I think I left one of my workbooks at her house. I can't leave something like this lying around."

"Do you want me to go with you?"

"I need you here just in case I can't find it. If I find it, I'll spend some time with Jundt. I suspect she'll be feeling a bit down today."

***

Jundt seemed to take forever to reach the front door. Sommer rang the bell again until she saw Jundt hobbling and puffing her way to the door, her hair unbrushed and looking feeble.

"What's wrong?"

"Just really tired. Some days are like that. My doctor says it's my heart. I think I enjoyed myself too much with you girls."

"Are you sure you're all right?"

"I've had these spells before."

"What do you do for it?"

"Sleep mostly. There was snow over Christmas, as you know, and the weather got decidedly colder. Tomorrow, I could feel completely different. Once I rest for a day or two, I'll be my old self."

To Sommer, she looked feverish and felt her forehead. It was burning, and she seemed to lapse into sleep. Sommer remembered her mother touching her father's forehead and going to the barn to get the old sleigh out, harness it to their only horse, and take him to the hospital in town.

Sommer made a decision. She called for a taxi, bundled Jundt in three blankets, and had the cab driver carry her to the taxi and put her in the back seat. Sommer slid in beside her, urging the taxi driver to drive as quickly as possible to the nearest hospital.

The taxi driver stopped at the hospital entrance and carried her inside. "This lady needs a doctor now," Sommer said in her loudest voice.

A nurse seemed to appear out of nowhere and directed another two nurses to lay her on a hospital bed at the end of the entrance. "And get a doctor here in a hurry," she yelled at them. She wet a cloth in cold water, laid it on her forehead, and slid a thermometer into her mouth.

The doctor, a man in his mid-50s with a greying mustache and a stethoscope around his shoulders and white coat, moved quickly to look at Jundt. "Get her to X-Ray as quickly as you can. We need to ensure she has not come down with pneumonia before treating her." He turned to Sommer. "Are you her daughter?"

"No. A good friend."

He turned to a passing nurse. "Get her to a room. She will need to spend the night with us so that we can monitor her progress."

"Don't leave me," said Jundt opening her eyes suddenly.

Sommer took her hand and held it until they wheeled her into a room. Jundt held her hand tight. "I want to be in my bed. Please don't leave me. I don't want to die here alone."

Sommer bent down and kissed her forehead. "I will always be here."

One of the nurses found her a chair and placed it next to the bed. Sommer sat, still holding her hand and using her other hand to feel her forehead as Jundt closed her eyes and went to sleep.

"Her temperature is going down, Thank God."

The nurse nodded. "Yes. We've given her Penicillin. It has worked miracles on just about everyone we've administered it to. "I also gave her a sedative to help her sleep. She will sleep the night through the night. So, try to sleep yourself. I'll find you a couple of blankets to keep you warm."

"I need to call home first."

"Follow me," said the nurse taking her to a special phone and their visitors.

"I won't be home, Lotte."

"Where are you? We've been worried sick about you."

"I am at the hospital with Jundt. Good thing I came. She had a burning fever, so I ordered a taxi and took her to the hospital. The doctor told me she was on the brink of Pneumonia and that it could have killed someone her age with a history of heart disease. They ordered her to stay overnight. Jundt held my hand all the way to her room and begged me to stay with her, telling me she did not want to die alone there. She's sleeping now. I'm spending the night with her and will call you in the morning."

Jundt's bed squeaked every time she moved. The room was small and painted white and bare of any ornaments. The quilts covering her were also white.

Sommer woke up just as the sun was rising. Jundt was already up and brushing her hair. I feel like my old self," she said, reaching for a hairpin.

Her nurse popped by. "You're looking radiant, Frau Fuhrman. The doctor will come by shortly.

"You look like the Jundt we all know now. I called Lotte last night while you were sleeping. She wants me to call her today about you. She was very concerned about you."

The doctor came by a few minutes later. He looked down her throat and into her ears, "How do you feel today, Miss Fuhrman? You gave us quite a scare yesterday."

"When can she be released, doctor?"

"Just as soon as you put your clothes on. But dress as warm as you can. It's very cold this morning."

The doctor was right. Even the heater of the taxi driver's car didn't give out much heat. Sommer wrapped her scarf around Jundt's throat and took a taxi to Jundt's home in about 10 minutes. The driver opened the door for Jundt and helped her to the front door. Sommer unlocked the door and led her inside, thanking the driver and leaving him a tip.

She helped Jundt to the sofa and wrapped her in a blanket.

"I'm not an invalid."

"I know. I just want you to regain some of your strength before you start thinking about going upstairs to bed. In the meantime, let me get you a cup of tea. It's always good on a cold day."

Sommer returned to Jundt's living room with a cup of tea with some cookies. "This will get you started. I have a couple of calls to make. I'll turn on the radio, finish your tea and have a nap."

Sommer called Professor Albrecht first.

"I was worried about you, Sommer. It's not like you not to show up."

"I visited the sister of Professor Fuhrman yesterday and found she had a high fever. So I got her to the hospital and stayed with her all night. They gave her some new drug that enabled her to come home today. I am with her now and will be until I am sure she is well."

"I will let Gretchen know you are on an errand of mercy. She has been worried about you. There was no answer t your home when she tried to call."

"Unless she gets sick again, I plan on being there tomorrow morning. Sorry about letting you down."

"Just make sure she is well. I recall meeting her once with Siegfried. Please give her my regards."

The next call was to Lotte. No answer. Steffen must be home, she thought, replacing the receiver.

Jundt was still awake when Sommer returned. "I just talked to Professor Albrecht, who sends his regards for a speedy recovery. He recalled seeing you with your brother."

"Bless you, Sommer," she said, edging up on the sofa.

"You never did tell me why you came yesterday. "I mislaid one of the workbooks and wondered if I had left it here."

"You did. I put it in the safe room, which gets us back to the room downstairs. Now is the perfect time to inspect it. Just remember to turn the key counterclockwise."

"If I need you, I will hammer on the floor with my shoe."

Sommer switched on the light and went downstairs. She found the fake wall without trouble and looked behind the vegetables to spot the keyhole at the bottom right. She inserted the key and turned it counterclockwise, and a new room suddenly opened for her. The opening automatically turned on the lights of the room. She looked at it in disbelief. It was far larger than her bedroom and featured a stove and wood beside it, two easy chairs, and a sofa. And her gift from Leisa, a transmitter receiver, which was hidden behind it.

She took it out and placed it on the table near the stove. She plugged it into the nearest wall socket. It lit up almost instantly. Then the key to receive and send messages. She couldn't stop her hands from trembling as she sent her first message and received one back almost immediately:

Relay this message to Myles Brookfield immediately. Tell him I am at a friend's home and have no idea how much longer I can send and receive. Ultra important. I have been chosen to work on a hush-hush project that sounds like a weapon of mass destruction.

The receiver came alive 15 minutes later:

Merry Christmas from Myles and Andrew. Please send all information you have on the project and any formulae you can remember.

Jundt was asleep on the sofa and woke when Sommer entered. "Did you find the room to your liking?"

"And then some."

"And your book?"

"That, too."

"You look much better, Jundt."

"Sleep, as my doctor keeps telling me, is the cure and a wonderful medicine if used moderately."

Sommer rose. "It's getting onto lunchtime. What about some eggs and bacon, a stack of toast, and some more tea to perk you up?

Sommer settled Jundt into her chair

"Let me get you a fresh cup of tea." Sommer shared a tea with her until Jundt finished the eggs and toast, talking about Christmas at Lotte's.

She had left the safe room door open and could the receiver for any new messages.

CHAPTER TWENTY

Steffen arrived back two days before New Year's in a foul mood. "Nothing is where it's supposed to be. Where's my pipe? It used to be in the ashtray beside my chair. That, too, has been moved. I feel like a stranger in my own home."

"Be reasonable for once, Steffen. The four of us had Christmas dinner and had to move a few things around. Besides, I sort of like it this way."

"You mean Sommer likes it this way. And what about that friend of hers?"

Gretchen's very nice and even provided a goose dinner for us. I know you'd like her. She's very attractive."

Steffen's face was flushed. He bit the cork in the bottle of Brandy and poured himself a full glass. Why can't it just be us, Lotte? Just you and me. The way it used to be."

Lotte put a finger to her mouth. "I hear her at the door."

Lotte took Sommer's coat. "How is she?"

"Better. In fact, a lot better. I brought her home from the hospital and decided to stay with her until I felt she could look after herself. I prepared lunch for her, made her nap, and prepared supper for her before I left."

"That was a fast recovery which you described as someone at death's door." Stefan's eyes were bloodshot, and the curl of his lip gave him a dark look.

"Yes, it was a fast discovery, Steffen, thanks to a new drug called Penicillin. I'm sure you've heard of it. They describe it as a miracle drug. I didn't believe it until I saw how she looked this morning."

He sat back in his chair and glared at her. It was evident, he hadn't, making him even angrier. "There's something not right about you, and I'll find out what it is before I'm done."

Lotte tried to quiet him by telling Sommer that Steffen was taking her to an SS Officers' New Year's party, at which the Fuhrer would be present."

"What a wonderful honour for you, Steffen. Everyone in Germany will be envious of you. You are obviously held in high regard by the Fuhrer," said Sommer.

He uncorked the bottle of Brandy and took a large mouthful, grimacing as it went down. "I understand you know Konrad Becker. He is also deeply suspicious of you. I know Konrad. Level-headed and rarely wrong. I trained with him. He's always fair," he said, slurring his words. "But he can smell a rat when he sees one."

Steffen had barely lit a cigarette when he began to nod. Lotte took the cigarette from his mouth and tried to get him to his feet. "I don't know what's got into him, but he's changed ever since he's been in Czechoslovakia. It's as though something is eating inside him, and he keeps trying to hide it."

"Let me help you," said Sommer. "I'll take his arm, and you take the other."

The next morning, Lotte decided it was time for them to talk about Sommer. Steffen's eyes, still bloodshot, looked tired, and his hands shook. He rubbed his chin and cheeks. "It's time for a shave." He reached for the bottle.

Lotte pulled it beyond his reach. "Nothing to drink until we talk about Sommer. "

Steffen didn't respond.

"I've lived with her for more than a year and consider her one of my best friends. I like her a lot. So does Zelda, who worked with her at Wehrmacht Headquarters, talks about how the British have been unable to crack her codes. She has never done anything remotely suspicious in any way. I would know it if she had. If Sommer is not at home, she is either with Jundt or at her church. If there were anything wrong with her, why is Gretchen her best friend? And before you say anything about Gretchen, her father was one the early members of the Nazi Party and practically worships the Fuhrer."

"What about this older woman?"

"She is the sister of Professor Siegfried Fuhrman, a friend of Professor Albrecht, whom the Fuhrer has chosen to lead one of his major projects. I have been to her home, and she has treated all of us as daughters."

"So."

"Professor Albrecht considers her his most brilliant student and has appointed her to work with him on a special project for the Fuhrer. So your friend, Konrad, is wrong, for once. Dead wrong. And I don't want to hear any more about it."

Sommer had entered the kitchen unnoticed. "If there is any doubt about where I was yesterday, you can check the hospital or the doctor who treated Jundt."

Steffen just stared at her, his mouth open. "I need a drink."

"You'll get coffee and like it," said Lotte

Steffen ignored her. "I agree with Konrad. I can smell what he smells. You're just too good to be true. You appear to be protected at the moment, but sooner or later, that won't be the case, and we'll be there waiting."

"While everyone is gaining up on me, I have bad news for you both. They'll be rationing everything soon."

"Everything?"

"Food, even shoes."

"How soon?"

"Very soon."

***

Sommer looked at Fritz Cullen and nudged Gretchen. "What's he doing here?"

"I gather Professor Albrecht had second thoughts over the holiday. He showed up yesterday and talked to Professor Albrecht before taking his seat."

Sommer headed for Professor Albrecht's office, knocked on the door and entered.

"I'm glad to see you, Sommer. Things just don't run smoothly when you're not here. How is Sigfried's sister?"

"Much better now, thank Heaven." Then after a strategic pause. "I see that Fritz Cullen has found his way back here." She paused again. "Before we begin talking about Cullen, I have news for your ears only. The government will start rationing very soon."

"When you say soon, Sommer, how soon?"

"Very soon."

"How reliable is your source, Sommer?" said Dr. Archecht.

"An SS officer who has to enforce it."

Professor Albrecht nodded and thought for a minute. "We were talking about Fritz Cullen before your announcement. His uncle, Col. Jager, whom you know, came to see me at my home last night and asked me to reconsider Cullen's case. I told him I would be happy as long as he behaved and obeyed my assistant in everything and me. I also made it clear that he lagged everyone else in the team and needed to improve dramatically if he planned to stay."

"That was very kind of you, professor. Do you think he will?"

"Probably for a while. I've seen his ilk in many of my classes, and eventually, they revert to form, often by creating a problem to justify their behaviour. So be careful around him. Do not meet with him alone. Always have one or two people with you whenever you meet."

"What about Col. Jager?"

"This is Cullen's last chance, as far as he is concerned. He called him a spoiled rotten child and hoped against hope that he won't do something wrong."

"I plan to see him for a chat right after work. I will let him know I would like you with me," Sommer said when she told Gretchen.

Sommer had been reviewing his work for the past week and couldn't believe all the mistakes she spotted – errors you would not expect someone with a master's degree. She checked his file and noted that he had received his master's degree at Ludwig-Maximilians University in Munich. She picked up the phone and called the university's registrar.

"I'm checking the credentials of someone who says he has a master's degree in mathematics from your university. Could you kindly verify that? His name is Fritz Cullen."

"Do you know the year?"

"1939, according to his application."

"Please wait." She left the phone for at least four minutes before she spoke again. "Sorry to keep you waiting. There is a record of a Fritz Cullen as a student but no reference in our records that he was in our master's program. Also, there is no record he ever completed an undergraduate degree."

"Could you kindly send me a letter about what you just told me? My boss will need it in case this individual disputes it."

She couldn't wait to tell Gretchen, who was going over his paper with Cullen.

"Do you plan to confront him?" said Gretchen.

Sommer offered one of her all-knowing smiles. "Let's just keep this to ourselves for the time being. There's always a right time for everything. "

Just before closing time, Sommer asked Fritz to remain

behind.

"You asked to see me," said Fritz, whose faded blue eyes looked more like the eyes of a dead man. He glanced at Gretchen, but it was clear that her presence made him uncomfortable.

Sommer didn't offer any formalities. "I've gone over your work for the past week, and, quite frankly, it's well below the standard you would expect from someone with a master's degree."

"In what way?"

"Simple mistakes that a first year wouldn't make. How do you explain that?"

Cullen didn't respond.

"We need people who will put their best efforts forward. Germany needs you to be the best you can be."

"Anything else?"

"Just that I'll be reviewing your work and the work of others every week to ensure that we meet the rigorous standards that have been set for us."

He listened to her comments with no reaction. Gretchen shivered every time, just thinking how he looked at Sommer. He rose and left without a word.

There was some improvement in the weeks that followed, and it was clear to Sommer that he was getting help from someone. It was still not up to the standards she had set, but it was getting better.

"I think Romy is helping him," Gretchen whispered.

"How? The only time is when they eat lunch, and nothing passes between them. They just talk."

"That's it, Sommer. You just told me how she passes information to him. He memorizes the equation and repeats it to her, and she tells him how to do it. To all intents and purposes, they're just having a friendly conversation over lunch."

Sommer smiled. "I don't know what I would ever do

without you."

"Do we tell Professor Albrecht?"

"There will be a time."

***

Professor Albrecht invited everyone for supper and after-dinner drinks after they finished for the day. The supper was brought in at the end of the day. Linens replaced pads and pencils on desks, and a bartender suddenly appeared and began to set up a beer keg, glasses and mugs and glasses for Schnapps, Cognac and Brandy.

"You all have been working very hard to create formulae that will hopefully bring us one major step closer to success. I just received a call from one of our partners in this project and what we provided them this week helped them make a breakthrough that had been eluding them for weeks. Congratulations to you all."

Jonas Stein asked Gretchen and Sommer if he could get them a drink.

"Some very cold water with ice would be appreciated, Jonas."

"She doesn't drink liquor," said Gretchen. "But I do. If they have it, I'd like a glass of Champagne."

"And if they don't have it?"

"Get me what you're having."

"You don't smile like that to me," said Sommer.

"You're not as cute as he is."

***

Lotte called to tell her that Jundt had telephoned her, looking for her. I told her you were at work. She's low on food and can't stand the cold. She was hoping one of us would come and do the shopping for her. I can't. Can you?"

Sommer put the phone down. It couldn't come at a better time.

Sommer memorized the breakthrough equation and

made her way to Jundt's home, stopping at the grocery store to pick up her order. She first needed to send a message to Brookfield with the breakthrough formula that caused such a stir the week before. She glanced over it and memorized it again.

"Time for supper," said Gretchen, swirling her dark hair around her neck and cheeks as she stood.

"Not today, Gretchen. Just got a call from Lotte. It seems Jundt has run out of food and wants to know if I go to the grocery store for her."

An hour later, Jundt opened her door. "It's you, Sommer. I wasn't sure who it was when I looked out. "Thank you for coming to the aid of an old woman."

"Do you want these in the kitchen?"

Jundt nodded and followed her. "I've also come to cook supper for us. Come to the kitchen so we can talk while I prepare the food."

"You certainly know where things are in my kitchen."

Sommer gave her a hug. "You forget, Jundt, that my mother and father are German, and our kitchen and yours are almost identical."

"Spring should be with us soon," said Jundt after supper, "I can feel it in my bones."

"I need to go downstairs for a few minutes," said Sommer as they finished tea.

It took only a few minutes to set up the radio transmitter and send the formula to Brookfield."

There was an immediate response from Brookfield:
Need more like this one. Keep them coming.

Jundt was standing, holding onto the table, when Sommer came up from the cellar.

"Can I help you to bed?"

"No need. I want to give you something." She opened her hand. "A key to my back door. You may need it one day when I am too weak to let you in."

CHAPTER TWENTY-ONE

Becker got everything he wished two months later when two members of Professor Albrecht's team tipped him off about a systematic program to sabotage and derail the Fuhrer's special project.

He acted on it immediately, arriving at Lecture Room 420 with an armed guard. You could hear the heavy footfalls of their boots as they approached the door and the sound of a rifle butt hammering on the door.

Lucas Stein rose to open it. Becker pushed him aside and strode into the room. He pointed at Sommer. "I knew you would show your real colours sooner or later." His eyes glistened in the sunlight streaming in from the windows on the left side of the room.

"You are all under arrest as enemies of the Third Reich."

"What's going on?" said Professor Albrecht in a thunderous voice that echoed off the brown wooden walls of the room. Sommer had never heard him use this voice before.

"Who are you?" Becher shouted back, motioning his guard to round up Sommer and other members of her team.

"Whatever you are doing, stop now and leave."

"Not this time, old man. Your little coven has come to the end of the road. Unless you want your head cracked, you'll join the other traitors in the van out front."

They crowded into the van, reminding her of the day they pushed Professor Hoffmann into the van that took him away. He was never seen again. Thinking about it made her shiver.

"We'll get to the bottom of this, one way or another," said Professor Albrecht, bumping his head as he tried to stand.

"Where are they taking us?" said Martin Koeln in a soft voice.

"To Gestapo Headquarters, where we will be questioned," said Lucas Stein.

Fritz Cullen twisted his lips. "You sound experienced."

Lucas ignored him and got ready to leave as the van suddenly stopped.

Professor Albrecht was the last to leave, brushing the dirt from the shoulders of his back suit jacket and patting down his grey hair. Sommer walked beside him into Gestapo Headquarters, up the wide staircase to the second floor and Col. Jager's office. Everything stopped at once. Sommer saw Jager's secretary out of the corner of her eye. Her hand was at her throat as she spotted Sommer.

Col. Jager heard the commotion and looked up, seeing Becker at the head of a small group of prisoners. He stood when he saw someone who looked like Professor Albrecht and walked out of his office. "What's this about, Becker?"

"We'd like to know, too," said Professor Albrecht in a voice that could be heard three offices away.

Becker drew up his shoulders and suddenly had a bad feeling about things. "I was simply acting on a tip from two members of the professor's team who described what their group was doing as sabotage."

"You should have checked with me first."

"You were in conference with someone, and I didn't want to disturb you."

"Did your informants happen to tell you their names?"

"Yes. Fritz Cullen and Romy Fischer. Both are members of the professor's team. They told me their work was usually changed and thrown out purposely."

"You're a food, Becker. Fritz Cullen is my nephew, who wouldn't know his elbow from St. Nikolas." He shook his head. "And you, Fritz. You're a disgrace to your family. And this is how you betray me. I went to Professor Albrecht before Christmas to ask him to give you a second chance and did so. He beckoned to one of his secretaries. "Take this fool to the enlistment office and tell them from me to send him to the Russian front."

Other members of the team moved away from Romy. "Sorry, Romy, but it would be impossible to you to continue as a member of our team," said Sommer. "We need to have confidence in each other."

"This won't happen again, professor. To you. Or anyone on your team. While you're here, I'd like to introduce you to one of our heroes."

Alex Greenfield appeared from behind Jager and extended his hand to Professor Albrecht. Sommer could feel her heart suddenly stop and felt sick to her stomach. She knew she had to do something but didn't know what. Her mind froze. "I'm going to puke," she whispered to Gretchen.

Gretchen put her arm around her and whispered to Lucas that Sommer was sick.

"The toilets are three offices away on this side of the corridor."

Gretchen led her from the room. "I feel queasy, too. You know, Sommer, I don't like it here anymore."

Neither do I, Gretchen. If it weren't for Professor Albrecht..."

Professor Albrecht looked around for Sommer.

"She and Gretchen weren't feeling well and left."

Jager put his arm around Greenwood and smiled.

"Some other time, professor. I have another appointment. I hope you all will excuse me."

"Are you feeling any better?" said Gretchen.

"Sommer nodded.

"Then let's get back before they send out a search party for us."

She opened the door just as Greenfield glanced at them as he walked by. He didn't look back.

"I see our wandering minstrels have returned." Professor Albrecht was the first to see them as they appeared in the doorway. He turned to Col. Jager. "Once again, Col. Jager, Germany is in your debt. I'm sorry it had to come about this way."

***

Sommer knew she needed someone to talk to about Greenwood. Her only choice was Leisa at the Beauty shop. She was careful about everything. Leisa would know instinctively what she should do. She made up her mind to see her at the end of the day.

There we no lights in Leisa's shop. She peered inside, and in the gloom, she could see it was empty. She went into the food store next door and asked the owner, a man in his 80s wearing thick lenses and who shuffled when he walked.

"I'm one of Leisa's clients. I wanted to get my hair done but see that her shop is empty. Do you know where she moved to?"

The old man had a gravelly voice. "Some secret service men raided her shop and shot her in the head where she stood. I have no idea why. She was such an innocent thing."

There was more bad news when she reached home. Lotte was waiting for her at the door. "I have to tell you something, Sommer." Lotte looked at her laced fingers. "Our friend, Jundt, has died."

"Dead. How?"

"The police think she died in her sleep. They called me

around noon. They think it was her heart."

Sommer felt like crying but couldn't. She felt empty inside, and nothing seemed to matter anymore.

"The police were alerted by her milkman, who noticed she hadn't taken in her regular bottle of milk for three days. One thing more. It seems she listed you and me as her next-of-kin to be notified in case of her death. You were closer to her. I feel sorry now I didn't spend more time with her."

"I feel the same way," said Sommer. She started crying for the first time.

"I called Steffen about it. He made a few calls and learned that she and her brother jointly owned her home but that the state had confiscated it. They will tear it down and have plans to build a temporary residence for soldiers recovering their wounds."

"Are you listening to me, Sommer? You seem lost in space. Just staring at me as though you didn't recognize me."

Later, when she was trying to drift off to sleep, she realized the secret room would be discovered when they tore down Jundt's home. It preyed on her mind, and she finally gave up trying when Lotte knocked on her door. "I can't sleep. Do you mind if I sleep with you tonight? I want to be alone tonight."

Sommer pulled back the blankets. "There's plenty of room for both of us."

***

"I thought I finally had her, but Albrecht is a friend of Jager's. How did I know that my informant was a nephew of Jager's and bore a grudge against Albrecht and his team? I also learned he was a liar and disappointed everyone he deals with."

"What happened?" said Steffen.

Becker told him, embellishing the tale as he went along. "As long as Jager and Albrecht are her friends, she won't be easy to take down. But I've seen all this before. Sooner or later, things will turn against her. They always do. That's when to take her down", said Steffen.

"You know, I'm actually beginning to doubt myself."

"Don't. You've got great instincts, Konrad. Trust them," said Steffen.

"Then, what's our next step?"

"Whatever it is, it must be as soon as possible. Like you, I believe she is a British agent and is doing incredible damage to the war effort," said Steffen.

"Do you know anyone in the upper echelons who might help us?"

"Leave it with me," Steffen said as he replaced the phone receiver.

CHAPTER TWENTY-TWO

It was time for her to disappear. It was only a question of time before they discovered the secret room when they tore down Jundt's home, found the transmitter and connected it to her. But where could she go and how?

With the radio transmitter available to her, Sommer has another problem. How to contact Brookfield and tell him she was closing shop and on the run. There had to be an answer. He had to know where there were safe houses, and he had to know where they were. She thought of Victoria Winters, but her gut warned her off.

There had to be a way. That's when she remembered the key to the back door of Jundt's home. She could get in that way. Her spirits rose and fell when she realized it would probably be under guard because the Reich was taking it over. And even if she did get in, there would be a problem finding her way to the cellar in the darkness. A light would be seen from the outdoors and be an immediate giveaway. There always is a way, she kept telling herself. She would think about it when she went to bed and let her subconscious work on it.

"You seem preoccupied, Sommer. Anything wrong?" said Gretchen, who placed a coffee mug in front of her.

"Thinking of home. Think about it a lot since that episode inspired by Cullen."

Martin Moeln approached her. "Professor Albrecht would like to see you in his office."

Sommer knocked on his door and entered.

"I hope you and Gretchen have recovered from our ordeal. It was incredibly disconcerting and unnerving. I don't mind telling you, it took a lot out of me. But our work must go on, no matter how we feel."

"We all feel the same way, Professor Albrecht. How may I help you?"

He rose and went to an olive green filing cabinet and handled Sommer a large file.

"There must be at least 200 other candidates in that file, and I would like you and Gretchen to scan them and offer me your top four candidates before the end of the day."

"You look a bit harried?" said Gretchen.

"You will be, too, once you hear what we'll be doing."

She planked the folder on her desk. "We have to replace the two we lost. There must be 200 candidates here. You take 50, and I'll take 50 until we get them done. Put the discards on the floor and place your choices in the folder he gave us."

They skipped lunch and lived off coffee. After three hours, they narrowed it down to 10 candidates, and it took almost 90 minutes to narrow it down to four. Part of the problem, it took Sommer longer than normally because her mind kept drifting back to Brookfield and how she could reach him.

At 3.45, they knocked at the professor's door and placed three folders on his desk with discards in one, the top 10 in another and their top four choices.

"I don't know what I'd do with you two." He studied their faces. "Did you work through lunch?"

They didn't respond.

"You've done enough today — both of you. Leave early, have supper together, and try to completely wipe what happened yesterday from your mind. I'm sorry we had to go through this ordeal, but some people are just plain evil."

"Come back to Lotte's with me. We'll have supper there. She won't mind. Steffen has gone back."

"I'd love that. I can also see that something is bothering you. If you're in some trouble, you know you can rely on me."

"It's just that sometimes I'd like to disappear and forget everything."

"Gretchen hugged her. "Some days, like yesterday, I wish I had never heard of this project."

Zelda and Lotte were listening to the war news on the battery radio and barely heard them come in. "We left early today. Professor Albrecht thought we deserved after reviewing the CVs of 200 candidates to replace Fritz Cullen and Romy Fischer."

"That can wait. I'm dying to see what's in that envelope from Jundt addressed to the three of us at our address," said Lotte, sitting on the sofa between the cushions and Zelda.

Lotte read it first and smiled. So did Zelda, passing it to Sommer. "Seems she's left us a few family heirlooms. She felt we were the only daughters she ever had. It was signed January 2, 1943."

"How wonderful for you," said Gretchen. "Just a few days ago. She would have had to go out to mail it."

"In all this, I forgot to mention that her death notice was in the paper," said Lotte. Sommer glanced at it. Her funeral is tomorrow morning. Are we going?"

***

St. Michaels was packed. "She had more friends than we thought," said Lotte.

Sommer looked around. She spotted Becker and a squad of SS troopers with him. Zelda nodded in his direction, and he smiled back. "He said he would be coming today, that he a tip than an enemy of the Reich would be present today," said Zelda.

"Surely not in church. The church has always been a place of sanctuary for centuries."

"Ridding the Reich of enemies is always a million times more important." There was a note of pride in her voice. "You know, he thinks there's something not right about you. I tell him every time he's barking up the wrong tree. I told him how much help you were to me in teaching me to create codes the British can't solve."

Despite all that, he has a one-track mind that never stops until he gets what he wants."

As the mass ended, Jundt's coffin was rolled down the middle aisle, where one of the pallbearers was removed so quickly you barely noticed.

As they left the church, Fritz Cullen, dressed in a SS uniform, stopped them. "Oberleutenant Becker asked me to look after you."

I thought you were on the way to the front," said Sommer.

"My father had other ideas."

***

Sommer felt the noose tighten and knew it was impossible to reach Brookfield. The atmosphere even felt different at home. Lotte was less talkative and brooding over something. It turned out to be the heirlooms Jundt had hidden them.

"Where do you think she held them?" she said finally.

"I think I know."

"Where?"

In the vegetable bin in her cellar, probably behind the

potatoes. What does she say in her letter to us:

I bequeath my heirlooms to Sommer Kappel, Lotte Kushner and Zelda Thiessen. Each individual piece is quite valuable and was given to my mother when our family had money. Wear them and think of me when you do.

Thank you for always being there when I needed help finding parsnips when we gathered for our Christmas celebration. You three young ladies were the only three daughters I ever knew. Thank you for helping an old woman find peace.

Signed: Jundt Fuhrman, January 2, 1943.

"I know," said Zelda, who had joined them for supper, bringing her bread ration. "Where the parsnips are."

"The next big hurdle," said Lotte, "is how we get our hands on them."

"That could be a problem. Since the state now owns her property, it will be guarded day and night," said Zelda.

Lotte's eyes brightened: "What if we take Jundt's letter to the guard and ask permission to enter? It's proof the heirlooms were bequeathed to us."

"I could ask Konrad to give us a letter of authority to enter?" said Zelda.

"Sorry, Zelda. I don't trust him," said Lotte. It may be just an excuse to charge us with theft. Better still. Steffen will be calling me in the morning. He'll know what to do. When there's money involved, he always knows what to do."

"I have another idea," said Sommer, who had been silent for the most part. "You, too, entertain the guard while I find my way in by the back door."

"How?"

"After Jundt recovered from her heart spell, she gave me the key to her back door, just in case she could not come to open the door for me."

"So when do we go?"

"Why not now?" said Sommer.

They finished supper and headed out to catch the tram.

"What about Cullen? He's following you, hoping to find something to incriminate you?"

"Then I'll leave first and head in the opposite direction of the house. When I can give him the slip, I'll head back in the direction of Jundt's house."

"You seem awful sure of yourself."

"He's really stupid. No one, certainly not Cullen or anyone else, will stop us from getting from what's ours. I have only one problem. I'm not sure this key will work. I never tried to unlock it."

***

Sommer knew exactly what she was looking for. She crouched as she made her way to the basement door, tripping over a box in the kitchen. Jundt used it to reach for dishes and utensils. She also kept her spices on the top shelf. She had come armed with a large bag and used her other arm to feel her way to the door to the cellar. It was partly open. She felt for the first step and closed the door behind her before turning on the light.

She rummaged behind the potatoes and parsnips before discovering them -- a diamond tiara, diamond bracelets, pearl earrings, necklaces, and eight gold diamond earrings. She stuffed them into the old flour sack and used her other key to open the door to the secret room. She entered and placed the flour sack beside the desk where the radio transmitter was located.

It took her only five minutes to tell Brookfield this was her last transmission because the Gestapo was closing in on her. She asked for his guidance about a safe place she could find. There was no response. That's when she added the last equations she was working on. Brookfield sent her a message just as she was ready to close down:

Leave Berlin soonest and hide out for a few months.

Let me know where you are, and I will have someone contact you.

She grabbed the bag with the jewels, hid the radio transmitter behind the sofa and turned off the lights in the secret room before locking the secret doorway and adding the potatoes and parsnips to her bag. She mounted the stairs gingerly, stopping at the top stair below the door and turning off the light.

On the top step, she crouched again and opened the door slowly before entering the kitchen. She stood slowly, picked up the flour bag and turned to face the shadow of someone. It was Cullen who shone his flashlight in her face.

"I thought I heard someone downstairs. What were you doing?"

Sommer held up her bag. He shone his light inside and felt among the potatoes and parsnips to find the jewels. "Is there more?"

"There may be. I was in too much of a hurry to get out of here to look for more."

He passed her the bag. "Wait here."

***

They giggled all the way to the tram, passing the bag among themselves and smiling dreams until they reached the tram.

"How did you escape? We couldn't warn you that Cullen followed you all the way here."

"I met him at the head of the stairs. I didn't know what to do until he asked me if more jewels were downstairs. He gave me my sack back and told me to stay put while he looked for more jewels in the cellar."

"Is he that stupid?"

"Will he talk?" said Lotte.

"I don't think so. Konrad ordered him to stay clear of us tonight, but he didn't obey."

"What if he does?"

"We have Jundt's letter, signed by her and dated, willing her heirlooms to us."

"Now that we have them, what do we do with them?"

"Hide them until the war is over," said Sommer. "Things have a way of disappearing during a war and could leave us empty-handed. Don't tell anyone about them, Lottie, even Steffen. The same applies to you, Zelda.

"I will hide them, just in case you let it slip. We shall meet at Lottie's one year after the war is over, and I will lead you to the jewels. I will write letters to you, and we can arrange a meeting place."

"You talk as though you're planning to leave, Sommer."

"Who knows where any of us will be a year from now? I would like to remain here forever with you two and my good friend, Gretchen. But war has a way of changing things. Just remember this. If we are still together at the end of the war, we will find the jewels together. If not, you'll hear from me within one year after the war."

Just then, the air raid sirens went off.

"Are you coming, Lotte?" asked Zelda.

"I want to wait here, Just in case Steffen calls."

Zelda and Sommer left to find the air raid shelter two blocks from Lotte's home. It was crowded with old men and women, and young mothers and children crying as the sound of bombs penetrated their shelter. The acrid smell of ash permeated the air, leaving the old people coughing and breathing hard. Some of them were crying and wiping their eyes with dirty handkerchiefs.

Zelda shook her head. "It should be this way. They will pay dearly for this before this war is over." She hugged Sommer and cried.

There seemed to be no let up as one wave of bombs

after another fell, some of them even shaking their shelter. They planned to stay there overnight.

CHAPTER TWENTY-THREE

Sommer took a deep breath. The building they had left the day before was now in ruins, with a fire still not under control that was eating up all their hard work and research. There was a rumour that Professor Albrecht had been in the building when it was bombed. No one would know for sure until the fire was out and the fire department and the professor's staff had a chance to see if anything were left in the rubble. The smoke and the smell of burnt flesh made her queasy.

"Everything. All our work up in smoke." Sommer didn't know it, but she was crying when Gretchen came up to stand beside her.

Gretchen held her close and brushed her hair with her hand. "We are like phoenixes, Sommer. We will rise from the ashes stronger and better than before. Maybe Professor Albrecht will be here soon. He will know what to do."

"There's a rumour that he was in the building when the bombs hit the building."

"I hope not. What will we ever do without him?"

"We'll have to wait until someone from the project comes to the university and decide what to do," Sommer said.

"Or do you think they'll kill the project? I hope not."

"I don't think so, considering it's a project launched by the Fuhrer. Let's find someone in charge at the university.

Maybe they can tell us what to do."

They found the registrar's office about 30 minutes later. They had set up shop in another part of the university, where they met Jonas Stein, who told them that Martin had been trying to find a bomb shelter when the wall of a house on fire collapsed, killing him instantly.

"We're trying to find out what's going to happen to the project," said Sommer after talking to two women and a man who had no word about it.

"I doubt if there will be any news today. Why not go home and spend the day trying to get over the nightmare. There's talk that the allies will be launching daylight bombing as well. When I was rushing to the shelter last night, I could hear the bombs whistling in the air just before they landed."

"Haven't been home yet," said Sommer. "Lotte decided to stay to assure her husband in case he called to see if she were all right."

"Let me come with you, Sommer."

Crews were trying to clear the tram tracks all over the city. The power was out, and here and there, food trucks stopped to hand out bread to people. They reached Lotte's home an hour later on foot.

They could see that her apartment was in ruin, with bricks and cement blocks strewn across the road. They stopped two soldiers who were patrolling the street. "The woman in that apartment," said Sommer. Her throat ached, and she had a hard time getting the words out.

They shook their heads. "No one survived. It was a direct hit."

Gretchen could see the tears in Sommer's eyes and grabbed her by the arm. "It's time to go. There's nothing we can do here."

Sommer stopped an air raid warden – an old man with tired eyes who shuffled when he walked. The lady from No.

38, Did she survive?"

"There were a few survivors from this street. You will find them at the shelter. "It's no use," said Gretchen, "not with a direct hit. You saw the rubble."

"Let's just make sure."

They entered the shelter and walked up and down the rows of wounded people. There were only a few nurses who were being run off their feet. The smell of burnt flesh hung in the air. A few of the soldiers who had been injured were trying to make their way out of the shelter to make room for the constant streams of new casualties. That's when Sommer spotted Lotte. A large bandage across her face hid a large cut gash that would forever scar her face.

"Lotte. Thank God, we've found you."

Lotte acted as though she did not know them and turned her face away.

"It's Sommer, Lotte. Sommer."

No reaction.

Sommer stopped one of the nurses. "She doesn't seem to know us. What is wrong."

The nurse, a young woman in her late 20s, had a deep matter-of-fact voice. "Besides the cut, she's in deep shock. They may or may not come out of it."

"Are we permitted to take her with us?"

"Yes, but on the condition, you don't bring her back."

✳✳✳

They had to walk all the way to Zelda's – past burnt-out trucks, around deep, large craters and picking their way around the rubble on the streets that made walking even more difficult. And around above it all, a stench of death and burnt bodies. Sommer and Gretchen grabbed one of Lotte's arms and helped her walk to Zelda's. It was a slow process as they had to stop every 15 minutes to give Lotte time to regain enough strength and carry on. They reached

Zelda's apartment two hours later.

Zelda put her palms over her face as soon as she saw Lotte's face. "I had a premonition something bad was going to happen to one of us. But not this."

"What am I doing?" she said, stepping back from her doorway. "Please come in and make yourself comfortable. My place is not as large as Lotte's," she said, helping Lotte to the sofa so she could lie on it. She turned on the radio to get the latest news. There's no phone service. No power. And no place where you can buy food. But you're welcome. You, too, Gretchen."

Zelda sat down alongside Lotte. "Can't she talk?"

"The nurse at the shelter said she was suffering from shock," said Sommer. "It's hard to tell how long she may be like this." She paused to catch Zelda's eye. "She has a long gash down the left side of her face. It needs stitching to reduce scarring. But the hospitals are filled with people who have lost limbs and or with burns all over their bodies."

"In fact," said Gretchen, "we were told not to bring her back to the aid station."

Zelda looked around. "I'll be a bit cramped, I'm afraid, but we'll make do. The only thing that matters is that we're still together."

***

The Registrar's office looked more organized than the day before but getting someone's attention was another matter. The noise level of excited voices made speaking and being understood almost impossible. The grey-hair woman who had talked to them the day before was trying to get everyone to line up.

"I have news for you," she said when she spotted them. "We received a telephone call this morning from the Science Council, which is in charge of your project. They said your project would continue and that you would report to this office next Tuesday. If you come then, I should have all the details for you."

"Do you know what I'm going to do?" said Gretchen. Sommer looked at her.

"I'm going to visit my aunt for five glorious days of peace and real food."

"That's what I'll do, too, Gretchen. Thanks for the idea. I'll go to see my aunt, Gerda. She lives in a small town in South Germany that's not worth bombing and where there is food. It will be good to get away from all this. You know I've lost everything in the air raid. I don't even have a tooth-brush."

They walked to Zelda's office to tell her they were going away for five days. "We'll try to bring you back some food."

"Where is this heavenly place?"

"In Munich and Southern Germany, where the phones are still operating and where there is still power," said Sommer.

Col. Schmidt spotted Sommer from his office and came out to greet her. "Good to see you again, Sommer. Sorry to hear that your project was bombed and your professor was killed. Just want you to know that if your project does get dumped, you're welcome back here any time."

Sommer thanked him and introduced Gretchen as a mathematical genius.

"You're welcome, too. Gretchen. Anytime."

Zelda, who was listening from her desk, tried to smile. "When will you be leaving?"

"There's a train to Munich at 6. I'll call you at your office to check up on Lotte. I will be knocking on your door five days from now."

Zelda tried to smile. "I talked to the woman who lives next door to me. She'll look in on Lotte to see if she needs anything."

"Before I forget, ask Col. Schmidt if he could get an

army surgeon to look at Lotte's face and see what can be done about it. She will be scarred for life if something isn't done about it now.

Sommer left Wehrmacht Headquarters with a strange feeling that she would never see Zelda again. She told Gretchen about it.

"I had the same feeling." Gretchen shivered and turned her face away from the wind."

When they reached the train station, they went to the ticket office. Sommer paid for a ticket to Engen. She met Gretchen in the waiting room. They found seats near the gate they would leave from. Gretchen's train left an hour later.

"What a handsome man," said Gretchen, nodding in the direction of a wounded airman who made his way on crutches.

"You will never change, Gretchen."

She smiled back. "You're lucky I don't."

Thirty minutes later, Sommer stood. "It's time for me to go to my gate. Let's plan to meet at Humboldt six days from now."

CHAPTER TWENTY-FOUR

F ate, thought Sommer, can play strange tricks on us when we're least expecting anything. Here she was in a panic, and what happens? An air raid destroys the building where they were working, killing Professor Albrecht in the process, and allowing her to travel to Engen, only 12 km from Switzerland, with no one thinking twice about it.

She looked out the train window, feasting on the green trees and flowers alongside the track and the evergreens in the background. She sat back in her seat and closed her eyes. She held as tough as a huge weight had been lifted off her shoulders.

And then it happened. Two hours out, two policemen entered the car, checking everyone's papers. The tall one with a watered left eye and a strong, no-sense voice said: "Where are you going?" Her heart started to beat faster as they stopped in front of her.

"To Engen."

"Purpose of your visit?"

"To see my aunt. She is feeling poorly and needs me."

"Her name?"

"Gerda Weber."

They looked over her papers and passed them to her. She swallowed hard and closed her eyes, hoping it would stop the pounding in her ears from her heart. She looked out the window. How green and peaceful everything looked. She closed her eyes and dozed off. She wasn't sure she had slept but woke to see someone tugging at her jacket sleeve.

"It was the wounded airman. "Hated to wake you, but they're taking orders for sandwiches and coffee."

Sommer smiled. A wave of loneliness swept over her. Wait until Gretchen hears about how she met the wounded airman. Then she realized, she would not be seeing Gretchen until the war was over.

"Do you mind if I sit down? My foot is killing me."

Sommer removed the book from the seat in front of her. "Make yourself at home."

The porter came by and was stopped by the airman. "Here, let me get this. A sandwich and coffee for the lady, and I'll have a Cognac and a sandwich." He turned to her. "Haven't eaten all day."

"Come to think of it, neither have I."

"What do you work at? In the Third Reich, everyone must work. Good thing, actually."

"I'm a mathematician. I have a degree from Bonn University."

"So what does a mathematician do in the Third Reich? "I started out creating codes that the British curse me for. They can't crack them."

"For the Luftwaffe?"

Sommer shook her head. Actually, for the Wehrmacht. I am now working on a special project under a very famous mathematician, Professor Albrecht. He was my professor at Bonn."

They laughed when she told him about life in Canada and recounted how she tried to get their horse to move when she tried to plough. The horse wouldn't budge. Her father had been sick; she was only 11 years old. To make matters worse, it was spring planting time. Her father had to get out of his sick bed to teach her how to use the commands. She tried to imitate his voice, and they started laughing.

"That's my story. I got a scholarship to study for two years under the great German mathematics genius Professor Friedrich Albrecht. I was working with him on a project at Humboldt. He was killed yesterday in the bombing. We're not quite sure what will happen next with the project. I have to be back five days from now."

"I guess it's my turn. My father was in the German army and spent a few months in a POW Camp in Northern England. He fell in love with one of the girls, who came to the camp with food and other goodies for the prisoners. He fell in love with one of the girls, and when the war was over, he decided to stay and pursue the young lady until she agreed to marry him. I was born in Manchester, where my father found work in one of the factories there. Eight years ago, I answered the call of the Fatherland. I had heard that Hitler was changing things and that there were plenty of jobs in Germany. There certainly weren't in England. I became a German citizen after a couple of years and joined the Luftwaffe when war broke out."

"My name is Gregor."

She smiled. "Sommer Kappel."

Before she knew it, the porter came by to tell them they would be coming into Munich shortly, where she would need to take another to go to Engen.

"That's where I'm heading. I've made the trip many times and never met anyone else going to Engen. Let me guide you to the next train."

"You know people in Engen?"

"A girl I once knew who invited me to spend a holiday with her and her family. I thought, Engen, no bombing and Berlin, a bombing almost every day. It took me three seconds to make up my mind."

The train came to a stop. He rose. "Follow me."

"Let me carry your bag," said Sommer.

"Thank you."

Sommer helped him off the train, and they walked slowly to the station, talking along the way. Sommer found them a coffee, and they sat near the gate where they would take their train to Engen. The station was filled with workers returning from working in the fields near Munich and soldiers with their girlfriends and wives. The loudspeakers above them played army marching songs and a few popular songs like *Lilli Marlane*. When their train was announced, Sommer helped him to his feet and made their way slowly to the loading platform. When they reached the train, she mounted the stairs first, taking his crutches on board before reaching down with her right arm to enable him to grab the railings on each side of the steps. He lifted himself to the platform, very neatly using them. "Let's find a seat where we can avoid the Sun. It'll be dark by the time we reach Engen."

The train headed west with a stop at Engen, which was on the opposite side of the tacks. Gregor had a bit of a problem navigating his way across them. She had to steady him from time to time as one of the crutches got locked in the tracks. Gregor stashed his crutches against the wall and lifted his foot to rest on the seat beside Sommer. "That feels a bit better. It hurts when I stand on it." He paused to change his voice. "I have a feeling I can trust you. Actually, I have a few friends in Engen. I want to cross into Switzerland."

"Why?"

"Because the Germany I came to is not the Germany that it is now. The Nazis have ruined it. And they have no chance of ever winning the war," he said in sotto voce. "I have a strange feeling you're also planning to leave. Maybe, we can pool our resources and make sure at least one of us gets through. If that is not the case, please forget what I just said."

Sommer didn't quite know what to say. "I'm not sure how I could help you."

"If the border guards see a wounded airman trying to get into Switzerland, they'll stop me even before I take the first step. But not if I am taking my wife, who is pregnant and needs the help of a Swiss specialist to help her save our baby."

"You're right, Gregor. I would like to get to Switzerland. The bombings yesterday and seeing one of my best friends with a big gash on her face that will always be there, and most of all, finding that my professor had been killed in the air raid, something snapped inside me. I wanted to leave it all and never see Germany again."

"If you need a message sent to someone outside Germany, I have a friend with a short-wave radio that I can ask to relay the message for you. He has done this for many people."

Sommer suddenly heard Brookfield's voice in her ears: *Trust no one. Not your best friend. And certainly not a stranger.* "I don't have any messages for anyone except my daughter in Canada, who is too young. I have not seen her in a long time."

"We'll talk some more later. Right now, I need to close my eyes. I haven't slept in 24 hours. Actually, " Gregor said, looking at his watch, 28 hours." He tipped his cap over his eyes and was asleep in minutes.

Sommer dozed off, too, waking when she heard the train whistle. They were just rounding the curve toward the station. She tapped him on the leg. "We're coming into Engen."

"Sorry about not being much of a companion. You should have awakened me earlier. You still haven't answered me about joining me in Switzerland."

The train came to a sudden jolting stop. Gregor, who had just stood up, almost lost his balance. Sommer rose and helped him steady himself.

"Well, what about it?"

"I'm thinking," said Sommer. "I would like to spend some time with my aunt. I must head back in five days."

"If we leave in two days, no one will miss you until you report for duty." He paused. "I have to report back to the hospital in four days. So, it's either in three days or never."

"I need to talk about it more."

Sommer got off the train first, taking his crutches with her before helping him land on each step squarely and then the last step off the train. She helped him steady himself as he fitted them beneath his arms. They walked slowly through the station and into one of the waiting taxis.

"Let me drop you off at your aunt's home before I meet with my friends. I'll pop by tomorrow morning around 11 and complete the arrangements."

"What arrangements." Sommer felt fear in the back of her head.

"For one thing, your passport. I'll come by with a camera and take your picture."

"What on earth for?"

"You need a new passport. You're supposed to be my wife, whom I'm taking to see a specialist about your baby."

The taxi suddenly stopped. Her aunt, who had been waiting out front for her, opened the door of the taxi as Gregor tipped his cap. "See you tomorrow."

"A friend of yours, Sommer?"

Sommer shook her head. "Please, Aunt Gerda. He is a wounded German airman who shared the same taxi with me."

Gerda hugged her three times and held her back to examine her face. "You're in trouble. The same expression your mother used when he had a problem. I have been sick with worry. What is it? Maybe I can help."

"Listen to me carefully, Aunt Gerda. It's better if you

don't know."

Gerda's face filled with sadness. "Except for my son and his daughter, I have only you left in my family. If anything should happen to you…"

***

Gregor's taxi rolled up in front of the house at precisely 11 o'clock. He used his crutches to open the door. Sommer heard the taxi and opened the door immediately, rushing to help him steady himself as he rose from the taxi. She helped him inside and introduced him to her aunt, using a new last name for Gregor. "Just in case the Gestapo decide to take you in for questioning and demand his name." Then, turning to Gregor, "You've brought a large bag along with you."

Gregor just smiled. "Just a few things to prepare for our journey," He said, reaching into his bag and producing a small bottle of hair dye – you need to get some new clothes and a new toothbrush."

His last item was a camera, which he used to take a head and shoulders picture of her. All you need to do is sign the passport.

Sommer went into the bathroom, applied the dye to her hair, and let it dry in the sun. Later, she tried on the black glasses he had given her. They certainly changed her look.

"Wonderful," said Gregor. "Even your mother wouldn't know you. I'll be back tomorrow with the passport and other items."

He left a few minutes earlier.

Gerda, who had been watching all this, shook her head. "What's this all about, Sommer? You and this man are planning something. New trouble. I can feel it in my bones."

"I didn't want to tell you this, but I have some kind of disease and need to go to a special clinic in Switzerland for a procedure that will cure it. "

In the afternoon, Sommer and Gerda decided to go shopping for a few things while she was at the clinic. Later, when they returned home, Sommer, with two changes of clothing, and Gerda, a toy for her grandchild, bought at a second-hand shop near the church. They walked along the cobblestone streets and by the white, green, and yellow walls of houses on the side streets. Sommer was never tired of seeing them. Gerda carried her grandchild, who had fallen asleep.

When they returned home, Gerda produced a small ham. "I've been saving this for a year or more, hoping you would visit me again." She lit a fire in her old wood stove in the kitchen and boiled a pot of water before putting the ham in it.

She struggled to get up, eyeing Sommer as she got to her feet. "What do you know about this man, Sommer? And are you sure you really want to do this?"

CHAPTER TWENTY-FIVE

Gregor arrived at nine o'clock on the dot. Sommer opened the front door, waved to him, and turned around to Gerda, who was crying.

"Please don't go. Sommer. I have a bad feeling about it, and you're all I have left in my old days. You remind me so much of your mother. I'm not sure I'll ever see my son again. When people go to these camps, you never hear of them."

Sommer kissed her hands. Outside, the taxi driver honked his horn. "I will return, Gerda. The war will not last forever, and everything will return to the way it used to be. But I must leave now. I will try to write you from Switzerland."

When she entered the taxi, carrying her clothing, the taxi started to roll away. The last thing she saw as it drove onto the road was Gerda standing before her front door, wiping her eyes and waving to her.

They reached the border post in less than 15 minutes. Gregor paid the driver and needed help getting out of the taxi. She carried his bag along with hers.

"Here's what is going to happen when we reach the guard post: I will go first, and when I get through, I'll entertain the other guards with a story of how I got shot down by a British plane and how a bullet from another plane smashed his ankle joint. It will distract them, and while I'm doing that, get the first guard to stamp your passport. Once that is done, we'll leave and head for the white-painted line that separates Germany from Switzerland. Once we step past that white line, we're in Switzerland, Got it?"

Sommer nodded and was amazed at how cool and authoritative his voice had become. Inside, she couldn't stop trembling no matter how hard she tried. Her heart was pounding madly, and she caught herself breathing hard.

"If I need to change the story, be sure to listen to what I say and play along."

Gregor went first. She could hear the guard ask his name, where he was going and for how long.

"I'm taking my wife to see a specialist. There is something wrong with her pregnancy, and I will do whatever I must to make sure my child is born healthy, strong and able to serve the Fatherland and the Reich when he becomes a man."

"When will you be returning?"

"In three or four hours. You never know with doctor's offices."

Gregor tried to take a step and fell forward. Two guards helped him to his feet and stamped his ID papers.

"How did you get your wound?" said a young, well-built guard with short blond hair.

"From not paying attention. I had a Spitfire in my sight, and after I fired on it, I could see smoke coming from his engine, and I followed him down, forgetting to check if there were anything on my tail. Another Spitfire fired on me from behind. I managed to get out when one of the bullets smashed my ankle bone."

Sommer took a deep breath and tugged on the arm of the first guard, who turned to see who it was while trying to listen to Gregor's account. Sommer passed her passport and ID papers. He stamped them after a glance. She moved forward to stand behind Gregor.

"Good luck," said one of the guards as they left the booth area.

Gregor turned and waved back and kept on moving. Ahead, they could see the white line. "Don't rush. Just walk normally. We can't afford to look like we've done something wrong."

At that point, Felix Wagner, now an SS officer and in charge of the border post, had been interrogating another traveller when he turned to see a wounded airman and a black-haired woman walking towards the Swiss border. Someone asked him a question. As he was responding, something made him look at the airman and the woman again. There was something about the way the woman walked that reminded him of someone he knew before. He realized then who it was.

"Stop that couple," Felix shouted at one of the guards." Run after them and bring them back to me." the guard raised his rifle. Felix knocked it out of his hands.

Two of the guards set out immediately, running as fast as they could, calling to them to stop where they were. One shot his rifle in the air to make a point.

"Ignore them. Just keep walking," said Gregor, who was walking as fast as he could.

A couple of minutes later, Sommer could hear running footsteps behind her. They were so close now she felt her heart would explode.

Gregor suddenly turned and swung one of his crutches to knock one of the guards off his feet while yelling to Sommer to run. Sommer was running as fast as she could. Her legs were aching as she gave one last burst of speed. The white line was only a minute or two away.

She lie on the ground, panting and out of breath, and seeing it was a matter of six feet to freedom. The white line was just a few feet away when she felt someone grab her

JIM CARR

ankles and drag her down. She felt like crying.

They handcuffed her and raised her to her feet. They walked back slowly, past Gregor, who lay lifeless on the road. In the distance, she could see an SS officer standing, hands on hips, waiting for them.

As she got closer, she knew who it was. Felix. His head cocked when he studied something.

"I thought it was you," he said as she approached him. "I'd know your walk anywhere." He suddenly stopped smiling. "What is this about, Sommer?"

"We were trying to escape to Switzerland."

"But why, Sommer? Why would a Luftwaffe pilot want to leave his country? And you, I never thought I would ever see you again." Then, after a pause. "Is he your lover?"

"No."

"How long have you been in Germany?"

"Almost three years?"

"Then why didn't you contact me?"

"I was busy."

"Doing what?"

"Working for the Wehrmacht and then for Professor Albrecht on a project for the Fuhrer."

"The war had already started by then. How could you?"

"It's a long story, starting with my father. He died."

"Yes, I recall he was very ill. That was the reason you went back to Canada."

"My father made me promise before he died that I would return to the Fatherland and help it achieve victory in any way I could." She paused. Their eyes met, and both looked away at the same time.

But Professor Albert. He brings back great memories. How could you leave him at a time like this? We all knew you were his greatest student. He always talked about you."

"You ask why I left and wanted to escape to Switzerland." Their eyes met again. "A few days ago, there was a massive air raid on Berlin. The telephones were knocked out, and when I went back to work with him the next day, I found that he had died when a bomb struck our building, killing him instantly."

Felix watched the tears form in her eyes.

"After that, I just wanted to leave and never come back newer again. Ever."

"I understand, but the Gestapo, who have been notified about your attempt to escape, may not be so charitable. I will do whatever I can for you, but I am just a lowly lieutenant at an unimportant border crossing in Southern Germany.

"In the meantime, I will do whatever I can to make your stay with us as comfortable as possible and make sure you have lunch and supper but don't expect too much. We're on rations, too. Later, I'll bring you my old record player with recordings you can play during my absence."

Sommer looked across the metal desk in his office, the olive-green filing cabinets, and the ragged curtains on dirty windows. A picture of Hitler that looked down on them. She started the phonograph player when he left and played some of her favourites. She had forgotten just how marvellous classical music was and how it uplifted her spirits, then as now.

An hour later, a cook brought her a plateful of potatoes and turnips along with a sliver of fish and two slices of bread.

After supper, Felix returned. "Got word an hour ago to warn me that two people from Gestapo Headquarters will be here tomorrow. It appears they want you back in a hurry.

After what she had gone through, all Sommer wanted to do was hide from everyone. What was the point of it all? Everything had somehow lost its meaning for her.

***

Felix decided to stay with her when the two Gestapo agents arrived. He knew many people disappeared when they were left in their hands. It was clear from the outset that they didn't appreciate his presence. "I just want to make sure that when she leaves with you, she arrives in the same condition."

Becker shrugged his shoulders. He and Cullen sat opposite Sommer. "I knew I was right about you." He tried to smile, but it came out looking the wrong way. "Now I know I'm right." He paused. "I have been instructed to bring you back to Berlin to work on the Fuhrer's project."

He tried on the smile he used while torturing suspects, which made him look evil. "You will not be permitted to stay with your friend anymore. Or Zelda, for that matter, either."

He got up and nodded to Cullen. "You will be handcuffed to Pte. Cullen, during your trip back. There is a train leaving in an hour. If you want to prepare yourself, I suggest you do so now."

"Can you tell me at least if Gretchen Moller will be back as well?"

Becker nodded to Cullen, who tried to imitate Becker's smile. "When I called her about you, she was disappointed but not surprised."

CHAPTER TWENTY-SIX

Gregor attempted to get to his feet as two Gestapo officers entered his room at Luftwaffe barracks near Berlin.

"Stay put. We know you've had a hard time," said the older one, a thin man with a no-nonsense manner and a gravelly voice. "I haven't talked to the Kappel woman yet, although Oberleutenant Becker has. I was hoping you could tell us if she indicated to you that she was a spy in any way. We have reason to believe that she is a British spy and well placed to do this country great wrong."

Gregor sat back on his cot with his back against the wall. "I tried every trick I knew. I got her to talk about why she wanted to leave Germany. She would only say that her Professor Albrecht had died in an air raid and that she no longer wanted to live in a place where air raids were common every day."

"We also need to ask you what would have happened if you and she had succeeded in escaping," said Becker.

"Before we left, I suggested I had friends who could send messages to anyone she would like to contact about hoping to escape, whether to Canada, friends in London or elsewhere."

"Her reaction?" said the older officer.

"She didn't respond."

"What about her aunt? Is she a real relative or a British sympathizer? She has a son in a concentration camp," said Becker, who rocked back and forth on his heels on the creaking floor. At a look from the older officer, he stopped.

"No. The familial bond was there, and it was real. I didn't know about the son, but I saw an older woman who begged her niece not to go. She kept saying that Sommer was the only family she had left."

"I'd like to go back to my earlier question," said Becker. "What would you have done if you had succeeded in escaping?"

"I decided early on that if she did prove to be a British agent after escaping or make any attempt to contact London to bring her back to Germany. Failing that, to arrange to have her killed."

"And if she did prove to be who she says she is?" said the older officer.

"I would have urged her to return to Germany to complete the work of Professor Albrecht."

Becker was about to say something when Gregor raised his hand. "I'd feel much more comfortable if you two would grab a chair and sit while we talk."

"I was going to ask if she knows you're still alive. For all she knows, you were killed or wounded in your attempt to escape."

"I'm not sure."

"Then you still have another role to play," said the older officer, who seemed to be in charge. "As you probably know, Sommer Kappel is a major asset in the project launched by the Fuhrer. She was highly regarded by Professor Albrecht, who treated her more as an understudy. So we must move very carefully."

"Everyone keeps talking to me about this professor. What was so important about him?"

"He was Germany's greatest mathematical genius."

Gregor whistled.

***

Back at Gestapo Headquarters in Berlin, Sommer was held in one of the cells in the basement. A week went by, and she saw several other inmates come and quietly disappear.

Col. Jager was the first face she saw that she knew. He said down beside her on her cot. "I'm sorry it has come to this, Sommer. Unfortunately, you somehow have made an enemy of Becker, who sometimes lacks common sense." He paused. "Are they treating you well?"

Sommer tried to smile. "I am all right, colonel."

"If you only didn't try to escape, give Becker an excuse to keep you under lock and key. You would have had a great future in the Third Reich."

"What will happen next?"

"You'll start work again in another building at the university next Monday. They have a new director, a mathematician like you. His name is Godfried Kaufer. He lacks Professor Albrecht's brilliance, but he is an excellent administrator. We're depending on you to provide the brilliance. So what do you think? Ready to give it another try?"

"Will my friend, Gretchen, be there?"

"Yes."

"Then I can't wait for Monday to come."

Then, in a more serious voice: "You'll be moved to another building where they keep political prisoners and be escorted to and from Humboldt every day."

Someone was singing *Lilli Marlene* a few cells away. Col. Jager smiled.

"Do you know who'll be escorting me every day?"

"That's up to Becker."

Sommer made a face. "He's not like you, Col. Jager."

"He has his uses."

She lay back, feeling better after Col Jager's visit, and looked out at the limestone walls beyond her cell for the millionth time. He had given her hope. Hope for the next time, if there ever was another next time. She felt thirsty again and rose to pour a cup of water from the cold water tap at the other end of her cell.

***

Becker appeared with Cullen two days later with smiles on both their faces. "We've come to take you to your new home," said Becker, signalling the guard to open her cell door. "Turn around," he said with a sadistic smile as he handcuffed her and pushed her in front of him. "What's this?" He opened the brown paper bag containing her clothes and looked up. "That's it?"

"That's everything. I lost all my clothes when a bomb hit Lotte's apartment. Talking about Lotte, how is she now? And was Zelda able to get a doctor to look after the gash on the left side of her face?"

"I can't tell you." There was a hint of bitterness in his voice. "I have someone new now."

It was still raining when they emerged from Gestapo Headquarters and into a black police vehicle. Sommer sat next to Cullen, who had a strange smile that never changed. No one spoke until they pulled up at the entrance of a grey stone building built like a medieval fortress with small slits in the wall as windows.

"Stay here," said Becker as he went to collect the key to a third-floor cell – No. 32. Cullen unlocked her handcuffs and threw her brown paper bag on the small cost next to the wall on the left. The bars extended along the entire length of her cell, giving her no privacy of any kind. There was a small sink on the opposite wall and a threadbare towel to dry herself. There was a pail at the end of her bed that she assumed was her toilet.

Sommer looked at the guards outside at the desk near the entrance and then at the light tan-coloured tiles covering her cell's walls. She wanted to cry. Above all else, she needed a familiar face — someone who loved her for herself.

***

She laid down on her cot and drifted off to sleep, dreaming of her mother and Gerda when they were younger, begging her to join them on a tropical island. She woke with a start. The sound of trays sliding into the slot in the bars meant supper and reminded her that she hadn't eaten all day. She rose and waited for the cart to reach her. When it did, the old man pushing the cart kept rolling past her. She called out to him, but it didn't seem to matter.

She went back to bed and closed her eyes. Ten minutes later, she heard someone stop outside her cell. It was Cullen with her supper, "I've got something special for you."

She got up as he started to push the tray through the space in the bars. The tray suddenly tripped from his hands, spilling her supper all over the concrete floor in front of her.

"Sorry. It slipped."

"What about my supper?"

"That was it, I'm afraid." He turned away with a smile.

She was starving by the time supper arrived the next day. Her stomach was making strange noises, and her lips felt cracked and dry. This time, Cullen took extra care to push the tray through the slot but tipped it before she could keep it from spattering over the floor.

"Sorry," said Cullen, walking away with a smile.

By this time, her cell was beginning to smell, and she banged her dinner tray against the bars. Five minutes later, the guard at the front desk came to see what she wanted.

"My supper. It has been deliberately spattered over the floor for two days in a row now."

"You must be mistaken, 32. Pte. Cullen understands exactly how hard our work is and is always happy to lend us a hand. We have no complaints from the other prisoners."

The guard had a broad face, light blue eyes that looked washed out, and a grey mustache. He was thin and quite tall and walked with a limp.

"Then how do you explain the food splattered all over my floor and the food stuck on the bars?"

"I suspect you have something against him and have done this yourself to create a problem for him."

"Then what about supper?"

"We do not have extra meals. You will have to wait until tomorrow." He turned to walk away, but she stopped him. "Before you go, can you at least provide me with a pail of water and a cloth so I can clean the floor?"

She went to bed feeling a bit better, but her mind kept returning to Cullen and what else they had in store. She turned her face to the wall to avoid the light from the front, where she could see the guard playing solitaire. Later, when she finally drifted off, she had no idea what time it was. Tomorrow, she was going to Humboldt and worried about being alert and sharp when she met the new director and seeing Gretchen and how she would react when she saw her.

She woke with a start, her heart pounding, when someone walked past her cell, beating each bar with a steel pipe. She tossed and turned for some time before finally falling into sleep, waking after one nightmare after another. All she could recall was seeing Cullen's smile and the blank look in his eyes.

All the lights went on at the same time, including the overhead light in her cell, with someone shouting: "It's 6 o'clock. Time to wake up."

Sommer put her feet down on the cold concrete floor and shivered. Cullen came by with her breakfast, but she shook her head. "Not for me."

"Then get ready. We leave at 7 o'clock sharp." He left without his smile.

Sommer hid her smile beneath her arm. She suddenly felt tired and lay down on her cot. She put her blanket against the bars so she could wash and dress in private. She closed her eyes and fell into a deep sleep.

She was awakened by one of the guards shouting. "If you don't get up immediately, you'll be drenched in cold water." There was no response. The guard asked for someone to help him. She could hear the two of them beating the person and then the sound of gushing water. And finally, an uneasy silence.

"He's dead."

CHAPTER TWENTY-SEVEN

Gretchen couldn't contain herself and could hardly wait until she told Sommer. "You'll never forget who I just saw in the lunchroom. That gorgeous airman we saw at the train station." She looked at Sommer. "You don't seem surprised."

"It's not that, Gretchen. I have other things on my mind."

"We talked briefly. Gregor said he recalled seeing me at the train station and couldn't get me out of his mind."

"I'm walking on air." She looked at Sommer. "Are you sure you're all right? You look pale."

"I'm fine, Gretchen. Go on with your story."

"Nothing doing," said Gretchen, grabbing her by the arm. "I'd like you to tell me what you think. He's there now. You know, Sommer, you and I are not getting younger."

He was sitting with his back to them. When they sat

down in front of him, he was stirring a cup of tea and looked up when they sat down. "This is my lucky day," he smiled. "I remember you, too. Gretchen was kind enough to tell me her name. What is your name? My name, by the way, is Gregor Krantz."

"I'm Sommer Kappel. I see you have lost your crutches."

"I traded them in for a cane. I can't fly anymore. The Luftwaffe doctors tell me my flying days are over."

"Is that what you were thinking of when we came in?" Gretchen was at her brightest. She didn't need to. Her skirt was still cut an inch or two shorter than others, and she could still twirl her blond hair when she shook her head to and fro as she was doing now.

Jonas turned. "We need you for a minute, Gretchen. "

"Let me go instead."

"No. I'll only be a few minutes. You keep Gregor occupied until I get back. But not too occupied," she laughed as she disappeared.

"I did not know you were here."

Sommer suddenly changed. "I thought you were dead. At least, that was how you looked when they marched me back to the guard post."

"So did I. At least, that's how I felt when I came to an army hospital three days later. To make a long story short, they declared me unfit for combat and assigned me as a caretaker at Humboldt. Tell me about you."

"I am working on a complicated mathematical project with Dr. Kaufer for the Fuhrer."

"Are you living close by?"

"No. I have an armed guard to take me from the university to the prison for political prisoners not far from here and also to Humboldt in the morning."

"I am sorry to hear this."

"Hear what?" asked Gretchen, taking her seat next to

Sommer.

"About my living quarters." I really have to get back. You stay for a while, Gretchen, and talk him into making sure he has two steaming cups of tea ready for us when we arrive in the morning."

Gretchen returned 15 minutes later with stars in his eyes. "He wants me to go to the pictures tonight with him. What do you think?"

"Fine, as long as he has our tea ready for us in the morning. But with one proviso. Tread carefully until you get to know him better. He looks fine, and there is no doubt that he's falling for you in a big way."

"You really think so?"

Sommer nodded and smiled before returning to her work. She couldn't stop talking about him and his exploits as a fighter pilot. She tried to put him out of her mind. Her stomach told her not to put too much faith in him, although it was clear that he had enchanted Gretchen.

Two weeks later, she met him in the corridor. "I was hoping to have another private talk with you again. If there is anything I learned, it's never to give up hope." His eyes looked as though he were trying to read her mind.

"How did you escape the wrath of the Gestapo?"

"I told them you convinced me that you had a fatal health problem and would die if she didn't receive a certain operation by a world-famous doctor in Switzerland. They seemed to believe me. Mainly, I think, because they wanted to." He looked at someone coming down the corridor. "I feel I've let you down and would like to make up for failing you at Engen. I've got a fool-proof plan to get us over the border. This one will work. It bypasses the border guards."

Sommer didn't respond. She had reservations. He seemed earnest enough, just as he did in Engen, but she had doubts about his explanation, which sounded rehearsed for her ear. Her experiences with the Gestapo had taught her they were anything but kind and understanding. Sommer knew she had to depend on herself if she were going to escape, and her ingenuity or someone she knew was on her side, like her aunt. Someone she could put her trust in. He was right about one thing. Never give up hope. What she needed now was hope. Someone like Perdita.

A month later, Gregor disappeared. Gretchen looked all over the university for him. No Gregor. She cried herself to sleep. "He didn't leave a note. Nothing," she finally told Sommer.

In the silence that followed, Sommer said, "I'm not sure whether I should tell you this or not,"

"What?"

"When we saw him at the train station that day, I discovered we were on the same train and going to the same place. He told me he planned to escape to Switzerland and told me he needed someone to make it work."

"Did you believe him?"

"To my regret, yes."

"You know," said Gretchen, "I thought he was really interested in you at one time. Not me. Every time we met, he asked me a lot of questions about you: Whether you were a British agent in disguise and even whether you had a boyfriend. He always brought the conversation back to you, even when I changed the topic.

"For a while, like today, I thought he was using me to get at you, that you were the one he really loved." A pause. "You're not, are you?"

"If you want my honest opinion, he's not someone I feel comfortable being around. Just a bit too smooth for my liking. Did I tell you I ran into Felix when I tried to enter Switzerland? He was the officer in charge of that border crossing, and we had a great chat. It was like the old days. He even played some of his recordings. It was nice hearing them. But he's in the past."

***

Becker waved Gregor into his office. "Back so soon? Don't tell me you've finished your assignment that fast."

"Sorry to tell you I failed. What little information I did get came from Gretchen, her best friend from her university days. It was almost as though she knew what I was after and became very guarded in those times we talked by ourselves. Sorry."

"Don't blame yourself. You probably got more information than we did. We have to play it very carefully because both she and Gretchen are working on this special project for the Fuhrer." Becker stubbed out his cigarette and looked out the window. There had to be something he was missing, he told himself. Someone thing that would bring her down.

He looked up at Gregor. "You were a distraction to focus her energies elsewhere. I saw Dr. Albrecht's death as an opportunity to slip two of our people into their next. They report only to me.

"I've also changed the guard who takes her to and from the university with orders to treat her with difference and care. I want to lower her guard. A false sense of security may do what we have been unable to do, even make her life miserable. I think we're on the right track, and only a question of time before she stumbles."

***

When Sommer returned, she was told they were moving her to a cell closer to the front. "There's a virus making the rounds, and we can't afford to have anything happen to you," said the young guard that took her to the cell.

"The inmate in the next cell to you came down with it yesterday and died in the night. We removed his body and washed every inch of the cell with disinfectant. It should be all right, but we'll wait and see. We were ordered to make sure you don't come down with it and to notify authorities at the slightest hint of a fever."

She awoke and washed in the new luxury of her toilet, no matter how small it was. The cell at the front was a bit larger and had a window and a small toilet beside her cot, which was a bit larger. The same guard, who looked as though he were trying to grow a beard, brought her breakfast when she finished dressing. It was the first good sleep she had had since being brought to the prison, and she dreamed about her mother and daughter again.

There was also a new guard to take her to Humboldt, quite young and courteous. "There was another raid last night," he said, pointing to the plume of smoke from the centre of the city. A lot of their planes were shot down. I watched a lot of it. My mother wanted me to stay in the shelter. I just wanted to see what a real air raid was like, just as it was happening. I didn't realize we had so many searchlights. They fix on a plane until our artillery shoots them out of the sky."

"Your mother is right. You are precious to your mother, and it would kill her if something happened to you." She looked at him closely. His helmet seemed too big for his head, and when he took it off to wipe the top of his hair, she realized she was just a boy, barely 16. She mentioned it later to Gretchen.

"I'm not surprised. Things are not going that well on the Russian Front, and all the able-bodied men are on guard in Greece, Holland, Belgium, or France and fighting against the Russians."

Sommer shivered. "I would not like to think the Russians are advancing on us."

"Don't worry, Sommer. Our soldiers will see they never set foot on German soil. It's what makes our work all the more important."

"In that regard, how are our recruits coming along?"

"There are two or three weak ones," said Gretchen, "but our old team is getting better by the day, and, what's more, they're helping the new members."

"All I really know is Clara. Do we have files on each of the new ones?"

Gretchen passed them to her. "I've gone through them, looking for anyone who looks like they might be another Cullen. They all seem fine from that point of view. But, as I said, the old crew is helping them along. Jonas has been a real asset."

Sommer smiled. "Then let's get to it."

CHAPTER TWENTY-EIGHT

Major Marius Von Bromen brushed back his hair. His greying temples were becoming greyer by the month, and he wondered if he should think about touching it up here and there. All the new commands were going to younger men, even though he was far more experienced than any of them.

Being the commanding officer of a group of misfits at a prison for political prisoners was not exactly what he had in mind. He thought it might be a command on the Russian front, where he could demonstrate his talents as a brilliant strategist of the first order. For the first time, he was glad his father was dead and did not know how the Austrian Corporal was treating him.

"Are you ready yet?"

His live-in girlfriend didn't respond. Why he wondered, does she need to take a bath and put on a new face just to tour the prison and take so long?

Lucia Rossi, a cabaret singer who intoxicated him from the first time he saw her, had been living with him for over two years. His family didn't accept her and ordered him never to bring her to their home again.

She opened the door and came out, swaying her hips as she walked and tossing her blonde hair in quick head movements. Her lips looked more intoxicating than ever. When she looked like this, he could refuse her nothing.

***

Captain Albert Guhr prided himself on running the prison like a place for lepers – simple, bare and lacking any amenities. A place where people could repent their opposition to the Reich and its leaders and emerge as its strongest supporters. He lifted weights almost every day and ran five kilometres every morning before breakfast. He looked at his boots, polished to perfection and gave him a sense of pride.

There was a knock at the door. One of the guards opened the door, and Major von Bremen walked past him with Lucia in tow.

Guhr raised his eyebrows. "Herr Major," he said, clicking his heels together and bowing slightly. "It is a pleasure to meet you. I've heard so many stories about you and never thought I'd ever get the chance to meet you."

"I 'd like to tour the prison from top to bottom and talk to some of the prisoners."

"Follow me them, Herr Major."

Lucia was getting tired by the time they reached the third floor. She stopped at the first cell. Sommer had just arrived back from Humboldt and was sitting on the edge of her bed.

'I'd like to talk to this young lady," said Lucia. "She's actually too young to be in a place like this."

"Go ahead," said Von Bremen. "Catch up with us when

you finish."

Only the bars separated them. "Bonfilia." Sommer smiled. "I knew it was you the moment I heard your voice."

"Why are you in a place like this?"

"I tried to escape to Switzerland but didn't quite make it. They brought me back to Berlin to work on a secret project launched by Herr Hitler that's supposed to be a new weapon of mass destruction that kills thousands of people in a single blast. That's everything. Brookfield needs to know about this. If you have a piece of paper, I could write an equation for him. It might give him an idea of what it's all about."

Lucia turned and asked the guard for a piece of paper and a pencil. She slipped them to Sommer, who wrote down three equations for Brookfield. "How can you remember something as complex as these?"

"I have a great memory. In math – that's what I'm good at – a good memory is everything."

"I'll send it to Brookfield tomorrow when Marius inspects the prison."

"I will not be here then. They take me under guard to Humboldt University every morning and back again at night."

"You never know with fate. Here I am, girlfriend to the new commandant of a prison for political prisoners, helping one of my fellow graduates from Beaulieu. It's a perfect set-up. Who would ever guess the major's girlfriend is a spy?" She laughed, a deep, throaty laugh that brought Sommer back to their days at Beaulieu.

Bonfilia reached through the bars. "You don't look well, Sommer. Is something wrong?"

"Not that I know of. But someone in the next cell next to me died from a deadly virus a couple of days ago."

***

195

"What happened to you? I've never seen you this gay before. You're positively radiant," said Gretchen.

"For one, there's been a changing of the guard at the prison. A new commandant. A Major Von something. There's already been a change. You can feel it in the air, and best of all, they've given me a new cell, with includes a small toilet." She wiped her forehead. "It's hot in here."

"I agree," said Gretchen, as two older men entered, carrying long poles and walking to the widow side of the room to turn the top panes outward to let in the air.

Sommer looked over the day's latest problems. "This one looks quite difficult. Let's get all the team working on it."

They made a circle of chairs and wrote down the problem for them to solve. "It looks deceptively easy but believe me when I tell you, it will test all our skills. Don't be afraid of trying a new approach. Let's get at it."

By noon, the wastepaper basket was full. It still taxed them by supper time, and the answer still eluded them by quitting time.

Gretchen wiped her forehead. "It's so hot in here."

"You don't look good, Gretchen." Sommer felt Gretchen's forehead with the back of her hand. "You're burning up."

"I'm all right. We have too much to do without worrying about something as trivial as a cold."

"Work can wait, Gretchen. Your health can't. You need to be in a hospital. You look the way Jundt did when she was admitted to the hospital." Sommer rose and waved to Jonas to join her. "Gretchen is not feeling well. I want you to take charge while I take her to the hospital."

She turned to the others. "I need to take Gretchen to the hospital. In my absence, you will take your orders from Jonas, who will be in charge in my absence."

She left to see Dr. Kaufer and asked for a car to take

Gretchen for help. Ten minutes later, they were at the entrance of the hospital, where two orderlies placed her on a stretcher and walked her to admitting. Sommer held her in her arms all the way, soothing her forehead and whispering in her ear.

Dr. Biermann, a tall young man with a black beard and thick glasses, took one look at her and ordered two nurses to take her to a private room.

"It's serious, isn't it, doctor?"

She's got a bad case of a deadly bug that's popping up all over Berlin these days. I won't give you false hope. There is a good chance she may die. We've already had three cases like this in the past two days. Two didn't make it." He turned to shout to one of the nurses to post a quarantine sign outside her room.

"None of our medications seem to work. Even Penicillin doesn't work. It's also highly contagious. None of you will be permitted to see her."

When she returned to tell Dr. Kaufer, she was beginning to feel a bit faint herself.

"Is there anything we can do for her?" said Dr. Kaufer.

"Pray and hope for the best."

She went to the toilet to cry. She couldn't handle the thought that she might never see Gretchen again. He asked Jonas to join her when she returned to the workroom.

"Gretchen is quite ill. I want you to take her place until she returns and sit next to me."

The others whispered among themselves. It was clear something was amiss, and they focused on the equations Jonas had handed them.

In the afternoon, Dr. Kaufer came down from his office to tell them that Gretchen had died.

***

An hour after she fell asleep, Sommer woke in a sweat.

Her lips were dry and felt cracked. She tried to raise herself from the bed. She felt sick to her stomach and fell flat on the floor. She staggered to her feet, falling and crawling to the bars, where she tried to call the guard. The guard entered and took a quick look at her before leaving to call the commandant.

"There will be hell to pay if she dies on us," said Von Bremen. "Call for an ambulance, and you and I will take her to the nearest hospital and hope for the best. It's that damn flu that's going around."

Dr. Biermann, who handled Gretchen, was still on duty and called for a stretcher to take her to a private room. Around three o'clock, when they were getting nowhere, the doctor ordered an ice bath, hoping to drop her temperature. Throughout the night, nurses kept replacing cold clothes on her forehead.

Sommer kept tossing and turning and uttering words that made no sense. Before he was ordered out, one of Becker's agents was in her room, writing down everything she said. They didn't mean much when he read them later.

Three hours later, her temperature started to drop, and Sommer went into a deep sleep. Everyone was smiling. "It must have been the Penicillin after all," said Dr. Biermann. He stretched his arms. "I don't know about the rest of you, but I'm beat."

***

When Becker heard the news, he gritted his teeth. The last thing he needed now was to have her die on him.

He called Zelda to tell her about Sommer. He kept tapping his fingers on the top of his desk and looking at the clock, wondering when Zelda would come. She didn't arrive until mid-afternoon, and when she did arrive, she took her seat on the right side of his desk, next to the window.

"What do you want, Konrad?" Zelda's voice was cold and business-like.

"Sorry to be the bearer of bad news, but I thought you should know that your friend, Sommer, is in hospital. She's caught that bug that's been killing many people."

"Where is she?"

"I'll check and call you unless you'd care to wait until I hear." He glanced up at the picture of Hitler and shook his head. It was the last thing he needed to do today. The first three hospitals had no record of Sommer Kappel. He kept shaking his head at Zelda every time he failed to find out where Sommer was. He found out where she wasn't until the fifth call.

The operator connected him to Dr. Biermann. "Konrad Becker, Gestapo. I'm trying to track down a Sommer Kappel. I understand you're treating her. How is she coming along?"

Becker nodded and hung up. He smiled and reached out for Zelda's hand. "I talked to her doctor. He tells me she is coming along, and they hope to discharge her before the end of the week."

Zelda thanked him, stood, and turned to go.

"I miss you, Zelda."

She didn't turn but opened the door to head out.

"Before you leave, you should also know Sommer's friend, Gretchen, died this afternoon."

***

Zelda and Lotte came the next morning, armed with flowers and chocolate. Each of them held her in turn and kissed her forehead.

Sommer tried to smile. "Gretchen. Poor Gretchen. She had so much to live for."

"You'll never guess who called me about you," said Zelda with a wide smile. "Konrad. He called again this morning to tell me where you were and told me to bring you this chocolate cake. All we had to do was pick it up from the store."

"Konrad. Sorry, that's hard to believe, and I'm the most gullible of us."

"I wouldn't believe it if I hadn't accompanied Zelda to the store."

"Lotte," said Sommer. "Bend down so I can see your beautiful face."

There was a thin line on her cheek. "I can cover it up completely with a bit of makeup. If it hadn't been for you hounding Zelda to get me to a doctor and her hounding up until he sewed the scar. It only took him a few minutes, but he grumbled all the time he was doing it. Steffen came back yesterday and asked me to thank you as well."

Sommer tried to sit up but sank back on her pillows. "Thank you for coming to be with me today. It means so much. Especially after we lost Gretchen." She paused. "I'm sorry. I feel very weak and tired suddenly." She closed her eyes and was asleep in less than a minute.

***

Dr. Kaufman. His thick, light brown hair over his fore-head suddenly appeared in the workroom. "I want you to know that Sommer, who also came down with the flu, is recovering in hospital, thank God. It may be a week or two before she returns. In the meantime, she has appointed Jonas Stein as her stand-in until she returns. Now, if there are any questions…"

Major Von Bremen heard about Sommer from her doctor at the hospital. "You say she's recovering. Is there any chance there could be a relapse?"

"I should not think so at this stage in her recovery. If there is any change, doctor, call me immediately. You may not be aware, but she is very important to the war effort." He was also acutely aware of what effect it would have on his career if she died.

He put down the receiver. "It seems that Sommer Kappel is in hospital. She came down with that deadly flu bug spreading all over Berlin."

"Which she are we talking about?" said Alicia.

"The one you stopped to talk to two days ago."

"Yes. She looked so hopeless. Did you know she comes from Canada?"

"Why am I the last to hear about everything." And then, in a softer voice: "Do you think we should visit her?"

Alicia nodded with a smile.

"You are always so kind, Marius. Always thinking of others."

Sommer was sitting up and looking far brighter when Von Bremen and Alica entered her room. Sommer tried to pat down her hair and pulled up the sheet in front of her."

"The major and I were anxious about you and wanted to make sure you have everything you need."

"I've talked to admitting," said Von Bremen, "and told them to give you everything you want, anything and everything to help you recover."

***

Ten days later, Sommer made a surprise visit to Humboldt. Jonas spotted her first as she entered the door and was at her side within seconds. "Thank God you're well and back with us."

Sommer looked around.

"The others ignore me, and quite frankly, aside from Martin and me, that's the only work that really gets done, they do a bit, but after an hour or two, they get bored and spend an hour or more in the lunchroom before coming out and putting in another hour of work. They spend the rest of the day either in the lunchroom or gossiping among themselves. I warn them, but they ignore me.

"If you were me, what would you do?"

"Get rid of those who don't want to work."

"You should have gone to Dr. Kaufer. I asked him to put you in charge."

"Dr. Kaufer came down the next day after they took you to the hospital and told them I was in charge until you came back."

"It's not your fault, Jonas. But they will. Kindly ask them to join us in the workroom."

It was almost five minutes before they all made their way back to their desks. No one spoke and sat at attention.

"Before I left, I made it clear to all of you that Jonas would be in charge of the workroom in my absence."

"We were just having a cup of coffee," said Karla. "It was the first break we've had in days. I don't know what Jonas has told you but ask the others."

Sommer looked at Jonas, who shook his head. "One last chance. Why were you not at your desks when I entered the workroom? Lunch time is noon." She looked up at the clock on the wall in front of them. "It is now 9.30."

No one spoke.

"Well, then, I'll do the talking. "We need people for this project we can rely on. Not people who try to take advantage of a crisis. The Fuhrer deserves better. You can be sure this will go on your record. Pack your things, and don't come back."

"We'll see about that," said Sofie Schafer.

Five minutes later, they left without a trace.

***

"She did what?" Becker couldn't believe what Sofie Schafer had just told him. "What happened?"

Five of us were in the lunch room when she made a

surprise visit. She told us to pack up and leave and not to come back because of that sneak of hers, Jonas Stein, ratted on us."

"What do the rest of you do?"

"I was the only one that spoke up. I told her we'll see about that."

Becker shook his head. "It seems I really can't depend on anyone."

He later sat back in his chair and started hatching a new plan. He thought about Sommer and smiled and couldn't help admiring her. He admired smart people, but he also knew he was smarter.

CHAPTER TWENTY-NINE

Sommer couldn't wait. Her guard was 10 minutes late. They barely spoke as they headed out to the cemetery where Gretchen was buried on the outskirts of Berlin. Zelda and Lotte were already there and joined her in laying a large floral wreath from the three of them.

Gretchen's parents were already there and introduced themselves. "Which is Sommer?"

Sommer raised her arm.

"So you are the Sommer our wonderful daughter talked about so much. You were her mentor and everything," said Gretchen's mother, who wrapped her arms around her as Sommer suddenly broke down, talking almost incoherently about the two Christmases they spent together and what it meant to her.

It was like a bad dream. It happened so fast, with no

warning. Gretchen was well one day and dead the next. It felt like a piece of lead in her stomach that she couldn't get rid of.

"Who's that?" said Zelda, nodding toward a woman dressed in a black raincoat and headdress.

"Probably one of Gestapo's operatives," said Zelda. "You know, Sommer, Becker has a fixation on you. It will be his undoing. Don't trust anyone."

Another young woman edged closer. He was wearing a nun's habit. Sommer motioned for her to come to her and threw her arms around her.

"I came with another nun. I hope you don't mind."

"Let me introduce you to Gretchen's parents. This is our old friend, Katrina. She, Gretchen, and I were together on our last Christmas in Bonn."

Later, as they were leaving the gravesite, Katrina said she had heard from Gretchen and that she was working with you at Humboldt. That's how I knew you would be here today. They told me you were attending a funeral and would be back tomorrow.

"We were waiting in hopes you would turn up. I am known now as Sister Agnetha."

Gretchen's parents invited them all for supper at the hotel where they were staying.

"I would love to, but I need to get back to the convent." She turned to Sommer. "Join me with a special prayer for our dear friend, Gretchen." Katrina took out her rosary and started.

**

Gretchen's parents brought food with them and had it cooked by the hotel and served in a private room. They were seated on both sides of a long table that could have seated at least 12 people. Sommer sat close to Gretchen's mother, holding her hand as Gretchen's father poured each of them a real coffee in oversized mugs.

"Where did you get this? I haven't tasted real coffee for years," said Lotte.

"I have a few friends from the old days who can get things for me." He poured a shot of Cognac into each mug and added: "I'm glad to have you all together at one time. It saves me from seeing each of you individually about a project we have in mind. I would like each of you to consider naming your first daughter Gretchen in memory of the Gretchen we all knew and loved."

"What a wonderful idea," said Zelda. "I certainly shall if I ever get married."

"Gretchen always said if she had a daughter, she would call her Sommer," said Gretchen's mother.

Sommer felt a tear coming and wiped her left eye with the back of her hand.

"For Gretchen's father and me, you are like another daughter to us. We know so much about you in all the letters Gretchen wrote us almost every day. In all her letters, she saw you as a sister. We have come to know you ever since you were with her in Bonn."

"Our son died on the Russian front, and, except for you," said Gretchen's father, "we have no one to leave our possessions and would like to pass them along to you if you agree."

"I am sorry about your son. Gretchen never mentioned that he had died. And thank you for your wonderful gift." Sommer took a mouthful of coffee and held it in her mouth to capture the taste of it for as long as she could.

***

"Jonas Stein. His name is Jonas Stein. Find out everything you can about him. Everything," Becker told the young recruit who stood at attention in front of him.

He had no sooner left when he had an unexpected call.

"Who is it?"

"He didn't say, but by the sound of his voice, I'd say it was an officer," said the young brunette at the switchboard, who was the new light of his life. "When I asked for his name, he didn't respond."

Becker picked up the phone carefully. "My name is Major Marius von Breven. I am the new commandant at the prison for political prisoners."

"I know who you are, Herr Major, and I was meaning to call you to introduce myself."

"I understand you have an interest in one of our prisoners."

"Yes. Sommer Kappel. I have been uneasy about her every day since she suddenly showed up one morning, saying her father made her promise on his deathbed to answer the call of the Fatherland. I didn't believe her then, and I don't believe her now."

"I gather you believe she is an Allied agent."

"Yes. And even more so since she tried to escape to Switzerland."

"I hadn't heard about that." There was a pause. "Whatever you feel, she is now our top person on a project launched by the Fuhrer. With the death of Dr. Albrecht, we have no other person to lead it."

"What are you asking, Herr Major?"

"Unless you have hard, inconvertible evidence to the contrary, we would prefer you abandon any investigations about her for the time being. The project will not last forever; what you do after that is up to you. Understood, Oberleutenant?"

Abandon my investigations, not very likely, he thought, lifting his phone to make another call. "

Sofie? Konrad Becker. About your friend, Jonas Stein. What can you tell me about him?"

"Not much. A bit of a loner. Self-taught and smart."

"Do you think Sommer Kappel may be attracted to

him?"

Sofie laughed.

"Then what?"

"He sucks up to anyone in authority. Doesn't have a mind of his own."

Becker smiled. He had found the weak link."

***

Jonas didn't quite know how to approach her. Dr. Kaufer came down twice to talk to you and would like to see you when you arrive."

He found Sommer changed. It was as though she no longer cared. "He seemed quite nervous."

Yesterday's meeting with Gretchen's parents seemed to revitalize her. She understood for the first time what was really important in life, and it wasn't Brookfield, The Third Reich or even Professor Albrecht but something more that went beyond borders or nationality and even time.

She rapped on his door and entered. "You were looking for me, Dr. Kaufer?"

He looked up, his thin face even thinner, and there was anxiety in his eyes.

"I had a visit from a Wehrmacht colonel yesterday, telling me that our work was falling behind and to double our output or they would replace us." His voice trembled, and he avoided looking at her.

"What aren't you telling me?"

"Those people you dismissed yesterday. They want them back on the project."

Sommer held his eyes. "That's not going to happen."

"You've become very sure of yourself."

"No, Dr. Kaufer. It is just that I know they have no one who can replace me at this time. Professor Albrecht would not have tolerated this intrusion for two seconds."

"You don't know what they're like, Sommer, or what they're capable of."

"No, I don't. But I do know that if they want to give the Fuhrer what he wants and when he wants it, they can't do it without you or me. And that they will be held responsible if they fail."

When she returned, the five she dismissed were sitting at their desks. Sommer stood facing them. "I told you never to show your faces back here again yesterday. So why are you here?"

"We had a call from Wehrmacht command to report for work as usual," said Sofie Schaufer.

"No one talked to me about it, and I haven't changed my mind. But I will give you another chance to answer the question I asked you all yesterday."

Sommer sat down and waited, her arms crossed and held their eyes in hers.

'What do you want to know," said an overweight young man, whose voice cracked when he tried to get his words out.

"Who suggested you ignore Jonas and spend your time in the lunchroom instead of working?"

"Sofie Shaufer and Horst Voigt."

She looked at them. "You two can go now, and if you ever come back again, you will have to deal with the Gestapo."

Sofie looked at Horst. "I'm not budging."

Sommer looked at Jonas. "Kindly call Col. Jager at Gestapo Headquarters and have these two arrested."

Jonas picked up the phone and started to dial.

"Never mind," said Sofie, "but we'll be back, and it will be your turn to be escorted out of the building by the Gestapo." The door slammed behind them.

***

"Tell me you didn't threaten her with the Gestapo," said Becker. "I had to pull in a lot of favours to get you reinstated. I think you and I are done. Sofie. Never seek my help again," he said in the voice he used on suspects.

Sofie looked out the window and ignored him.

"Should I have someone remove you?"

"Not if you want me to tell Sommer Kappel it was part of your scheme to get rid of her."

Becker's mind returned to Major Von Bremen's warning and felt like gritting his teeth.

Later, Sofie waited for Jonas to leave the building and followed him all the way to a two-storey house about 20 minutes from the university. A second-floor light went on, and she could see him hang up his jacket a couple of minutes later.

It's now, or never, she thought, entering the building. She felt her way up the darkened stairs and knocked on the door.

***

Jonas seemed unsure of himself as he sat beside Sommer, who saw something troubling him.

"You'll never guess who knocked on my door last night."

"Sofie Schaufer."

"How did you guess?"

Sommer just smiled. "I gather she wanted you to intercede for her with me?"

Jonas nodded.

"Did she offer any incentives of a personal nature?"

Jonas blushed. "It was clear that would be part of the exchange." He paused. "In case you're wondering, I kept my distance and asked her to leave."

"I have a better idea, Jonas. Call her around quitting time and ask her to drop by your place if her offer still stands."

"I'd rather not."

"I think that someone in the Gestapo's office is the author of all the problems we've been facing, and I think they've put her up to it and will threaten to tell me unless you agree to spy on me for them."

Jonas looked at her open-mouthed.

"Instead, we'll turn the table on them. After you meet Sofie two or three times, tell her that she must have had very powerful friends to show up for work the day after being dismissed. I will bet you it's Becker in the Gestapo's office. Once we know that, I can pull the plug on him and keep him away from us forever."

"I don't feel comfortable about this."

"I know, Jonas. It's me they're after. Do it for me."

CHAPTER THIRTY

"Are you ready?"

"No."

"I'm coming in."

"I don't want you to see me like this," said Bonfilia as she finished sending an urgent message to Brookfield and scrambled to fit the radio transmitter into the outer shell of her beauty cabinet of creams and perfumed powders.

"What is this?" Von Bremen caught her as she put the outer shell over her radio transmitter.

"My beauty cabinet."

"I'm not blind, Alicia. "There is obviously more than just beauty creams hidden in that cabinet." He grabbed the outer shell and lifted it to expose the radio transmitter. "You forgot to pack these," he said, tossing her earphones on the toilet seat cover.

"How long has this been going on?"

"I can explain."

"I do not want to hear any of your explanations. I just want to know how long you have been deceiving me."

Bonafila didn't know what to say and tried to smile.

Von Bremen slapped her hard across the face, sending her against the sink and hitting the side of her face on the taps. Blood oozed out of her right eye, and she felt like vomiting.

He removed his sidearm and aimed it at her face. He

turned away and pulled the trigger.

Tears rolled down his cheeks.

A few minutes later, his guard opened the door and peeked in. "I thought I heard a gun being fired. Is everything all right, Herr Major?" He looked at the blood spots that spattered his tunic and his cheeks.

"I was trying to show Alicia how to hold a gun before aiming it at anyone when it suddenly went off in her beautiful face." His words came out haltingly, and he sounded unsure of himself.

"I am sorry to hear this, Herr Major, but you do not look well," he said, edging Von Bremen out of the toilet and to an easy chair in the living room. "Let me call the doctor for you, Herr Major."

Von Bremen nodded as the guard wiped the blood spots from his face and tunic with a damp cloth. "What is your name, private," said Von Bremen suddenly.

"Jurgen. Jurgen Zimmerman. Let me call the doctor."

Von Bremen nodded, took off his tunic, and washed his face and hands. The soap slipped from his hands. He still trembled as he wiped his face and hands with a towel in the kitchen and returned to the living room to wait for the doctor, who arrived a few minutes later.

"You're in shock. Let me give you something to help you get through this."

Bonfilia's body lay in the bathtub, and the radio transmitter stood beside the toilet cabinet. The doctor, a young man with a dark face and a cleft, kept sucking in his bottom lip as he examined Bonfilia's body. He glanced at Jurgen's face. "Any idea what happened here?

Jurgen pointed to Von Bremen's gun on the floor beside the toilet. "The major told me that his lady wanted to know how to use a gun in case she was attacked. He was shocked when I saw him but he did manage to tell me that the gun went off when he handed it to her. Later, I helped him to a chair he's sleeping in now. He kept repeating over and over that she should not have been seeing someone else."

The doctor looked at the radio transmitter and nodded.

"Is there anything else we can do?"

"Arrange for an ambulance to take her body to the morgue. I'm interested in her eye wound."

"Cause of death?"

"Gun accident. And have someone come in and clean up the bathroom. I don't want the major to see this when he wakes up."

***

Becker heard about it almost immediately. "Seems his lady friend was a spy and caught her red-handed trying to hide a radio transmitter, which fitted into her beauty cabinet," the guard from the prison told him. Becker's mind was going in all directions. He was able to connect dots that often escaped others.

"Did the major's lady ever talk to any inmates?"

"A few."

"Was Sommer Kappel one of them?"

"Often. More than she did to the other inmates.

Becker smiled as he hung up. Finally, the break he had been hoping for. There would be no way out for her this time. All he had to do was connect the transmitter to Sommer.

Becker smiled as he hung up. He knew in his heart of hearts that there would be no way out for her this time.

***

"We are sorry you had to go through this, Marius," said Col. Anton Palus, a Prussian like Von Bremen.

Von Bremen just looked straight ahead.

"Terrible accident but, perhaps, for the best. She would never have fitted in." Palus paused. "If you would prefer to be transferred, everyone would understand."

"Whatever you think is best, Anton. Is there any prospect of a command on the Russian front? That's where I'd like to be right now."

"Let me see what I can do. You may have to stay put for a bit, but we'll see."

An hour later, at his apartment, Von Bremen made a few decisions. The first was to have Pte. Zimmerman transferred to France, on the coast, just in case Hitler decided to invade England after all. The second was to have the toilet changed completely -- a new bathtub, sink and toilet, and have the walls repainted and a new floor put in as well. He never liked the old one anyway.

"You have a visitor, Herr Major. Do you wish to see him? It's Oberleutenant Becker from Gestapo."

Zimmerman escorted him in and left. Von Bremen pointed to the chair opposite him. "What's this about, Oberleutenant?"

"I came to offer my condolences and help, should you need it, Herr Major."

"What did you have in mind?"

"I was given to understand that a radio transmitter in the hands of the lady -- the kind spies use."

"Get to the point, Oberleutenant."

"It's about Sommer Kappel. We talked about her before. Do you think there is a connection between her and your lady? And that your lady was sending messages to London on her behalf?"

"Where did you get that kind of nonsense? I know exactly who she was trading messages with. So, unless you have something more concrete to offer, good day," said Von Bremen, standing up, signalizing the end of their meeting.

The chance of a command on the Russian was within his grasp now, and he was not about to ruin everything by condemning someone the Fuhrer had placed his trust in, certainly not for Becker, this woman, or anyone else.

***

"Sofie tells me she's pregnant with my child," said Jonas. Sommer laughed. "Maybe she is, and maybe she isn't."

"What do I tell her?"

"Tell her you'll think about it – but before you decide, you want a test to determine whether you are the father."

"What good will that do?"

"My hunch is you'll never see her again once you tell her that. And if you do, insist that you want Konrad Becker checked as well. But at the moment, we have a lot to accomplish today. Here," she said, "give this to your friend, Horst Voigt and tell him we need his equation by the end of the day."

Jonas watched Horst copy down everything Sommer said and bet it was going straight to Becker. He told Sommer, who decided to start each day with a prayer for the "health, safety and continued success of the Fuhrer." Later, Jonas caught him stirring something in her coffee.

"What was that you stirred in her coffee.?"

"Some powdered milk to make this so-called coffee more palatable."

Sommer laughed and tasted her coffee. "He's right," she said to Jonas, "it does make the coffee a bit better."

Sommer heard about Bonfilia when she returned to the prison – that he was handling a gun that went off accidentally and killed her instantly. The news hit her hard, and all the confidence she had built up in the past week ebbed away. Sommer knew better than to accept the story about the gun accident. She remembered their training at Beaulieu and that Bonfilia was better than the rest.

She heard whispers from other inmates that the major's

lady was a spy. She had come to the end of the road. But she had enough stubbornness not to panic or admit to anything.

***

Becker could feel that things were about to unravel one way or another. He was sure he finally had her where he wanted her. His instincts told him that stiff-necked Prussian major would not last long, and he would be ready when that day came.

Sofie was waiting for him when he returned. "I'm pregnant. I told Jonas, but he wants a blood test and a blood test from you before he would decide anything."

This was not going the way he had planned. He regretted that he had become familiar with her despite his better judgment. It was all part of the end of a cycle somehow. Strangely, he could feel the walls closing in on him. He had one last alternative, which he didn't feel comfortable using.

CHAPTER THIRTY-ONE

"What about your star, Sommer Kappel?"

The minister had invited Brookfield to the underground headquarters Churchill occupied during the early war years. The passageway was not well-lit and made him feel uneasy as he was led to the office the minister occupied.

"Well, Brookfield. You haven't talked about her for some time. I hope all is well?"

"There have been problems. After she tried to escape to Switzerland, she now occupies a cell at a prison for political prisoners and is escorted to and from Humboldt University every day."

The minister's office was small, large enough for a desk and three small folding chairs. The concrete floor was painted a bright grey, and a used Indian rug at the door led you inside. Two large paintings of 18th Century figures made up for the lack of windows. The black phone on his desk lit up. The minister raised his hand and picked up the phone. He didn't say anything and replaced the receiver a few seconds later.

"Where does that leave us?" The minister, a short man with a pot belly, had a sore throat, and his voice seemed ready to crack at any time.

"From what she is working on would indicate the Germans are working on what we have been working on. If anything, I'd say they're a bit ahead of us."

The minister sat down and drummed his fingers on his

desk. "I feel you're leading up to something. What is it?"

Brookfield glanced at the map of Germany on the wall behind the minister. He had lit a cigar and rolled it in his mouth.

"At Humboldt, Sommer worked under the great German math genius, Professor Friedrich Albrecht."

"Never heard of him."

"Sommer was one of his students. When he discovered she was back in Germany, she was sidelined to work for him on his project. When the professor was killed in one of our raids, Sommer became the de facto head of the project, even though she reports to a normal head."

"Does she know what she's working on?"

"I suspect not. She was told it was for a new weapon of mass destruction that would help Germany win the war and take over Great Britain and the rest of the world, with Germany at its helm."

"All well and good, but you still haven't told me what you've got up your sleeve."

"One of our agents, an Italian lady, lives with the officer who heads the prison garrison. She trained with Sommer at Beaulieu. She tells us that Sommer could crack under all the pressure. Evidently, her best friend from Bonn days died from a super bug making the rounds in Berlin. She thinks Sommer should be retired before she becomes a danger to the others who trained with her."

He paused to catch the minister's eye. "We must rescue her and bring her back to London as soon as possible. She could be a gold mine of information for us as well as an enormous help in speeding up the completion of our project."

The minister sat back and glanced at the light that was flickering insanely before stopping. "I think that's a pretty tall order, Brookfield, given the fact that she's in prison and under guard night and day. But that's your problem, Brookfield. You came here hoping for my support, and you've got it. But I'm curious. How do you plan to pull it off?"

"I have an idea, but first, I want to pass it by the people who will have to do it and get their input."

Brookfield made his way up the stairs and unto the street. There was a cool breeze, and he could see smoke rising from the docks and seagulls wheeling in the grey sky in the distance. He took a bus to his office to find firemen trying to put out the flames from a direct hit. Nothing was left. Everything went away in that one blast – his books, his painting of Churchill and all his files. Even his private storehouse of cigars. He shivered and made his way to St. Ermines, where he had an alternative office and acted as a host for special occasions.

He decided to have dinner sent to his private room and to do some hard thinking. When supper came, he turned on the radio to hear the latest war news. It was followed by a radio adaptation of the *Count of Monte Carlo* right through to his escape from the Chateau d'If. If someone could escape from an island prison, why not a prison on the third floor of a prison? He would try it out on young Bartlett, who had recently been promoted captain of a new commando unit formed by the Royal Marines.

***

Andrew Bartlett hadn't heard from Brookfield in weeks and wondered what it was about as he made his way to St. Ermines. He alit from the taxi and was immediately saluted by the doorman, who had been in the Royal Marines in the Great War.

Brookfield was waiting for him at the entrance. "Let's have tea before we get down to business."

"What's this about, Myles?"

"In due course, my boy. But first, tell me how you're

getting on with the Royal Marines."

Andrew stirred his tea and took a sip. He preferred a bit of sugar in it and never got quite used to having tea without it. "Still in the training stage. Right now, we're learning Judo and how to hit a moving target 100 yards away."

Later, when they sat down in Brookfield's hotel office, Andrew lit a *Craven A* and was about to speak when Brookfield stopped him.

"It's about Sommer. She's in serious trouble. If we don't rescue her, there's a good chance we may never see her ever again. Don't remember when I updated you last, but she's in a special prison in Berlin for political prisoners and taken to and from Humboldt every morning and evening. At night, she's locked up because she tried to escape to Switzerland but failed."

Andrew's eyes were glistening, and he waited for the punch line.

"She is working on a project to help the Germans not only win the war and leave the rest of us to kiss our freedom goodbye if they succeed."

"I know Sommer, and I know she wouldn't do something like that unless there's a gun at her head, and even then, she wouldn't," said Andrew.

"Ordinarily, I would agree. But she doesn't know what she's working on. In fact, none of the others working with her know either. They call it Hitler's secret to end the war. She was able to send a few equations they're working on now – so we know what they're doing and how far advanced they are."

Brookfield lit one of his cigars stored in his hotel office and got up to walk around the room. "I can only stand sitting for so long,"

"I gather you would like me to drop into the middle of Berlin and bring her back here."

"You were always a quick study, Andrew. I met with

the Minister before coming here. I told him she needed to be rescued, and he agreed before something happened to her. I hear from another source she is starting to fail and is losing weight." He paused to see how Andrew was taking it. "All I can say is if the Nazis get it first, God help the rest of us."

Andrew didn't respond. He knew the word what Brookfield was going to say next.

"We need you to lead a small, hand-picked group of commandos to break into the prison and rescue her. "What do you say, Old Man?"

Andrew just looked at him.

Brookfield could see the wheels turning in his head. "Report back to me in two weeks with a plan worked out on how you plan to do this. It's for the Minister. Not for me, just in case you're wondering."

Andrew went back to his barracks. He had hoped for news about Sommer, anything, rather than this. How could he devise a plan to reduce the danger Sommer and his men would face at every turn, no matter how well planned?

After a sleepless night, he had an epiphany. He would spend the weekend in Surrey with the one person who saw everything and everyone differently from other people – Perdita. It was one of the reasons why his mother felt it necessary to make excuses for her.

But first, he needed permission from his colonel to spend the weekend away to clear his head for a special mission Myles Brookfield had asked him to undertake. "It's dangerous and would involve six of my men."

"What's this about Bartlett? No one has called me about it."

"I agree, sir. May I call Mr. Brookfield now and let him talk to you about this?"

"I must say, Bartlett, this is somewhat irregular."

He picked up the colonel's phone and dialled the number given to him at St. Ermines. "Myles. It's Andrew Bartlett. "I'm with my colonel. That's correct, Col. Morris. I have told him you would like me to undertake a special mission for you."

"I gather his nose is out of joint," said Brookfield. "Pass him over."

Col. Morris listened for almost five minutes before he suddenly came alive. "No problem. Count on my full support."

When he hung up, he nodded to Andrew. "I don't envy you for what Brookfield describes as a mission that no one may return from – but must be carried out to stop the Germans from creating a new deadly weapon. You have my full support, Bartlett."

It was noon when he boarded the train for Shere. He kept thinking about the mission all the way and how to arrive unnoticed and leave the same way. Before he knew it, the train was slowing down for Shere.

"Captain Bartlett," said Angus, a Scot who had come to Shere when Bartlett was a boy and drove one of the town's two taxis. "Good to see you back. Where to first?"

"I want to spend a day with my Aunt Perdita before I see my mother."

Ten minutes later, he grabbed his travel bag and tossed Angus two shillings. He rapped on Perdita's front door. No answer. He rapped again, this time a lot louder, and shortly heard her shuffling towards the door. She opened it immediately, and he stepped inside and hugged her.

"I didn't expect to see you again so soon. Were you here two weeks ago? Is anything wrong?"

"Not really. But I need to chat with you about a mission I will undertake soon."

She sat him down at the kitchen table and poured him a cup of tea, adding a thick cream and a dollop of honey. "Just as you like it." She sat opposite him and passed him a cookie. "Does this involve Sommer in any way? I have been thinking about her a lot lately. Is she in any danger?"

Andrew didn't answer her question directly. "I have been asked to go to Germany and find a way to bring her back to London. It seems she has a lot of knowledge that could help the war effort, maybe even shorten it."

"I gather it's very dangerous."

Andrew nodded. "Very. It involves rescuing from prison for political prisoners and getting her back safe and sound to England. It's going to be tricky. But one thing. Please do not mention what I've told you to anyone. Not even to the Vicar. It could end in my death and Sommer's if the enemy ever gets wind of it. These days, you never really know who is a German spy.

"You've always had an inventive mind, Aunt Perdita. What would you do if you were me?"

"I would carry it out in the middle of a big bombing raid when most people will be in air raid shelters and their soldiers busy trying to shoot down our bombers. But you need not pay attention to me. I'm just an old woman with a lot of fancies."

***

"You don't look well these days, Sommer. "And you seem quite tired. Sometimes, I can see you nodding off, and I ask you a question to keep you awake."

"Thank you, Jonas. You have been an incredible friend to me in every way. Between you and me, I have a hard time walking back to the prison many days now."

"Ask your guard to find a military vehicle to drive you back from now on."

When her guard came for her at 9 o'clock, she told him she was too tired to walk back. "Could you send for an army vehicle to take me back?"

That night, she was so tired she could hardly take off her clothes and slip between the covers.

CHAPTER THIRTY-THREE

Bartlett was in his office, reviewing the files of his best 14 recruits. He wanted to check their psychological profiles and ability to follow orders under extreme pressure. He thought it was always the simple things that tripped everyone up at the end of the day. He decided to trim the number to seven. Getting a plane large enough to handle seven people and their weapons, ammunition, and explosives would be easier.

The first thing was to ask each of the seven how they would rescue someone from a prison guarded night and day.

"The first thing I'd do is learn everything I could about the prison, its exact location, when there is the fewest people around, how many guards are on each floor and their weaponry. Then I'd plan each step – how I'd get there without drawing attention or the best way to enter the facility and where the person I'm supposed to rescue is located in the building."

"You're quite a strategist, Cpl. Humphreys. I see that as the hardest part of the exercise. But what about Part Two: Escaping successfully from prison. I'd like to hear your comments on that."

"I'd like to think about that one for a bit, captain."

"You're a wise man, corporal. One thing before you go.

Please do not discuss our conversation with any of your friends or other NCOs. A person's life may depend on it, including yours."

"Is it that dangerous?"

Andrew nodded. "And then some. Getting back to my question: Once you've freed the individual, how do you plan to escape if the building is surrounded?"

Jeremy Hawkins, a private undergoing basic training, kept feeling the top of his shaven head as if trying to find his hair somewhere else on his head.

"If you had to rescue someone from a well-guarded building, how would you escape, especially if you've alerted everyone by firing your gun and the enemy places machine gun nests on all building exits."

"Got it," said Humphreys. "I'll go to bed thinking about it."

Harry Greene, a career soldier, had a slightly different take. "If we're talking Germany, I'd ask the underground to help us find a truck that would hold all of us and our equipment. I think a couple of the lads should be dressed in German uniforms so that they can cozy up to the guards outside and kill them as silently as possible."

The four others had similar ideas. Andrew had a few of his own.

Later, when they got together to discuss the mission, it was to see a scale model of the prison to review exits and the location of each prison room, as well as an enlarged map of Berlin and the surrounding countryside.

"This," said Andrew, is where we will land. We will be met by a small group of anti-Nazi protestors, who have been asked to provide a truck for us. We will use the truck to transport us to the prison."

"Won't we be noticed?" said Humphreys, a big-boned young man with sandy-coloured hair and a broad, flat face.

"We're working on that. We want to arrive in the middle of an all-out bombing raid. We expect to slip in and land without being noticed. The Germans will have their hands full, just trying to deal with our bombers, and most civilians will be in bomb shelters."

"What happens after we liberate our prisoner," said Jack Sinclair, a regular army sergeant who transferred to the new commando unit with Andrew.

"Hopefully, we'll be able to do this without setting off any alarms."

"And if we don't?"

"We'll have to fight our way out."

"We'll have to do that anyway. We need another diversion. What about setting all the prisoners free, and we mingle among them?"

"Great idea, sergeant. Any other ideas?"

"Then let's look at a scale model of the prison," he said, pointing to it at the back of the room. They surrounded the model and peeked into the corridors as well as they could and what was on each floor. There was also a diagram of each floor, starting with the entrance, showing where guards were located. There was also a cut-out of the third floor where the prisoner was located. "She's in Cell 3," said Andrew, using his pencil to underline the entrance, and the guard station opposite.

"What do you think, Jack?" said Harry Greene.

Sgt. Sinclair stroked his chin. "We need to use the other prisoners to cause confusion once we board the truck by getting them to run in all directions to avoid capture.

"Add that to our list of objectives," said Andrew. "Before we head out for lunch, I want you to think about how we can make our plan even better."

They got up to leave.

"A word, sergeant."

Sinclair followed him into the company office. "I need your on-the-ground expertise to work with me to break down each part of our mission and what we need in terms of manpower as resources for each phase. I've already arranged for an Armstrong Whitworth to fly us to Berlin and a ground support group of anti-Nazis to have a truck ready for us that could take us to the prison.

"Once we reach the prison, we need to decide and train who will kill the guards on the outside without giving them time to sound the alarm?"

"What about Manley and Godfrey? They've seen action up front and are not squeamish about slitting someone's throat."

"Then we'll need two Nazi uniforms large enough to fit over their own," said Bartlett, glancing at a black and white picture of Sommer and him the night before she left for France.

"Is that the lady we're going to rescue?"

Andrew nodded.

"She looks too pretty to be a mathematical genius.' Then, in a business-like tone: "Once we proceed, how do we proceed?"

"I suggest securing the first and second floors first. They'll block our way out if we don't, should the alarm go off." Hopefully, we can do this without having a shot fired by us or at us."

"That's when things will get a bit sticky. What do we do with the prisoners while they wait to leave from making a noise and alerting the other floors?"

"Good question, sergeant. We will need to train your marines to make sure they do it. I'll leave that in your capable hands."

"One thing, if I may, sir," said Sinclair. "If there is one thing life has taught me is this: If anything can go wrong, it will."

"Remind the men that every day." Then, after a pause: "We leave in 10 days. There will be no moon that night."

***

Bartlett stood and raised his glass. "Watching you in your training over the past few days, I feel privileged to fight shoulder to shoulder with the best the Royal Marines has to offer. Thank you for being with me. In case I forget, there's a party to end all parties at the Savoy when we get back."

There were a lot of surprised smiles as they left, laughing and singing. Sgt. Sinclair raised his hand. "Captain Bartlett deserves all the support we can give him."

Later that day, they boarded the Armstrong Whitworth around 9 o'clock. They were to join over 150 bombers on a major raid on Berlin and find their way once they reached the outskirts of the city.

Sinclair sat down next to the three newest marines who had never been in combat before and closed his eyes. You could hardly hear his voice above the sound of the bomber's two engines. There was a sudden drop and he grabbed an upper steel railing to keep from falling. Two hours later, Bartlett returned from talking to the pilot and the navigator and then proceeded to speak to the top gunner.

"We'll be landing in a few minutes. Grab onto something solid. It's going to be a rough landing. I don't want to lose you to a couple of bad fractures."

The plane landed with a big bang and bumped twice before coming to a stop.

"Stay put until someone opens the door and sets the ladder down. Sling your gun over your shoulder, step down carefully until your feet are on the ground. There should be a friend there to help you."

Cpl. Humphreys was the first to descend. "We've been betrayed." He managed to get out before being shot. Bartlett got the top gunner to train his guns on the figures below. "You're clear to go," he shouted.

Bartlett was the first to hit the ground, followed by the

others. In the distance, an armoured car turned on its lights and headed toward them. One of the armoured car's soldiers rose and aimed his machine gun to send a rain of bullets that made holes in the fuselage in the darkness. Bartlett, who had ordered everyone to lie down, aimed his machine gun at the gun still firing and killed him instantly. He ran to the armoured car and climbed aboard, shooting the driver and another soldier.

He returned to the plane.

"So much for our help on the ground," he heard a voice say.

"Couldn't agree more," said Bartlett, who left to talk to the pilot. "Our taxi will take off in seconds – so we're on our own."

"I guess we can kiss the truck they promised goodbye as well," said Sinclair.

Bartlett started in the direction of the forested area. "We need to get out of here."

The edge of the forest was littered with bodies, but the truck they promised was still there, the driver slumped over the steering wheel.

"I'll never jump to conclusions again, " Jeff Greene said.

"Remove the driver and stow the ammunition and explosives with you." Bartlett climbed beside his wireless operator to tell London we're on our way to Berlin."

Overhead, they could hear explosions from bombs from the 150 bombers.

"Sgt. Sinclair. It's time to roll."

***

One of the bombs had crashed into the fifth level of the building. The panic was real and palpable. Everyone knew an unexploded bomb could go off at any time and kept pleading with the guards to let them out of their cells and relocate them on the bottom floor. Captain Friedrich Roth, the new commandant, ordered his guards to quiet the prisoners.

Roth shook his head. "We're staying put, and so are you," he shouted to them.

Sommer was too sick to see or understand what was happening and spent much of the time in the toilet vomiting. She could still taste the vomit in her mouth and tried it wash it away, using mouthfuls of water.

When she felt well enough, she staggered to her cot, turned her face to the wall and went to sleep.

CHAPTER THIRTY-FOUR

They parked a few yards away from the prison on the other side of the road. "You two," said Sinclair, pointing to Robertson and Holmes, "stay put. You're going to be our insurance. Set up two machines, and if you see a lot of German soldiers ready to fire on us when we leave the prison, open fire when I give you the signal."

"What will that be, Sarge?"

"See this flashlight? I will flash it three times when I want you to fire on them. We plan to let the inmates escape first. So don't get confused. And wait for my signal. Remember, three flashes." He shone it in their eyes three times.

He glanced at Manley and Godfrey, looking somehow taller in their German uniforms. Manley put a cigarette in his mouth, approached the guard and pointed to the end. The guard said something in German as Godfrey quickly slit his throat in front of the other guard while Manley

230

slipped behind and stabbed him through the heart.

"The rest of us will follow Captain Bartlett."

Bartlett led them inside, suddenly facing another two guards trying to free their machine guns from their shoulders. Sinclair stepped in and stabbed both in the heart before they could do anything.

As he came to call them, Bartlett's privateers entered the first-floor cell block, catching the guard on duty half asleep. They disarmed him, unlocked the cells, and locked the guard in one of them.

Bartlett held up his hand. "We need all of you to be quiet. We are here to liberate all of you and will lead you out of the prison. But you must be silent. If you aren't, they will put us all behind bars. So please be quiet," he said in German.

"Permission to speak," said an aristocratic woman. "You should be aware that an unexploded bomb crashed into the fifth-floor cell block. We're all worried whether it will explode and take the entire building with it. I understand they have sent for an expert to disarm it. But in the middle of an air raid, that may be days from now."

"Sgt. Sinclair, take two men and take over the second floor and free the inmates," said Bartlett.

Sinclair nodded and pointed to Harry Greene to follow him.

Bartlett headed for the third floor. He was spotted the minute he opened the door. An officer was talking to one of the guards, saw them first and told the guard to shoot. The commando behind him killed him. The officer tripped the alarm and raised his arms. "You won't escape," he said to Bartlett, who ignored him and took the keys to the cells. Sommer was sleeping when he entered her cell. He raised her, but she shivered and withdrew herself from him.

"Sommer. It's me. Andrew. I've come to take you home."

"I feel sick."

He helped her walk into the guard room. The only light was still swaying from a bomb blast nearby.

Andrew emerged from the guard room. "You," he said to the officer. "Put your side arm on this desk and open each cell." He gave him a fierce kick that sent him sprawling. Haven't got all day."

The officer looked back at Bartlett and called him a dog in German.

"I should tell you I understand German. So, unless you want an early grave, you'll keep your opinions to yourself and do exactly what I tell you," he said in German.

The inmates surrounded Bartlett. "Before you do anything, "he said, "pointing to a young half-shaven young man at the edge of the circle, I'd like you to lock the guard and his officer in separate cells and keep the key. If they cause you any problems, just kill them."

When I set the alarm, I alerted every guard in the prison and the nearby army camp. The officer looked at Bartlett. "You'll pay for this. You will face them when you open the door."

"Perhaps. But then again, we won't be the only ones. I will leave one of my men behind to kill you if we are not able to make our escape."

The room fell silent. There was a knock on the door, and Sgt. Sinclair stuck his head in the door. "We're ready to go."

"The other floors?"

"All secured, including the fifth. We've freed all inmates, and they're ready to lead the parade."

The inmates started down the stairs. Bartlett was with them. "Remember, once we open the door, run in every direction. Run as though your life depended on it, and don't look back."

"What about our men at the front?"

"Both dead," said Sinclair. "There are two squad cars out there packed with soldiers armed with machine guns and ready to shoot us down as soon as we pop our heads out the door."

"What about the marines we left in the truck?"

"So far, so good. They haven't shown their heads.

"Give them the signal to shoot anything that moves as soon as we open the door."

Sinclair pointed the flashlight at the truck and gave it three quick bursts of light. Bartlett made his way down the stairs to the front of the line with Sommer.

"Now," he said, opening the door.

It took three or four minutes before all the inmates left. The German soldiers stopped shooting as soon as they saw they were shooting at inmates and turned to direct their fire at the truck. It was too late. All the soldiers in the first squad car had been gunned down. Only a few were left in the second.

"Time to go," he said, grabbing Sommer and heading out into the darkness.

"Finally," said an officer standing in the second squad car with an SS officer. "I was right all along." Becker raised his luger and pointed it at Sommer.

The other officer suddenly wheeled around and shot him in the back of his head.

It was Felix. He looked at Sommer clinging to Bartlett. "Go now while you have the chance."

They ran to the truck and were on their way. Bombs were still going off in the city as one wave after another dropped their bombs, filling the air with the smell of ashes and burnt flesh."

They hadn't gone five miles when the truck hit a hidden crater and died. Sinclair got out to check and returned a minute after. "The axle is broken. We're going to need to walk." He looked at Sommer, who still clung to Bartlett.

"Then let's get started," said Andrew. "Our taxi leaves at 4 o'clock. With us or without us. That's it."

Andrew had to help her take every step. By 3.41, when he looked at his wristwatch, they still have another mile to go.

"I think the other two should run ahead and tell them we're coming and may need another few minutes," said Sinclair.

Bartlett nodded and kept on plodding ahead. In the darkness, they failed to see a large pothole. Sommer fell headlong into the hole and began vomiting. Sinclair shone his flashlight at her and helped her to her feet.

"I'm not sure what it was, captain, but whatever she vomited looked black and had the smell of death. I experienced something similar at Dunkirk."

Behind them, they could make out a motorcycle heading towards him in the distance.

"It might be one of the prisoners."

"Far from it. Sergeant. We want them to see us as they get closer. We'll stand a few yards beyond the pothole. Hopefully, that will distract them just long enough that they won't see the pothole."

Three minutes later, the motorcycle hit the pothole and sent the driver and his sidecar passenger flying across the road.

"I'll take care of them," said Sinclair. He returned a minute later and worked hard to right the motorcycle, hampered by the sidecar.

"Here, let me give you a hand," said Bartlett. Two minutes later, they were able to straighten it out. Bartlett helped Sommer into the sidecar and hopped on the motorcycle.

"You and Sommer take it and head for the plane. I run the rest of the way,"

"There's another seat behind me. Get on and put your arms around my stomach," said Bartlett.

Five minutes later, they turned into the landing field. The plane was ready to go. Greene and the others helped Sommer and Bartlett get aboard. Sgt. Sinclair was last.

Bartlett went ahead to the navigator. "Time to take us home."

CHAPTER THIRTY-FIVE

"We're not out of danger yet", said the navigator. "We've got a lot of German territory to cross before we can relax. The pilot thinks the safest route is northwest towards Denmark. But it also means flying low to avoid German radar. It should be much easier once we reach the North Sea."

An hour later, they were dodging flak and running away from the sudden appearance of German fighters. The pilot suddenly changed course and headed for some low-flying clouds.

They had lost three commandos, and the three left were asleep on the floor when the plane emerged from the clouds into clear skies over moonlit waters. The navigator crawled back to talk to Bartlett. "In 30 minutes, we should be over the North Sea and home in time for tea."

An hour later, they are spotted by a squadron of German ME109Fs, who zeroed in on them immediately. The top turret gunner was shooting and yelled down. "Just got one." His gun went off again. Silence, and then his gun rattled again. More silence, Then the sound of bullets hitting the fuselage outside. The top turret rattled again. "Got that one, too. Only one more left."

Bartlett fell and skinned his knees as he made his way to the cockpit. The pilot was killed instantly in the next pass, and the co-pilot was wounded badly. He was having a problem keeping the plane steady. "The pilot's dead, and I'm not sure how long I can keep her up."

Bartlett motioned the navigator to help him remove the pilot from his seat. Bartlett squeezed behind him and sat in the pilot's seat. "What do I do?"

"Just hold the wheel the way I do."

Bartlett grabbed the wheel.

"Just hold it steady. The navigator will tell you when to change course."

On the next pass, the German fighter hit the starboard engine. It suddenly burst into flame, and then, the second one, as the plane suddenly went into a tailspin.

"Pull back the wheel," said the co-pilot. His head suddenly went to one side, and it was plain that he was dead.

Andrew pulled on the wheel immediately and helped to level it. But they were losing altitude.

"I didn't know you could fly a plane, captain," said Sinclair, leaning over the co-pilot's seat.

"I don't. We will be crashing into the sea shortly. I got last-minute instructions from the co-pilot before he died. Get the navigator to send out an SOS with our position."

"The navigator has already done it and is heading back of the plane with the others. He told me that if you somehow get trapped, there's an escape hatch on the upper left," said Sinclair.

"See to Sommer. Whatever you do, make sure she survives."

The plane suddenly crashed into the water a minute later with a jar that almost tore the plane apart. Anything not bolted down went flying into the air. Two marines suffered broken bones. Sommer felt her head and panicked when her hand was covered in blood.

The navigator took charge. "First, those of you who can strap on your life preserver. Second, we can all escape if you do what I tell you. Third, I am going to this door. The water will rush in and fill the plane immediately when I do. Now get in a line and get ready." He opened the hatch door.

Sommer was the first to leave, followed by the two commandos, Sinclair and the navigator. The wireless operator and the top turret gunner escaped from the turret hatch and dove into the water. Greene could see Sommer flailing the water, trying to surface, and headed in her direction.

Andrew was slumped over the wheel and slowly raised himself, looking out the windshield that was partially covered with water. He spotted the escape hatch and pulled the level. The canopy suddenly opened, and he climbed out on the top of the aircraft. He could see the navigator throwing dinghies into the water and yelling to everyone to swim to them.

Andrew jumped and swam to the dinghy where Sommer and Sinclair were sitting. The navigator and wireless operator sat with the two commandos. "We need to tie them together."

"Does this thing have any paddles?" Sinclair said to the wireless operator.

The navigator managed to smile. "Yes. Along with three flasks of water and a couple of chocolate bars. Just look under the flap."

"Where to navigator? Guide us home."

The navigator pulled out his compass. "Steer southwest. Let me lead the way."

The navigator and the wireless operator started paddling almost immediately. The commandos suffered from broken ankles and had a hard time staying long in one position but insisted on taking their turn.

Sommer hallucinated, crying for her mother, Gretchen, and Dr. Albrecht. Andrew gave her a bit of water, which she vomited overboard. He wet her lips and helped her to find a comfortable position. Sinclair nodded at Bartlett and pointed at the water. Bartlett looked back to see a black patch in the swirling water behind them.

By dawn, everyone was tired and hungry. They decided to stop paddling and rest to regain their strength and hoped that London was already searching for them. The wireless operator spotted land first, and they went back paddling with new vigour.

"Where do you think we are?" said Bartlett.

"Because of the currents, it could be anywhere, but if we stayed on course, it should be Scotland.

An hour later, Bartlett stood and ordered them to stop paddling. "The current has taken us to France."

"Are you sure?" said the wireless operator.

"Absolutely. I can see a German patrol boat being launched and headed in our direction."

"I don't want to go back. I'd rather die here." Sommer's voice was weak and tired.

As the patrol boat drew closer, they failed to hear approaching planes. Sommer looked up, tapped Andrew on the shoulder, and pointed to the three Spitfires approaching them. The lead Spitfire passed overhead and fired two rockets into the patrol boat, which exploded seconds later. Sommer hid her face as one of the Spitfires dropped a red flare near their dinghies.

About 10 minutes later, a Canso flying boat landed, skimming the water before stopping near them. Both dinghies padded furiously and touched the Canso, which opened its side door. Andrew stood and pointed to another approaching patrol boat.

"They will soon come in firing range," said Bartlett. We need to hurry and get aboard. In two or three minutes, we'll be sitting ducks."

The Canso had revved up its engines and started skimming the war as soon as the side door hatch was closed. The patrol boat started firing at them as they glided across the water and slowly began to lift into the air. One of the shells ripped into the side of the fuselage. More shots were short of their mark as the plane gained altitude.

"Next stop," said the navigator," London."

Thirty minutes later, they landed in the harbour, coming to a stop near one of London's main wharves. A boat was sent to ferry them to the pier, where they climbed a rusting iron ladder to the top. Brookfield's hand was there to help Sommer to her feet, followed by Sinclair and Andrew. The two commandos had to be lifted by sling and then by stretcher to a waiting ambulance.

"You did it," said Brookfield when he saw Andrew.

"It was touch and go, but she's back where she belongs. She's gone through a lot. I think she should be taken to hospital and given a thorough check-up, x-rays, blood tests, the works."

"Is there a reason?"

'Yes. I think someone was slowly poisoning her. She didn't know me when we raised the prison, but it got increasingly worse on our way. She vomited a lot. Black vomit and the smell of death, as one of the commandos described it."

Brookfield waved to his assistant and spoke to her before turning back to Andrew. "I gather you lost a few of your men."

"Four. Four hard-to-replace marines, who gave up their lives bravely so that Sommer could live."

"By the by, I've let your colonel know that you're back from your mission and will report for duty in a couple of days after you have rested from a very tough assignment."

The ambulance arrived, and Sommer called out to him. "Are you coming with me?"

"Yes. I will be with you all the way. I didn't go all that

way to abandon you now."

She squeezed his hand. He stayed with her all the way to the hospital, going with her as they took x-rays and did blood tests.

Three hours later, the doctor came into her room. "I think I can tell you what is wrong with Sommer. As you rightly guessed, she was slowly being poisoned. It was mixed with heroin, so she would not be aware of the poison. A pretty potent mix."

"How long will it take for her to recover?"

"Hard to say. It depends on how long she was being fed this cocktail. If she recovers, it could take a week or even less. Any ideas?"

Bartlett shook his head. "You said *If she recovers* a second ago."

"That is always a possibility."

"When will we know?"

"The next 24 hours will tell us everything."

"I haven't slept for 36 hours, doctor. Could you get someone to find some kind of chair I could sleep in here? I don't want to leave her side in case she needs something."

Dr. Clifford smiled. "I'll see to it."

He checked her pulse and gave her an injection. " This will help to purify her blood."

***

Sommer opened her eyes around 11 o'clock the next morning. She looked out the window at the harbour and, farther afield, the Tower of London. She turned to see Andrew sprawled on a chair next to her bed.

"Andrew. Wake up."

He opened his eyes.

"Am I really back in London?"

"We rescued you from the prison in Berlin where they had you locked up."

"I've been in a haze for so long that I can't tell you what I saw and remembered and what was just a dream. I can remember being in a small boat and water everywhere. And gunfire. And crowds of people."

"Someone was trying to poison you. How do you feel now?"

"Phenomenal. I haven't slept like this in a long time."

"That's good news," said Dr. Clifford, who had slipped in unnoticed. "It means we were successful in flushing out all or most of the toxins out of your system. Who would have done this to you?"

"A Gestapo officer called Becker, who shadowed me all the time I was in Germany and made life miserable for my friends and me."

"I think it was Becker who tried to kill you when you were escaping from the prison. I heard him say something like *I was right after all.*"

"He harboured evil in his heart, although not all Gestapo officers were like that."

"He was shot by an SS officer, who looked at you and told me to leave while I had the chance."

"Felix."

"I guessed as much. Will you miss your life in Germany?"

She looked at him. He hadn't shaved in two days and looked it. His eyes drooped, and his dark brown hair pointed in all directions.

"I will miss my friends, Lotte and Zelda. Lotte is married to an SS officer, and Zelda was Becker's girlfriend before he dumped her. But most of all, I will miss Gretchen for the rest of my life. She was the first person to speak to me in Germany and became my friend in Bonn. Later, we both were seconded by Professor Albrecht to work on a special program with him. She contracted a bad case of the flu and died. I will always miss her." She paused to say a prayer for

Gretchen. "But I will not miss Germany."

A young nurse popped her head inside the door. "If your name is Captain Bartlett, there's a phone call for you."

CHAPTER THIRTY-SIX

"I'm afraid it's not going to be much of a party. With Humphreys, Robertson and Holmes gone, it'll seem more like a wake," said Sgt. Sinclair.

"What would you suggest?" said Andrew.

"What about having a farewell party to them for the entire company?"

" It was supposed to be a party of parties for the group that went into Germany not knowing whether they'd return or not."

"I was thinking of it as a kind of memorial for the three who didn't make it back."

Bartlett smiled. "Go ahead. And where would you like to hold it? The Savoy would be out of place for an entire company."

"What about the Officers' Mess? It gave us quite a charge before we left on our mission."

"I'll have to square it with Col. Morris first. It may be a bit of a stretch for him and the other officers."

Sinclair had a broad smile. "We can do anything. We flew into Germany, entered a prison, freed prisoners, and lived to tell the tale. One other thing. Do you think Sommer would join us?"

"She's still a bit shaky. Someone in Berlin was trying to poison her. But we'll see."

Sinclair turned to go.

"I'd like to commend you on your bravery during our mission. You're a very smart man, sergeant, and I believe the mission would not have ended the way it did without you. I'm putting you up for a special commendation."

***

Col. Morris extended his hand. "Congratulations, Bartlett. You've pulled off a very difficult mission under impossible odds."

"A favour to ask, sir. I promised our group a party at the Savoy when we got back. But with half the group failing to be with us, the men would like to hold a memorial party for them in the Officers' Mess."

Col. Morris didn't respond for almost a minute. "I have no problem with it, but some other officers may not feel the same way. Tell you what, Bartlett. I'll fly it past them and see what they think. But understand one thing. This will be the last one."

Bartlett smiled.

"Anything else, captain?" The colonel was becoming a bit wary and bit at his greying mustache.

"I'd like a special commendation for Sgt. Sinclair. And while we're talking about him, I'd like to recommend him for promotion as an officer."

"What is his background?"

"Not Oxford or Cambridge, of that's what you mean, but he's a natural-born leader, always putting his men first and a superb strategist. The men admire and look up to him."

Col. Morris rubbed his chin. I'll look into it."

Bartlett saluted and headed for the door.

"Check in with me in the morning, and I'll let you know about the Officers' Mess. But understand, it can't happen again."

***

"When I told them what your group did and the loss of your men, they agreed to a man but with one proviso – there is to be no fighting, no smashing of furniture, no ill manners and never again. One last thing, If there are any damages, it will come out of your pockets."

Later, he met with Sinclair in his office. "The colonel made one point clear. If our men do not act as civilized gentlemen, there will be hell to pay. And it will come out of my hide."

"Don't worry about them," said Sinclair. "I've laid down the law and know better than to get on my bad side."

An hour later, they marched into the Officers' Mess, two abreast without a word, boots shined, and buckles and buttons polished. They sat down quietly at 30-odd tables and waited for Bartlett to enter. When he did, they waited until Bartlett, Sinclair, Greene, McCall, and Bartlett took their seats. Behind them were large pictures of Humphreys, Robertson, and Holmes.

One of the soldiers stood. "No offence, Jack, the Officers' Mess would be a grand place for a funeral, but we're here to honour three of our friends who sacrificed themselves to ensure the success of the mission. Well, the lads would be much happier knocking back a few beers at the Anchor. They've got a great bar there, two dart boards, and all the beer you can drink."

Sinclair looked at Bartlett with a big smile. "What do you say, captain?"

"I go where my men want to be. So, let's get the hell out of here."

There was a big cheer as men stood. They looked at Sinclair, who had a finger pressed against his lips. "We're not at the Anchor yet. And remember, walk out of here two abreast, the same way you walked in. Anyone who doesn't will be banned from the Anchor."

The Anchor was a 20-minute brisk walk away. They sang all the way there, with Sinclair leading them. Bartlett disappeared and returned with Sommer, wearing a blue dress and a string of pearls.

The Anchor had two floors. The basement floor was where the dart boards were and where most of the biggest beer guzzlers liked to hang out. The noise level was horrific, with laughter and loud voices. There were three or more pitchers of beer on almost every table and a barmaid who couldn't keep up with the shouts for more. She was forever slapping hands that reached out from many of the tables, trying to pinch her behind.

Ladies and their husbands preferred the main floor, where the tables were far apart and where many City people liked to enjoy their evenings after a busy day in the stock market. It had stained glass windows and a recently sanded and painted hardwood floor. There were two male waters dressed in blazers and red bow ties. The main bar was located at the entrance. Behind it was a large mirror, bottles of Whiskey, Gin, Cognac and Brandy, and a lone bottle of Champagne in the centre.

There was an ear-splitting cheer and raised beer glasses. The beer was flowing, and a lot of the men were singing bawdy songs. Sinclair, who arranged for a microphone, introduced Bartlett and Sommer.

Looking like a cinema actor in his new uniform, Bartlett waited for the noise to ebb away. "It's great to see you all tonight. I value every one of you. The death of any one of you diminishes us all. We are all here for each other, as well as our fallen comrades. Because of him, Sgt. Sinclair and Harry Greene are here tonight. They also died to rescue a Canadian-born mathematics genius forced to work on the development of a new German weapon of mass destruction. So let me introduce you to Sommer Kappel."

He adjusted the microphone to a lower level. Sommer stood and was greeted with whistles and clapping. "I feel small in the company of brave men like yourselves. Without brave men like you, I would be dead now. I will never forget the sacrifice of your three comrades. May they always be in our hearts."

She wiped her eyes and started singing, *We'll Meet Again*. Before she finished, everyone had joined in, and the applause rocked the room like a bomb blast when it ended.

Later, walking back to her hotel, Sommer grabbed his arm. "That was a wonderful party. They'll all remember that long after the war is over."

***

Brookfield was waiting for them at the hotel with a drink in his hand. "Just checking to make sure Sommer gets everything she needs to completely recover from her ordeal. We're going to need her when she feels better."

Sommer, who always admired Brookfield's cleverness, smiled. "Actually, I'm ready now. What would you like to know?"

"Before we get into that, do you know why that great brain of yours was so important to them?"

"I was told it was for a weapon of mass destruction."

"It was certainly that and much more. It can destroy civilization. It's called the atomic bomb. Just one dropped on London would wipe it out forever and kill everyone in it."

"*Mein Gott.*" Sommer shivered, and her face turned pale.

Brookfield leaned closer. "We need you to provide us with all the math equations you can remember."

Sommer stiffened. "I will work with you on one condition – that this atomic bomb of yours is never dropped on Berlin or Bonn."

"You have it. We are not interested in using it in any city. What we plan is to demonstrate its power in a remote area. That will be enough to demonstrate what it could do if Germany does not surrender."

"And if they choose not to, what then?"

I can't, in all honesty, tell you all I know. All I can say is that Germany is working on developing an atomic bomb, too. And I don't need to tell you that they will have no hesitation of using it on London, or any other city for that matter, not just here but all over the world. Right now, it's a race.

"They want to dominate the world, and this bomb will give them the power to do it."

Sommer didn't respond. When she did, it was to ask Andrew if he knew about it.

"He didn't," said Brookfield, finishing the last of the Brandy. "

"Sorry, Myles." Then looking at Sommer in the eye, "I wished I didn't, but it made me understand the urgency of getting you back now and why the Germans kept you under lock and key."

When your professor died in the bombing raid," said Brookfield, "they put all their hopes on you, which puzzles me somewhat why they were poisoning you."

"I think I can tell you about that. It was Becker, Konrad Becker, a lieutenant in the Gestapo. He had suspicions about me from the moment I landed in Germany and never let up. Even his superiors told him to back off. But no, with him, it became a duel to the death."

"You can take comfort in knowing that your departure will put them back months, if not a year," added Brookfield."

Sommer looked at Andrew. "I have to tell you, Sommer and you, Myles, that you were the main reason why I jumped at the chance to rescue you."

She squeezed his hand. "When would you like me to start with the equations?"

"Now, if you're up to it," said Brookfield, rubbing his hands.

"Then get me a pad and a pencil and leave me alone until I finish." She looked at the pad for almost a minute and then started writing, not stopping for nearly 20 minutes.

"I knew you had a prodigious memory, but this is incredible. I'll make sure it reaches the proper people tonight."

"What happens next," said Andrew,

"We'd like to hold an informal dinner in Sommer's honour to let her know how much we admire her courage and how happy we are that she's back where she belongs."

Andrew looked at her. "Be careful, Sommer, but that's how they sucked me in."

"Tomorrow at 7 o'clock at the Savoy."

"I don't know, Mr. Brookfield."

"Call me Myles. That rascal of yours does."

CHAPTER THIRTY-SEVEN

Sommer felt self-conscious when Andrew helped her out of the limousine, and she took his arm. She wasn't used to high heels and had to grab him a few times as they walked into the front hall with its black and white tiles that led to the lobby, holding his arm even tighter as they entered the elevator to the Savoy Grill.

She had spent the afternoon shopping for a new dress with Andrew and to have her hair done, and her face made up.

"You're really stunning," he whispered in her ear. She responded by holding his arm even tighter as they approached the room. In dress uniform, two commandos from his company stood guard and saluted him before opening the door.

Brookfield, dressed in a tuxedo, held her hand. "Let me introduce you to the Minister."

"I am very happy to finally meet you, Miss Kappel. I'm sorry it took so long."

Next were two senior members from the ministry, who oversaw Brookfield's office, and then a surprise – Col. Winslow from Beaulieu.

"Well done, Sommer."

"I saw Bonfilia before she died. I was locked up in prison, and she was able to send messages to Brookfield for me."

"I was sorry about her death as well. Her real name was Angela DeLuca. She was one of our best."

"She looked more beautiful than at Beaulieu. She had attached herself to the commandant of the prison I was in. He doted on her, she told me, but he shot her to death when he discovered her radio transmitter. Also, on one occasion, I also came face to face with Alex Greenwood."

"Yes, he fooled all of us and created a lot of trouble. It meant reassigning agents in some areas."

Then, almost out of nowhere, Perdita, looking better than ever, suddenly was standing beside her.

"How bad was it for you, Sommer? I prayed for you every day. Worst of all, I didn't know where and if you were in trouble." She relaxed her arm and looked at Sommer's face.

"It was very hard for me at one point. You didn't think I'd ever see you, my mother, or my daughter again. When I felt really down, I kept repeating what you always said to me."

"There's always tomorrow?"

"Yes," said Sommer with tears in her eyes.

"Talking about tomorrow," said the Minister, who had been chatting with Brookfield. "We want you on a plane to Canada tomorrow. We've already alerted the people there that you're now in safe hands. They want you working with some people in Washington before the end of the month."

It was time for dinner. Sommer wasn't sure which fork to use when the first course arrived. Andrew, who had been watching her, lifted his soup spoon. Sommer nodded and smiled.

Brookfield, who sat next to Andrew, whispered he would like to see them after dinner.

"It's going to be a longer night than I expected," said Brookfield, who caught up with them on the way out. Sommer was getting used to the heels and laughed when she clutched Brookfield's arm. Perdita supported her other arm.

"You need to get to bed early. You're going to have a very busy day tomorrow."

Andrew picked up his ears.

"There's a plane leaving for Halifax tomorrow in the morning. From there, you'll board another transport for Toronto."

"What time?" It was Andrew.

"8 o'clock, I'm afraid."

"You have reservations waiting for you at the Royal York in Toronto, where your mother and daughter will be waiting for you. On the 30th, you'll be picked up by a U.S. transport plane and flown to Washington, where you'll be welcomed by fellow scientists and armed forces personnel. They're looking forward to meeting you."

Brookfield looked at Andrew and smiled. He was staring off into the distance.

"You'll make a lot of friends there," added Brookfield. "They already know much about you and will be at home with other mathematicians, physicists, and engineers. And now, Andrew, this concerns you. You're being seconded to accompany her to Toronto and Washington and ensure that nothing happens to her. You're the only one we trust to make sure that nothing does. You'll also act as our liaison should any problems arise."

Sommer glanced at Perdita, who was smiling at her.

She was right, thought Sommer. There always is tomorrow.

Epilogue

"Sommer?" I don't believe it. But it's you. Really you."Zelda was smiling as she relayed the news to Lotte later.

"How did she track1 us down? We've both moved. Twice," said Lotte.

"Her husband is a captain in the British Royal Marines. He asked one of his buddies to track me down. Once they got my phone number, she called me from somewhere in England and asked to meet you and me at my apartment at lunchtime today."

"I thought she was dead. So did I, I told her. She escaped from the prison and made her way back to England," said Zelda.

"Why at your place? She stayed with me when she was here," said Lotte.

"I'm sure we'll know in a couple of hours from now. Grab your coat and remind me to stop and get some coffee. I always remembered she always liked coffee."

Sommer's heart was pounding wildly in her ears as she knocked on Zelda's door.

Lotte opened it and threw her arms around Sommer. Zelda joined them, putting her arms around both of them. Zelda started to cry first, and a few seconds later, Lotte and Sommer joined her. They tightened their grip on each other and didn't want to let go.

Andrew appeared in the doorway suddenly. They unlocked their arms slowly.

"Who is this gorgeous man?" Zelda gave him her widest smile.

"My husband. The man who rescued me from prison and saw that I got back to England."

"The father of your daughter?"

Sommer ignored the question. "Whatever happened to Felix?"

"Last I heard, he was teaching mathematics at some small university," said Lotte. "My husband keeps in touch with him once in a while."

"And Becker?"

"He was killed trying to stop the prison break by another officer."

"Someone you knew?" said Zelda.

"I think I can answer that for you," said Andrew. "It was Felix."

"Felix?"

"I'm not sure, but he took one look at Sommer, but when he saw that Becker was pointing his gun at her, he turned and shot Becker in the back of the head before Becker could pull the trigger."

An uneasy silence followed. "Good thing," said Zelda suddenly. "Dumped me for some nitwit in his office who hung on every word that came out of his mouth."

"How do you know it was Becker?" said Zelda.

"He said something like *I was right all along*. And from what Sommer tells me about Becker, it can only be him,"

"Let's celebrate," said Lotte. We're all back together again, and that's all that matters. There's a great restaurant down the street, my treat," said Lotte. "We'll have coffee and then go there."

Zelda left to make coffee. "Here it is. Real coffee. Not that make-believe stuff we drank during the war."

"Before we do anything," said Sommer in a business voice, "you've forgotten something very important."

Lotte and Zelda just looked at her.

"Gretchen?" said Zelda.

"No, our good friend, Jundt."

"You know, with all the things that have happened in the past three years, I think we all forgot about her."

"What else?"

"I know," Zelda said with a smile that would charm any man who showed interest in her. "Her jewelry."

"And what we planned after the war?" said Sommer.

"We would meet, and you would show us the hiding place, and we'd divide everything," said Lotte.

"We'll. I'm here to tell you where I hid them." She smiled before adding: "The last place you or anyone would look for jewellery."

There were puzzled looks on their faces. "Do you recall I left my Bible and Missal with you, Zelda, for safekeeping?"

"You know, I was going to throw them out last October when I moved here, but something I can't explain stopped me. Wait a sec, and I'll get them for you."

Zelda returned with a cardboard box and laid it on Sommer's lap.

Sommer opened the box and invited Lotte to pass the Bible to Zelda, and you take the Missal and, on the count of three, open them."

"Everyone, including Andrew, stared at the Bible and Missal.

"Three," said Sommer in a loud voice.

Jundt's diamond tiara, necklaces, rings and bracelets glittered in the morning sunlight.

About the Author

Jim Carr's adventure with words began as a teacher of Latin grammar for the first five years. He studied Latin for seven years and holds a degree in Classics and English. He has written a Latin Grammar called *Lingua Latina, Latin for Beginners.*

It was followed by a lengthy career in print journalism at two daily newspapers as a reporter, copy editor, columnist and editor. He left journalism to become a communications specialist for a number of national and international corporations and institutions.

In retirement, he returned to journalism and now acts as associate editor of *Spa Canada* magazine and a freelancer for other publications. He writes a blog about Thai Retreats and spas, which is featured on Spa Canada's website.

He has also written an ebook about 50+ outstanding Thai resorts, and their spas in Bangkok, Chiang Mai, Chiang Rai, Pattaya, Hua Hin, Koh Samui, Krabi and Phuket called *Spa Magic Collection.*

Four mystery novels, *Abbot's Moon, Gravediggers The Door,* and *Death Star* and his book of short stories, *Betrayal,* are available as ebooks and print books. His other books include *There's Always Tomorrow,* and a historical romance, *Yesterdays* while *Forget-Me-Nots* takes place during the Second World War and *Femme Fatale* in Soviet East Berlin.

www.ingramcontent.com/pod-product-compliance
Lightning Source LLC
Chambersburg PA
CBHW030405020726
47493CB00003B/948